# Illuminated

A Heaven and Earth Novel

VICKI WILKERSON

# ILLUMINATED

To Preston,

The baby I miscarried in 1990.

I promised you that I would never forget you.

# PREFACE

Readers should be aware that *Illuminated* contains subject matter that implies a sexual assault has taken place in the story. The novel also deals with the sensitive subject of abortion. Readers who may be offended by either topic should not read this novel.

*Illuminated* is a fictitious tale of a woman who finds herself caught between Heaven and Earth and is challenged to reexamine her earthly choices after she meets her babies' souls. The story is an allegory of lights and enlightenment and symbolically addresses what may happen to those tiny little souls who never take a breath. It is also an allegory of faith and the Christian journey, and even when the name of Jesus is not written overtly on the page, He is implied between the lines of this story. The fictional settings are earthly, heavenly and in between. This novel is not doctrine or theology, and I pray that it is not received as judgement because it was never intended as such.

The idea of *Illuminated* had been placed upon my heart years ago, and I had been pondering it for a very long time—ever since I had miscarried a baby that I had wanted very badly. That loss preceded many other loses, and I found myself overwhelmed with graduate school, teaching, and raising my two children alone. Throughout it all, however, I kept a calendar, marking the age of my precious, lost baby. My heart turned black with guilt when I thought about how much more difficult my life would have been to have managed with an infant—that little baby that I had so desperately wanted. Throughout the years, I never lost the hope that one day I would be reunited with that little soul.

As I grieved over the years, I also grew to feel compassion for women in the many situations they sometimes find themselves in and the difficult decisions they make under pressure and without all the guidance, education, charity, and support they would need. I ultimately wanted to explore the complexities of a story like that because that is where God can love people and provide mercy, grace and healing—in those most difficult circumstances. I also pray that this story inspires compassion in readers for these women.

This story's surface is meant to provoke thought, like a parable. For some, there will be no lesson to glean because their minds are made up, and they are closed to the possibility of life after death—especially for those baby souls. For others, I pray it to be illuminating, filled with hope and healing because our God can cover all things, and Jesus' love offers grace through repentance.

I understand that some Christians are led to march in the streets or in front of medical facilities or to present their convictions about abortion in the media and in the courts. However, I feel that my ministry is to attempt to change the hearts and minds of those looking for illumination about the reality of abortion. It is my prayer that this story may save the lives of these tiniest of souls.

VICKI WILKERSON

# CHAPTER ONE

## Falling From Upon High

*How has it come to be that I am going to die on such a breathtakingly beautiful fall afternoon?*

Autumn had always been a season of ironies for Cotton Rivers—especially in the Lowcountry of South Carolina. Almost as if she were moving in slow motion, she unhurriedly fell through the air after losing her grip on the tall ladder. The breezes were temperate…and cool. As she grazed the branches of the broad sycamore tree, the leaves falling with her were gold…and green. The light through the trees was a mix of sun and shadow. The scent in the air was a heady combination of burning leaves and the sweet, orange-citrus fragrance of tea olives. Fall had always been the season for beginnings and endings with her. Especially today.

In her head she said a silent, sliding prayer. *God, help me save this little boy in my arms.*

How could she have the time to be praying for the small stranger in her grip and contemplating such esoteric concepts as she was falling to the pine straw-littered pavement below? Somehow, she understood the tranquil answer. Time was inexplicably falling with her, too. Ever so slowly.

For the briefest of moments, she wondered if she should be trying to protect herself and all that was hers, but she couldn't hold onto the thought as she fell, and it tumbled away from her like the paint can at the top of the ladder she had just recently climbed.

The crash was going to hurt. She certainly knew that. Buddy was gripped onto her waist like an opossum onto the belly of its mother as Cotton instinctively tucked her head over his to protect his small skull. The momentum curled her platinum blond hair around his face. White paint floated through the air in bright, wet ribbons of cool streams and streaked across their clothes and arms as they passed through it.

It was nearly accomplished—her fall from upon high. In so many ways.

*Plop.* Something heavy and hard pushed the breath out of her chest from her back, and at the same time she heard what sounded like the crack of sticks. But she knew it to be bones. The funny thing was that she didn't hurt at all. Not one little bit.

Liquid dizziness enveloped her in a warm numbness. The sun's red rays colored the backs of her eyelids, and Cotton kept them closed because it felt so comfortable.

Slumber crept in on black slivers, moving the red rays aside, eventually turning her dim perceptions black.

She was confused and was no longer in control of understanding simple things. Sounds, senses and time seemed...transfigured. Muddled thoughts and warmth and fall and falling and obligation and escape came in waves that she couldn't determine as imaginings or reality. It was a sort of *sur-reality*.

After an undetermined tendril of time, she was suddenly awake, unusually awake. *Thank goodness.* But she was still unable to open her eyes...or move. It was as if her eyes were bandaged shut and her body bound to the ground.

Where was Buddy—the little boy she'd met a few hours ago—the one she'd climbed the ladder to save—the one who'd held on to her waist for dear life in the fall? Had he survived, too?

She had no idea how long she had slept. A while, she guessed, judging by the way nothing cooperated. Something had to be broken, but who knew in her altered state? She'd broken her ribs as a child, but she couldn't touch that feeling of...pain. Right now, she just felt...distant and transformed.

*Where's Buddy?*

She knew there to be noise all about her, but what were those sounds? Most of the clamor was...*red and white*. But how can that be? She must have hit her head. Her thoughts felt...weary and wavy, and they were hard to keep from moving. She'd been dizzy on the ladder for many reasons, partly because of her fear of heights. All the brilliance of the white paint and the radiant fall sunshine had gotten to her even before she'd made the mistake to climb.

*Where is Buddy?*

Her head radiated a cool spot that seemed to be growing in the center of her brain. Her stomach tumbled in a weird warmth, and Cotton felt nauseous, like she needed to throw up, but she couldn't. Nothing in her body was working the way it had before her fall.

Guilt, in tiny trickles, trailed into her thoughts. She'd ruined so much in her fall. And she hadn't had the time to make things right with Caleb, the virtuous man that she'd let walk out her door months ago. She'd developed a plan to win him back—no—earn him back, but she hadn't had time to implement it fully yet. Would she even get that chance now? And how about her other projects—her special project?

What was going on around her? And why was her body locked? She concentrated on forcing her eyes open to try to explain the sounds and sensations. Eventually, somehow, her vision returned...in a curious way. Was her trouble seeing from her inability to open her eyelids fully...or—perhaps—she was looking *through* her eyelids? She couldn't determine which. But now that she somewhat had her vision back, she wished she hadn't. A new phenomenon lay before her, and she was puzzled. All the colors around her emitted...vibrations and sounds.

People stood at a distance all around her. Just above her, a paramedic was pumping on her chest. Hard. But why? And why couldn't Cotton feel it? Fear made her want to slurp in a deep breath, but she couldn't do that either. Another paramedic was pressing on Cotton's thigh really hard for some reason—so hard that the woman's face was red. She seemed panicked as she kept looking behind her and calling out something to the small crowd that had gathered. But what was she saying?

Cotton could see The Pumpkin Patch—a sea of artfully arranged pumpkins directly in front of her under the ancient live oak tree. It was the annual charity event for her childhood church. Miss Tree, otherwise known as Miss Theresa, who'd been her Sunday school teacher long ago when she'd been a child, was standing on the edge and had her back turned to her, blocking the scene from a child she had her arms around. Was it the small boy?

It *was* little Buddy—a paint-streaked little Buddy. *Thank God!*

Beside Miss Tree, some in the crowd had formed a small circle and were holding hands with their heads bowed. They must have been thanking God, too, for Buddy's safety.

Above Cotton little lights flickered intermittently in her peripheral vision, but as she tried to focus on them, they darted upwards. Maybe she had damaged her optic nerve in the fall. Great. Now, she was going to have to get her vision checked out, too. That would be another day she'd have to take off from the television station and another day she wouldn't get to work on her new project.

Cotton felt wet and warm under her head and under her thigh. And in some sense, she felt…red. Abruptly, they pushed her on her side, shoved something under her, and almost as abruptly, they let her fall onto it. If they'd just let her up, she might feel more…normal. But they kept pumping her chest. That was odd. Certainly, they could see that she was okay—well, almost. If they'd stop with all the rough handling.

She attempted to open her mouth to tell them she was fine, but it wouldn't cooperate. Something was amiss, as if her mouth had…locked. Maybe she'd wave them away. So she endeavored to lift her hand. It was locked, too. For some reason that she didn't understand, she knew she wasn't paralyzed. It was as if her body was...inert. She couldn't understand any of the sensations.

Then she saw the female paramedic who'd been pressing hard on her leg wrap it with something and cinch it...hard. Some of the white paint that Cotton and Buddy had fallen with was on the paramedic's uniform. With both hands free, she proceeded to move them over other parts of Cotton's body. Cotton supposed that the woman was trying to assess if anything else was wrong. The woman palpitated Cotton's arms and neck and then ribs and abdomen, and then she looked at her watch. The woman lifted up her head and looked at the man who was pumping on Cotton's chest. Surprise in the woman's eyes. She was opening her mouth like she was talking, but Cotton couldn't decipher the words. The red and white lights whirred about her, making a defining din. That was the only sound she heard—if the vibration could be called sound.

*Why do the lights make noise?*

Cotton wished she could look at her phone to see what time it was, but who knew where that had landed? It had probably cracked into a million little pieces—and just three weeks after she'd purchased it. See, she wasn't selfish as Caleb had once pronounced. She'd sacrificed her brand new, expensive iPhone to save Buddy.

Everything was going to be fine. Her body was probably just in shock, and she needed to snap out of it. She was not about to panic over a phone and a broken leg, as long as all else was okay. Everyone just needed to calm down. She was beginning to calm herself, and she was the one who should have been upset.

The paramedic pushing on her chest kept shaking his head as the woman who'd wrapped her leg kept tapping her watch, telling him something that apparently was time sensitive. She barked something at the crowd. Suddenly, everyone backed up, except the man pumping on her chest.

*Thump.* Her heart jolted with what had seemed like all the jagged lightening in all the dark skies that had ever rolled through her beloved Lowcountry. She felt a swoosh of warmth in her body. Though she couldn't hear through all the lights, she read the woman's lips. *She has a pulse.*

*Of course, I do.*

The large yellow leaves of the sycamore tree, burnt umber pine straw needles, and the narrow auburn-brown leaves from the willow oak nearby floated down all around her, They looked like a kaleidoscope of fall, making mottled leaf art on the ground near where she lay. In the distance, Miss Tree's Pumpkin Patch glowed orange. Cotton could smell the freshly hewn hay that covered the ground under the fall harvest of pumpkins.

From the corner of her eye, she saw Aaron Brown, her fellow reporter who was going to do the personal piece on her for the television station. Concern covered his usually unemotional face. Great. Now, her accident had become the day's story, instead of her connection to the community piece. She had called him away from the television station to help her film the segment. It was supposed to be a personal interest story—her personal interest story. One couldn't get more personal interest than this catastrophe. Hamilton Fox, her station manager, should be really pleased about this one. Surely, her chance at the anchor desk job would be increased now, especially if she could get up and do the reporting herself. That would show real dedication. And strength.

Imagine if she could simply stand up and say, "Reporting for WHLY, Channel Seven, this is Lawton Rivers."

If anyone could do it, she could.

She needed to get to Aaron before anyone else got to him to tell him that the people here—at the church—called her by her old nickname. She did *not* want that on videotape. Professionally, she was known as Lawton. Lawton Rivers. Cotton was what everyone in the town of Summerbrook, South Carolina, had been calling her since childhood, since she had been born with hair as white as cotton. It didn't help that—as a child—it was somehow easier for her to pronounce Cotton instead of Lawton. "Cotton Wibbers," she would say. Many of the older women would call her tow-headed when she was really young, but she didn't like that at all. She'd have to straighten out the moniker later at the station when he would edit the piece.

If only she'd been able to continue to apply her lifelong mantra to the situation at the station. *Ignorance is its own reward.* Cotton had feigned ignorance again and again to get out of chores and responsibilities throughout her life, but Hamilton had approached her numerous times, asking about what she was going to do for her personal promo piece that would act as one of his station advertisements. If only she'd been able to invoke her practiced ignorance, her fall would have never happened. But she was trying to change some of her old ways—her entitled ways.

Another problem cropped up into her head. When this would all be over, Cotton was probably going to have to find another little church to attend, not that she attended regularly, like she had when she was small. People, even churches, get weird over things like this—like they would worry that they might get sued or something. Cotton didn't want any more weirdness than she'd already felt after coming back to church to do this story—after nearly fifteen years of being away. She felt kind of bad for that—especially because she'd always loved attending church with her grandparents. She loved when she'd enter a new Sunday school class each fall as she grew a year older. The thing she liked best was learning all the Bible stories because Cotton was a storyteller at heart. It had been the thing that had made her join her high school newspaper staff and study journalism in college. She loved the art of storytelling—the angles, the characters, the crafting of the details in just the right order and tying it all up with a satisfying conclusion—a bow, if you will.

Autumn had always been special to her—a new season, a time for new school clothes, new school supplies and new classes. It had always excited her that she'd get to spend more time with her old friends. The five of them had been through school and through church together since they were children. Charlene, Jenna, April, Hanna and Cotton. Though they all still stayed in touch with one another, she'd fallen away from them over the years because of her career. For over a decade, she'd figured they'd forgotten about her. Recently, however, Cotton had called each to reconnect. It was all a part of her plan—to return to her softer self—to change.

But right now, she had more pressing concerns—even though

they seemed hard to corral. For some reason she felt like she'd taken on the weight of the parking lot, heavy, thick and dark. If she closed her eyes, she could rest a bit, so she did. Maybe this experience would be over soon. She felt the wetness from her head spread over the entire back of her body. Was that liquid the white paint that had fallen with her? Or something else? She didn't know, but then she felt the same cold feeling spread over her body, and it radiated inward from her fingertips, like the feeling in her head. All but the very center of her was chillingly cold. Something was very wrong.

She'd never felt so leaden before, nor had she ever been this tired before, so she gave into the thick, drowsy feeling that overtook her body. A little rest might reset things.

⁜

When she finally opened her eyes again, no one was there. She then realized that the cold had intensified throughout her body, replacing the nausea that had been in her tummy. Cold rags had always helped her overcome nausea when she was sick, but no one had offered them when she had needed them earlier. Thank goodness that sensation had disappeared.

Something more important had changed, though. This time, she was able to move her head. From behind her, she heard the sound of water approaching, splashing off the asphalt, so she turned to see Mr. Earnest, her grandfather's old friend, coming at her with a garden hose. What the heck. How dare he!

Even though her clothes were still covered in white paint, she didn't want them splattered with cold water, too.

She immediately got up in a most awkward crab-like way,

turned and sort of scampered toward the tree that seemed alive with the golden colors of fall. Good. All her body parts worked. Nothing was broken, like she'd thought. But shouldn't the paramedics have taken her to the hospital—to get her checked out? All of her, inside and out? Who would just leave someone to rest on the ground after a fall like that—even if they did determine that she was okay?

"Mr. Earnest," she called out. But he couldn't hear over the splashing water, spilling onto the asphalt.

Her legs were a little weak, and she still felt light-headed, so she sat under the sycamore tree and watched the older man feverously attack the parking spot. All his attention was focused on the dark pavement—more than it had ever been on that rail he had been sanding earlier when they were all working on the church building. What was he washing with so much commitment? A streetlight flickered and glittered in the waning light, making little glares twinkle down around the pole. Her vantage point under the tree was not good, and the shade it cast with the company of the heavy setting sun had painted red shadows everywhere. She stood up to get a better look.

The water hit the pavement hard, and the red shadows lifted into the air, along with a few large yellow leaves. Only, those were not exactly shadows. They were crimson sprays.

And then she realized the loose sprays were splashes of blood—her blood.

12

# CHAPTER TWO

## Before the Fall

Cotton had never truly fainted before, but this was what she'd always imagined it would feel like—an irresistible sinking of consciousness and encroaching darkness.

*Thump.* She woke suddenly. She didn't know how long she'd been out, but when she realized her surroundings again, she was even more confused.

She was painting the church, just like she'd been earlier in the day.

But what about the fall? Had she simply remembered some nightmare she'd had the night before? No. She didn't think so. Because something else was different.

*Something really peculiar is going on. And the light is...different.*

She put down her paintbrush and stared at her surroundings. What was up with the iridescent light? If it were possible, the light was even brighter than she'd noticed earlier. And more than that. There were no shadows. Everything was illuminated. From above and somehow from below.

An overpowering sense of *deja vu* enveloped Cotton. Maybe this would be a way of changing what she'd thought had happened. Or maybe the fall had never happened in the first place. Maybe her earlier remembrance was some sort of...warning. She'd heard of people—especially at churches—having premonitions or prophecies.

*What is going on here?*

Then it all came flooding back in the strange shadow-less light.

⁂

Her station manager had dictated that all the personalities in front of the cameras get involved in the community in some personal way, hopefully endearing each personality to the station's viewers. Everyone would have to do pieces on their public contributions, ideally from the community of her youth. This would look good on film, right? *Local television star goes back to hometown church to help restore building in preparation for their annual Pumpkin Patch Carnival.* She could see the promo now with all the fall colors and the pumpkins. All that would look great on camera. Though she'd resisted helping at first because she was busy with her regular duties and with planning a special reporting series, this just may help out with getting that anchor desk job that she'd wanted for years, too. At the least, it couldn't hurt. At first, she had evaded the station manager because she thought the task tedious and boring…and it required manual labor—something Cotton had not been used to doing. Ever.

But her ideas about it changed after Caleb had left, and she found herself utterly alone. She had a lot of thinking to do, so she did some reassessing of her life. Things in her life needed transformation. One by one, she reconnected with her friends from school, and she worked tirelessly on a charitable project that would bring some needed assistance to children in crisis in the Lowcountry. It was the first time she'd been truly excited about a project in a very long time. And it wasn't going to hurt that she'd garner some notoriety and brownie points at the station, too. Two birds with one stone, right?

Going back to this little church seemed to be a step in the right direction, as well. She simply needed to keep herself on task—on this uncreative, pedantic task of painting the ancient little tabby church she'd attended with her grandparents and learned about Jesus. She had her doubts now that she was actually doing physical work because she didn't feel so well. Yes, she'd been feeling out of sorts lately. Yes, the sun shone brightly, making her feel excessively warm. And, yes, she was not physically in the best shape of her life, but she'd promised herself to add additional cardio to her workout when she could get some of her work off her plate.

While she slapped paint on the hard, stone-like surface, she waffled between calling in the crew for the story and coming up with her own story to get herself off the hook for this manual labor. She really didn't feel like herself. If she chose the first, she needed to get a little more paint on her clothes and body. The small splats just weren't enough to show up on camera. It was painful, but she dipped her brush into the can of paint, held it at her shoulders and let it drip down her red Ralph Lauren t-shirt. That ought to do it. It was a small sacrifice for a great photo opportunity. She could order another later and—possibly—even claim it on her expense account.

Doing a story about her helping her old church was challenging in many areas. The church she'd left long ago needed more updating than just a paint job. It operated like it had since before most of the Lowcountry had even been settled. It definitely did not keep up with progress. It was a risky career move, aligning herself with such an old-fashioned group as they, but she had a knack for telling a story so that it highlighted the good and left out the…culturally insensitive stuff. In her field, image was everything. And facts. She could never forget about facts. But they could be…manipulated. Of course, she'd highlight the Pumpkin Patch, the event that would bring in thousands of dollars to the little church that would be spent on outreach and charities in the local community. Miss Tree would be happy about that.

Cotton looked up at the clear skies and the great light—the unusually great, lustrous light. This promo piece needed to be shot. And working at the church imported an additional benefit—it would prove Caleb wrong, and he might even be proud of her—when he found out about it.

The leaves shimmered on the willow oak tree about thirty feet away, but when she looked underneath it, no shade was to be found. The same was true for the Pumpkin Patch under the expansive old oak.

*That is exceeding odd. The light on this amazing day is*

*nothing like she'd ever seen before. It was almost as if she is watching a...a memory that is enlightened.*

*Thump.* Something had hit her back. She saw a soccer ball roll away from her. A small boy of about five or six put up his hand, squinted at her in the most adorable way and said, "Sorry."

She knew him from earlier—during the tumble she had somehow already taken—but was watching again. It was Buddy. But she also realized it was *supposed* to be the first time she'd ever *met* the little boy.

*How is that? Am I re-living this entire day—in this unusual light?*

"No harm done," Cotton said. She watched as Buddy ran toward his friends. "Children are cute...in an arcane sort of way," her mother had said so many times. So many years ago. Her mother had never planned to be a grandmother. And Cotton really never had a reason to make her one, and then it was too late—for many reasons.

"You kids had better get out of here before Miss Theresa comes," called Mr. Earnest, who had been sanding the rails on the steps, his hands as wrinkled and as abused as the sandpaper he was holding. "Buddy, don't kick the ball toward the church again."

"Yes, sir," said the little boy whose eyes were as blue as the cerulean sky above him. His beige sweater fit a little too tight, and his blond hair had grown a little too shaggy.

Cotton felt kind of bad for him. A little neglected. Or a little poor. She had never been either. She had been the centers of her parents' and grandparents' universes. She owned legions of fancy little smocked dresses and matching bows when she was small. When she was a bit older, she took all the right lessons, dance, piano, manners. Her mother, especially, took great joy, planning out most parts of Cotton's life—that is until she graduated college and got her first job. Then, one weekend, everything was irrevocably altered.

Her parents had been on one of her father's friend's yachts in the Charleston Harbor, partying, and, somehow, her mother had fallen off during the night, after she had gone above deck for another drink while everyone had been sleeping. No one had known until the next day. They didn't find her body for three days. Nothing was ever the same after that—especially Cotton's father. It was as if he was…ashamed of what had happened, like it was all his fault. He was a professor of English at a local college, and his poetry and his "musings," as he would call them, took a somber, solitary turn.

Her mother would never be a grandmother, even if Cotton had wanted her to be.

Cotton turned her attention back to the white paint and wished she'd brought her sunglasses. *Deja vu? Again?*

That was one of the peculiarities of autumn she'd liked best in the Lowcountry. The sun was far more brilliant than the season it was ushering in felt.

A note of burning leaves whirred about her and then was gone. That was also one of her favorite things about fall. Fires and leaves. Smoke and pine straw. At that moment, one of the huge yellow leaves from the sycamore tree floated past her on a light breeze, and at the same time she caught the scent of the tea olive trees that were growing all about the church yard.

*The same as before.*

The gleaming white on the stone-like façade seemed to wave, and she thought she saw a flicker of light glisten or move off it. The whole thing made her a little off balance, so she paused to get her bearings. Why couldn't she have taken the time for some breakfast this morning? Because she wasn't a breakfast kind of girl—usually. Obviously, she had needed something in her stomach since she was doing actual physical labor. Anyway, she had been working on her pet project, like she did every spare moment lately when she wasn't at the station. One big thing still bothered her about it. She couldn't come up with a good name for the children's project or the planned awards ceremony that would accompany the project. Usually, she was really good at putting a name to things like that, but every time she tried, she created great, big stink bomb names—Kids in Crisis Series, but who'd want to be associated with a name like that? The Orphan Awards. Yuck. Going It Alone segments. Not.

But the whole project was in its infancy, and it wasn't ready for her big reveal. When she'd lie awake in bed at night, the whole thing made it seem worth giving up her Saturdays. This little church project was a quickie story that could be done in an afternoon and would satisfy Hamilton Fox. For now. The big project, however, would be ongoing and would be her big stamp upon her community and her career—and Caleb—eventually. And who knew who else—maybe even little Buddy, if he qualified.

*The eerie light still surrounded her.*

It was as if the day was on repeat—kind of like that old

movie. What was it? Oh, *Groundhog Day*. Yeah, it was her very own *Groundhog Day*. All this had already happened—before she had fallen from the ladder.

She looked back at the children playing, kicking the soccer ball toward all the things they shouldn't have—especially the Pumpkin Patch. Children. Seemed like they'd never even been a real *possibility* for her, and ultimately, that had given her the idea for her big service project. During her career, she'd reported on enough kids, with their proud parents beaming beside them for whatever laudable thing they'd done. She sometimes wondered what that might feel like—being proud of someone else—some little person she had been responsible for or had created. Her mother had certainly experienced that feeling with her.

Cotton and Amanda Winningham, a woman she'd met while doing an investigative story about the Department of Social Services, were discussing some of the agency's staffing issues after a child had gone missing while in foster care—only to turn up later at a friend's house. During the interview Amanda kept redirecting the discussion toward the amazing things children in her care were achieving—honor roll, college, volunteering, art, overcoming physical and emotional disabilities. It was then that Cotton conceptualized a series of stories on each achievement and then throwing a huge awards program at the end of the year for kids who didn't have parents to beam at their sides over their accomplishments. Cotton eventually bought two binders to help her organize—one for the children's project, and one was for something she hadn't wanted to address…quite yet…but eventually would because the empty notebook would be a constant reminder. Notebooks were her organizational superpower. She was gathering names and ideas for the pieces and was writing grants with Amanda, who was quickly becoming a friend, so they'd have money for the awards and scholarships. For the first few months as she worked on the project, Cotton thought that it was as close as she'd ever get to being proud of her own children.

When she had been a cub reporter in Greenville, South Carolina, her insides had stopped working like they should have, and she gave up the little idea about having a family her grandmother had placed there when she was so young. Her initial thought was that little project would have to suffice. But ideas evolve, and things don't always stay the same.

Cotton moved down a rung on her four-foot step-ladder and brushed some more paint on the little tabby church. Three steps were about as high as she would climb. Her fear of heights had always stopped her with a gut punch to her belly. Falling out of that live oak tree when she was small had affected her abilities and desires to do many things—and it had steeled other things in her. It had been her first experience with time seeming to stop. Immediately after her childhood fall, she had lain under that tree, concentrating on the twisted limbs and trembling leaves for what seemed like seconds and hours at the same time, struggling to breathe, unable to call out and listening to the wind rustle through the massive tree above her. In those moments, she determined that she was going to live, that she was going to achieve great things, if she didn't die.

Later, when she had healed, she would return to stand under that old tree, over and over, to trace that steely determination again. That tree was a touchstone for her. Suddenly, a different scene flashed in her head—another horrendous experience under another old tree that had caused time to freeze. But she quickly blocked that buried nightmare. For some reason, trees had always acted like sentinels in her life—for good—and for evil.

*The light around her glowed.*

Her friend, Charlene Hughes, climbed down from the scaffolding she was working from and walked over. "Cotton, I can't tell you how much we appreciate you helping us today—especially since my babysitter bailed and Aiken had to stay home."

"Not a problem. I'm glad I didn't have to work my reporter beat this weekend," Cotton said as she picked up more paint on her brush. When she lifted it, more paint drizzled on her red designer t-shirt. That was a good thing. The paint would show up even more on camera.

"You're a lifesaver. Now, I just have to get the rest of our high school crew to pitch in at some point," Charlene said. "Even if they came out to simply support the Pumpkin Patch Carnival. I'm bringing my children, and I'd love for you all to meet them. They're amazing." Charlene chuckled. "Hey, remember when we all used to meet up at the Pumpkin Patch Carnival as kids. We'd run and hide from one another between the piles of pumpkins under that same old tree." She glanced at the tree and grinned like she had when she was small. "We've got to get the whole gang together again. We've all missed you."

Cotton smiled. "I hope so. It's been too long since I've seen them. If we can't get them to come to the carnival, maybe we can do lunch or something." From the corner of her eye, she sensed lights twinkling above her, but when she gazed up, they were gone.

*What's up with this crazy light?*

Charlene nodded. "Absolutely," she said as she walked over to the two guys on saw duty.

The thought of lunch, however, made Cotton's stomach feel weird and warm, and it made her nauseous. Paint fumes always made her feel that way, too. She tried to put the sensation out of her mind, like she had before because she had more important things to think about—her project, her promo piece and, one day, patching things with Caleb—the amazingly unselfish man she had fallen in love with more than she'd even realized—if she still had a chance with him. But Cotton had lots of hope because she had lots of confidence. She could accomplish anything...almost. Her mother had drilled that into Cotton's very fiber.

Her very fiber was growing weary, however, because this whole painting thing was not going to win her an Edward R. Murrow Award, no matter how much she got involved with the community. Her life was overly filled with reporting, telling human interest stories and broadcasting...oh, and occasionally shopping.

When she was young, like the kids kicking the ball, she didn't even know who Edward R. Murrow was, much less what a communications degree was. And had never cared about shopping, even though her mother had been a professional at it. Life had changed. Life had changed her. For the worse, she'd been told. But she was in the process of redeeming herself and repairing all that. Today was a step toward her...redemption.

*Clang.* She heard aluminum echoing against itself. She shuddered and looked up at the tall ladder that was a few feet away. She stiffened at the height of it, and her stomach lurched again. It didn't take much to remind her of her childhood fall out of her backyard tree.

Mr. Homer startled at the movement of the ladder and grabbed the fascia to steady himself. A younger man should have climbed that ladder, but there were none of those helping today, just her, Charlene and the old men…and the older women, cooking inside the fellowship hall.

*Thump. Wait. Aren't I supposed to be on that ladder?*

Reality and nightmare blurred, yet she was drawn into all that was going on around her in the odd light. She seemed both participant and observer. But why were things so different this time?

Mr. Homer looked down at the parking lot from nearly twenty feet above. "You guys were told to go play on the athletic field over there," he said, pointing. "If that ball had landed in my bucket of paint up here, Miss Theresa would paint the backs of your pants 'til y'all looked like a zebra and walked like a sloth."

When Cotton and the other children were small, they had trouble saying Miss Theresa, so Miss Tree was the name that had stuck. Hearing the older adults still call her by her real name was jolting for her. The nickname they came up with was apropos because Miss Tree was as immovable as the huge oak under which she set up the Pumpkin Patch each year. Not only was she the pumpkin tsar, she was the enforcer, and the kids had better listen to her commands. Or else. It would take a few years yet for them to learn that Miss Tree was fueled by her love for Jesus and her compassion for them.

A little boy of about nine spoke up. "It's wet out there, and we can kick the ball farther on the pavement."

The two men who were cutting boards for Charlene to replace the rotten sills had stopped what they were doing, as well, to look at and listen to all the commotion. Cotton leaned her head back as a temperate breeze swept over her face. She shivered, though, trying to shake the confusion.

*And the shadow-less light that engulfed her.*

Then Miss Tree hobbled through the door of the fellowship hall. "Hey, listen to what you've been told, or there won't be story time and dessert after lunch today," she yelled. "You could hurt someone with that ball. And if you guys get near my pumpkins, I'll make pumpkin pies out of you."

"Yes, ma'am," a girl of about ten called back. "We'll listen. We want to finish hearing about that guy with the lions."

"And I've made lion cupcakes for all the good listeners who can answer my questions after our lesson," Miss Tree said.

"Yaaaayyy!" came the cheers from the kids.

Miss Tree raised her hand. "Who can recite our bible verse from last week?"

One of the older girls yelled the answer, like Miss Tree apparently wanted, but without raising her arm. "So Daniel was taken up out of the den, and no manner of hurt was found upon him, because he believed in his God. Daniel Chapter Six, Verse twenty-three."

The words and the citation came out so quickly that Cotton could barely understand. All those recitations of chapters and verses had always turned her off. Probably because she was never a fan of math and numbers and probably because—to her—the numbers always detracted from the meat of the story. Cotton was a storyteller, not a mathematician.

Miss Tree and the children clapped at the rapid-fire recitation.

"Rilla, you get an extra cupcake."

"Do we get a story and cupcakes, Miss Theresa?" asked Mr. Fred, one of the old men working with the table saw.

Miss Tree turned and threw up her hand to say she'd had enough. As soon as she brought her old knees to cobble a walk, she wobbled back into the fellowship hall, certain that her authority had been heeded and apparently too exhausted to double-check. The group of young athletes continued to kick around the soccer ball on the pavement between the athletic field and the Pumpkin Patch, and the men went back to work.

The saw whirred, and Charlene climbed the scaffolding again with her contractor's belt and the newly-cut board. Cotton admired the way Charlene handled power tools and wood. They were not Cotton's cup of tea, but admirable nonetheless.

Mr. Earnest said, "Hey, Cotton, do you remember that joke your grandfather used to tell about where the lion lived—every time he heard about Daniel?"

The children were close and stopped to listen.

Of course, she did. "Yes, Mr. Earnest, the lion lived on Mane Street."

All the men laughed. She could tell that some of the younger kids didn't get it.

One of the older kids said, "That's lame. You must mean Lame Street." The older kids giggled.

"Yeah, I used to love to go fishing with Oscar. We'd sit in that old boat of his, and he would tell jokes practically the whole time. No matter what was going on around us or what we were talking about, he'd find a way to slip in a joke that pertained to it. My face hurt by the end of the day. He'd pull the fish in one after another until he'd reached his limit—the whole time, telling those tired, old jokes. And after he'd reached his limit, he'd pull out his old pocketknife and some piece of wood he'd had stored in his tackle box, and he'd start whittling." Mr. Earnest chuckled at the remembrance.

Cotton remembered Poppy carving little animals from wood for her. She'd had an entire menagerie that she'd displayed upon her dresser in her bedroom at home—until she'd gone off to college. She remembered her grandfather always smelling of wood…and coffee. Then a sad memory—one that she'd tried hard to put out of her mind. Upon her first visit home from Clemson University, she walked into her room, and they were gone. Her mother had thrown them all away—all the dear little animals that had become oiled with love from her hands were gone. Her mother had turned her familiar childhood room into a sophisticated space, and—in her mother's words—"for her sophisticated daughter."

Cotton had always felt caught between two worlds, both filled with people who loved her, both filled with entirely different expectations.

Charlene stopped nailing the piece of wood on the window casing upon which she was hammering. "I still have my little lamb that Mr. Oscar carved for me when he was working with my Pa-pa on a project. I love that little thing. I let my children play with it sometimes, but they know to be careful with it because it is very special to me." She went back to tapping a nail.

Oh, if only Cotton had one of her own now. She would treasure it even more than she had as a child.

Mr. Earnest continued, "I hardly ever caught a thing when I went fishing with him." He chuckled and pointed skyward. "I bet he's up there fishing and telling jokes to anyone who'd listen."

Cotton doubted that, but then again, she didn't spend much time thinking about stuff like that because…well, he was gone…and she had been so busy with her career.

"I hardly caught fish with him, either," said Mr. Vern, one of the old men working on the step rails. "I don't know how he even pulled them off the hooks near the end—or how he carved those little animals of his. His old eyes were so covered by those cataracts. But no. He said he'd never let one of those teenaged doctors put a knife in his eye," said Mr. Vern, chuckling at the memory. "I don't know how he kept whittling, but he did. I suppose he just felt the carvings in the wood." He paused. "Did he ever tell you the one about how Lake Marion and Lake Moultrie became friends?"

Mr. Earnest said, "No, but I bet I'm gonna hear it now."

Mr. Vern chuckled, even before he told the punch line. "They kept waving at each other when it was windy."

Moans erupted all around. Cotton just smiled. Her grandfather was infamous for his corny jokes. She'd give anything to hear him tell one again. She wouldn't roll her eyes this time, if she ever had that chance again. But her grandparents had passed when she was in high school, her grandmother, her freshman year, and her grandfather, the year after.

Cotton loved hearing the old stories about her Poppy. She continued to break—to take a few deep breaths, while absorbing the stories about her grandfather and to watch the smallest boy play soccer. *Again. Only in the strange light this time. Why was she reliving what happened before she fell?*

Buddy seemed shy and reticent to steal the ball as the others did boldly. She remembered being wary in school at first, and look at her now—prancing around in front of a camera all the time with her platinum blond hair and her red high heels with matching soles. With her mother's help, she grew out of her bashfulness and grew confident. He'll probably grow out of his shyness, too. She had a feeling.

A tall boy kicked the ball hard, and it went sideways. "Hey, Buddy, get the ball from under the car. You're the littlest," the older boy called out.

She almost felt like interfering, but no, she wouldn't. The children were none of her business. Her mother had wanted to see to that fact during Cotton's first fall semester at Clemson University. But she couldn't entirely blame her lack of children on her mother, now, could she? After all that had happened afterwards.

Cotton gingerly stepped to the ground, carrying her bucket, allowing more paint to drip onto her red t-shirt and jeans. She wiped her hands on a rag she had draped on the handle of her step-ladder, walked a few feet away, took out her new cell phone from her back pocket and checked the time. One o'clock. Should she call the crew? Why not? She was sufficiently covered in paint now, so that would look good on camera. She pressed the numbers, and listened to it ring.

"Channel Seven, Aaron Brown speaking."

In a low voice, she said, "Hey, Aaron. Lawton here." She hadn't yet thought about how she was going to soften the blow of everyone calling her Cotton here at her old church. She would pull him to the side when he would arrive and then try to explain. "You know that project Hamilton's all jacked about?"

"Of course. That's all he talks about. He's fulfilling some station mandate thing from the owners," Aaron said.

"Well, I'm at the Summerbrook Christian Church, doing my time. You got a crew free?" she asked, setting down her brush.

"Yeah, mine. And absolutely nothing is going on downtown. You want us to come?"

"That would be awesome. We've got some great sunshine out here today. I'm painting my childhood church, and they're getting ready for a fall carnival," she said, looking toward the sky to check on the light for the cameras.

"Okay, great. That'll look good on film. We'll be there in under an hour."

"Perfect." She walked back to her short ladder.

After she put her phone away, and dipped her brush back into the can of paint, she began to slap it on the building again. She and Charlene had been the only people there under forty on the work detail. Everyone else had left behind their active years and productivity and brought with them their limps, and their canes, and their arthritis and their gray hair to the job. The church needed healthy people who worked out and had enthusiasm for doing physical labor. Charlene was truly the only one that fit in that category today.

Cotton was merely there because she saw an opportunity—a couple, in fact. Inhaling a deep breath, she shook off the impatience she felt creep up in her. She needed to work on her attitude, as well as her life. She inhaled to breathe her impatience away. She needed to stop being so selfish, and this project was great practice. And she needed to film a promo spot. This was a step toward achieving those objectives and connecting with her childhood friend. She could accomplish all those things at once. A sprig of satisfaction sprang up in her.

*In the strange light. In the reliving of what she'd already lived...or dreamed. Maybe this is the way she could change the dream.*

Change. Change was what Caleb had told her she'd needed. Just before he'd walked out on her, he turned and said, "I've never met someone so self-absorbed and shallow in my entire life."

The accusations struck a secret chord deep inside her when he'd indicted her. She knew she had been all that...and more. How did she ever get to that place in her life? Confused about where she was going. What she wanted out of life. With a job that devoured all her free time. And she was protective with the little time she had left over from her career.

*Slowly.* That was the answer to how she had gotten here. Mostly, her mother had been her greatest encourager...enabler. Cotton had been the center of her mother's life, her greatest accomplishment. Charlotte Rivers had lived vicariously through her daughter, and Cotton felt she could do no wrong. Well, until her mother had died. Unfortunately, she had no other fans, unless one counted those who'd become enamored with her TV personality, the smart and sassy reporter who dressed to the nines in red heels and red lipstick. Her polished image was rather hard to accomplish—to procure designer outfits that always went with her signature red heels. She especially liked wearing a touch of leopard print with the heels. To Cotton, it showed flare. It had all been her mother's idea.

Miss Tree came back, stood in the door of the fellowship hall and called, "Lunch is ready." With her hands on her hips, she stared at the young soccer players on the border of the parking lot and the lawn on which she had told them to play. A light breeze blew her soft gray curls around. Cotton wondered if the children would come in to face the church's judge and jury to get reprimanded again. Miss Tree had a formidable look on her face.

Charlene and the men unplugged their power tools, brushed off the flakey sawdust and headed slowly toward Miss Tree.

"Didn't I tell you guys to play on the field?" Miss Tree yelled again at the kids. Her voice was harsh to those who didn't really know her, but to those who did, they knew her heart was a marshmallow.

"We are. Sort of," a young girl in a pink sweatshirt called out.

"Well, you can't sort of get into heaven or sort of eat lunch. Do it now, or I'll call your parents to come pick you up early. The athletic field is an extra-credit privilege. You're actually here to listen to Bible stories and to eat a healthy lunch." Sternness shot from her voice. Miss Tree had once been a seventh-grade teacher and still behaved as such. They don't make them any tougher. Or more compassionate.

"Yes, Ma'am," another boy of about twelve called out. He tucked the soccer ball under his arm. "We just need to make one more point."

She shook her head and turned to Cotton. "Come in and get some lunch" she said, relaxing her arms by her side. "I've made your favorite from when you were a little girl. Apple pie."

Cotton felt her eyes widen. She couldn't believe it. She'd thought that everyone who knew that apple pie was her favorite had left her. "Let me get this last section completed, okay? I'd love some pie." Even though her figure for the camera wouldn't want the extra weight of it. A tiny sliver couldn't hurt—if she could stomach it.

"I thought you'd like the pie. I even made it with honey crisp apples. I can't tell you how much we appreciate how you're helping us. Thanks for volunteering," Miss Tree said.

"Oh, it's the least I can do," Cotton said, still marveling that Miss Tree could remember that honey crisps had been her favorite, too. "I'm nearly finished with this corner."

Miss Tree nodded and yelled toward the children. "Lunch is now. Come wash up." She turned and walked inside.

This was going to make a decent story, and this might even help her to show Caleb that she was serious—about helping others, like he did. She appeared selfless giving up her Saturday, right? Maybe he'd see the piece if they ran it after the news tonight.

She had been selfless once, as a child. She imagined she could be again. With practice. If she tried really hard. It had simply been a long time, but she knew she had it in her.

All the adults were inside, and the kids continued to disobey Miss Tree. Cotton, determined to finish painting the last section, heard the ball hit the ladder once again, but her attention stayed on her paintbrush and getting the white paint into the rough surfaces. If she was going to do something, she was going to do it well—school, reporting, painting.

One of the girls called out, "Go get the ball, Buddy."

Cotton picked up even more paint on the brush and continued to cover the last area by the steps in bright white. The wet paint shone lustrously in the fall sun, and then a flash of light darted left at the edge of her vision. She closed her eyes for a moment. The paint combined with the sun was the only reason she'd been confused earlier. Right? She saw reddish-pink flickers of light behind her lids, and her eyes felt hot.

Suddenly, one of the kids shrieked a blood-curdling scream, and Cotton glanced behind her to find all the children looking up. At the top of the tall ladder was little Buddy, his right arm wrapped around the ball, which was dripping white paint. He was precariously hanging on with his left.

*Everything is repeating itself!*

Cotton didn't think. *Again.* She didn't have time to think. *Again.* She dropped the paint brush in her hand and sprang up the ladder as fast as she could without experiencing the kick in her gut that had always kept her from heights. The metal made clinking sounds as she took each rung. Her head spun. She shouldn't be doing this. *Again.*

She looked down at the kids. "Go for help!" she yelled. One of the older girls dashed away. The other kids looked frozen. Like her. But she had a few more steps to take before she could reach Buddy.

*The shadow-less light made her feel off balance. Again. Wait. Is she really doing this again?*

But she was caught up in it all, and couldn't think—shouldn't think—and she couldn't really back down now. Could she? Little Buddy could die. This was an emergency!

The kids below continued to scream. She heard an "Oh, my God," come from somewhere down below as she took the final step. She grabbed Buddy's leg that was now hanging and pulled it onto the ladder.

Something bright and sparkling—a rung above her head caught her eye. This was no time to be distracted. "Hold on tight," she said. She pulled the body of the little boy toward the ladder. He was safely between her arms, but everything got slippery and white with paint. *Oh, no.*

*This couldn't be happening again. She'd be careful so it wouldn't. Holding on with all her might, she was not going to move. Surely that would stop the chain of events that had happened earlier. She breathed in hard to fill her lungs to yell for help. They'd be saved by some of the men inside, and this whole nightmare on repeat would end. They'd be safe.*

And then she felt it. Something shifted. Hard.

She heard the metal rattle, almost echoing.

Buddy screamed.

One of her feet slipped and pushed against the ladder that was leaning hard to the right, and her other foot got tangled in a rung, and it seemed to her that they were leaning left. "Don't let go, Buddy," she said slowly in the strange light. She stiffened and braced the little boy between her arms because she knew this couldn't possibly turn out well.

*This is how everything had started.*

# CHAPTER THREE

## Touching Light

Suddenly Cotton was under the silent sycamore tree again, where she'd scampered to in order to avoid Mr. Earnest spraying her with the cold water. The little twigs on the ground poked at her legs, but they only caused numbness where they stuck. The weird light had disappeared, and things had shadows once again. Only a twinkle or two twitched in her peripheral vision.

Everything could be explained if she put her mind to it. She could always do that...because she was a journalist. No matter what had ever happened, she could figure out a way to make it make sense, to make it go her way—turn it into a proper news story with facts and photos.

That was the job of a journalist, and she had learned her craft well at journalism school. If someone had an unusual response to her questions, or if they filled it with their feelings and opinions, well, Cotton devised a way to make them answer her questions directly and would then edit the interview to still get her desired result, according to the angle she chose. She was really good at what she did. And she never allowed anything to get in the way.

And Caleb could call her self-absorbed for that, but she was the one with the brand-new BMW and the condo on the golf course—even though she had never played golf. Because she'd never had time.

She looked around the empty parking lot. Hey, where was that fancy car of hers? The parking lot was completely empty—except for one old sedan.

Her BMW and all of those other things were extraneous right now because the problem she faced at this moment was seemingly insurmountable. She had to figure out a way to get from here to home without her car. Who in the world could have moved it? She reached into her pocket. Her keys had been removed. Darn. Who would do something like that? It must have been when she had her eyes closed and took that short rest.

As an old pickup passed on the road, she tried to follow it with her eyes, but as she did, little sparkles of light twitched around the borders of her vision. "Hard Day's Night," an old Beatles tune, blared and then disappeared as the truck drove away. She hated the Beatles music, but that was attached to a story that she'd worked hard to forget about long ago. She had more pressing matters at hand.

Surely, Mr. Earnest could help. Her legs were still wieldy and wobbly, so she called out, sort of, she thought. She wasn't sure he'd heard her over the spray. She'd wait until he'd finished to get him to help. People who lost a lot of blood were supposed to be weak, and there was still a huge pool of blood on that pavement. She'd had a bloody nose when she'd tripped on the sidewalk at school once, and she'd thought that was a lot of blood, but it didn't compare to the scene in front of her.

It was still inconceivable to her that no one considered taking her to the hospital earlier. The weary weakness came upon her like lead once again, like it had before. The little lights twinkled as her eyelids became heavy. She'd rest and close her eyes for just a little while—until she would hear the hose go quiet. Maybe then she could figure something out—figure out a way to get home...or, perhaps, even to the hospital.

⚜

Suddenly, the silence and stillness woke her. She struggled to sit up but had great difficulty. Everything was strangely stagnant, no people, no sounds. The wet weight of the fragrance from the tea olive was overpowering. The twilight was wrapping around her like a heavy fog.

In the periphery, she thought she caught three little flashes of light. This time, they seemed almost...tangible, tamable, touchable. But each time she turned her head toward them, they'd disappear. Probably a result of the fall. She'd make the appointment for the optometrist on Monday.

For a moment, she wasn't even sure she was still at the church. She straightened herself and propped her back against the trunk of the sycamore giant. She glanced around. Yep. She was still there, but she felt like she weighed a thousand pounds. What was up with all the strange sensations? She'd been taught to take note of observable facts to construct a news story; however, there weren't many of them to be found. In their stead were impressions, thoughts, feelings, vibrations and senses.

Just then, the lone car at the end of the parking lot rumbled. She tried to lift her hand to Mr. Earnest, but he couldn't see her. He backed out of his spot, pulled up to the road, waited for a car to pass and then pulled out onto the street and disappeared. Mr. Earnest was gone. That was an observable fact. This was the last straw. So, these are her circumstances, and this is the place she'd landed by being selfless. Could she ever be selfless and help this church and any of its members ever again? It had been a struggle in the first place, but she'd been determined to help them, even though in the process she was helping herself.

She felt completely helpless in the old churchyard. No one was there for her like they had always been in the past, waiting, even if she didn't need them. She was glad—at least—the church's little graveyard was on the other side of the tabby sanctuary. In that solitary garden of stones were her parents' and grandparents' overgrown graves—the ones that she'd been planning to visit for some time now. Her dear family would help if they could, of course. In some strange way, she felt closer to them here. Somehow, it was more than simply physical proximity. It felt like time had somehow wrapped itself back around her and she thought she might somehow be able to see them if she could walk around to the other side of the building. How foolish! She really must have taken a serious hit to her head.

Reality hit her as she felt a gut punch to her stomach. Guilt flooded her insides and covered her in a tight cocoon. With all that her parents and grandparents had done for her, she was sitting here looking for more. Why hadn't she done more for them—before they died—and after?

Her thoughts also wrapped around to the past and to Caleb.

After he had left her the night they'd argued, she'd toyed with the idea of rejoining the little church her grandmother had taken her to years ago—the little church where she had given her heart to Jesus when she was so young. She could hardly remember that little girl any longer.

Caleb's accusations about her self-centeredness had nibbled away at her consciousness and had exposed something raw and thorny. But this was as close as she had tangibly gotten so far to changing her life in some meaningful way. Painting the church…and doing this story. But she knew this was a place that she could help people and do good work for the community. That was her goal. She wished, however, that she felt something more—more than just accomplishing a goal. A desire maybe?

Somewhere inside, she knew that coming back to this church where people once knew a childhood version of herself wasn't going to be the complete answer to her…loneliness. She'd abandoned all hopes of close friendships long ago in lieu of her career. Everything had been sacrificed to her profession—family, love, children, and now she had no one to even call, if she'd even had a cell phone. It made her want to repair the damage with Caleb all the more, but she still had a lot of work to do on that front for him to see her. She so wanted to feel sincere and real.

The sensation of aloneness was dense and smelled like…dust, and the darkness smelled a little like…fear.

When she got her bearings, she'd try to walk, but that weighty feeling was growing again. Her arms felt like the limbs of the solid sycamore tree above her, and her legs felt like the trunk that had been planted for a hundred years. Her lashes pulled her lids down, so she helplessly gave into the sensation once again. She'd done some of her best figuring when she used to close her eyes as a child under that old live oak in her backyard where she used to play with the menagerie her grandfather had carved for her. Her imagination would create all sorts of silly scenarios with her little friends, and when she allowed it, her little spirit and heart would feel and see the rest of the world through them. The entire world seemed to make complete sense to her under that crotchety old tree.

There had to be a solution to make sense of her current situation, as well, even though she was under a different tree, and even though she was older and more educated. If there was ever a time to be self-absorbed and selfish, this was it. *Think, Cotton, think.* But her mind didn't work like it had earlier in the day, like a journalist. In addition to her loss of blood, she was growing ever more certain that she may have a concussion. She'd done an investigative story on concussions in high school sports last year. Now, she had first-hand knowledge of a head injury. She'd have to do a follow-up story—if she ever got her life back in order—which she would...because she had no other choice.

As she lingered, time seemed alien and friend alike as she rested under the oppression of the October tree as the occasional yellow leaf floated down around her. It was growing cooler now that the sun had set, much cooler, but somehow the temperature she sensed wasn't the temperature she…felt. The sensations of cold and warm she'd experienced earlier were somehow a mere memory. That twenty-foot fall from the eves of the church must have caused more trauma than the others had assessed. Cotton knew she had always come off to others as perfection on the outside. She'd gotten really good at faking that she was okay—in every type of scenario. If only she could have told the paramedics or the news crew or the church people how she'd felt. How she feels. But her mouth had been locked.

Being under this tree reminded her of more serene times, napping on the moist ground in the fall under that large live oak tree in her backyard, its crooked arms bending down to hide her, to protect her. It had somehow comforted her. This, however, was not comforting at all. She felt exposed in a way she had never before.

Though her eyes still felt heavy, she forced them open. More time must have passed than she had realized because the stars had all come out and were more dazzling than she'd ever seen them. In fact, little stars seemed to glitter all about her. But that couldn't be. Stars at her fingertips? It was almost as if she could reach out and touch the otherworldly display of twinkling lights through the clear night sky.

So, she did. And when she reached, she felt her body speed toward them as if she were a shooting star herself. Only, the distance seemed negligible. As she squinted her eyes once again to stop the dizzying sensation, she glimpsed the smaller twinkling lights she had noticed all about her earlier. Somehow, they seemed to be traveling with her.

As she sped through the clear night, she pulled her arms toward her to keep them from floating away because they felt so suddenly…unlocked and feathery. As her body moved through time and space, she lost her former understanding of fear, so she refocused her eyes. Some of the stars seemed streaks of white as she sped through the garden of celestial bodies, while some of the little not-quite-white lights that seemed to be traveling with her kept themselves at a safe distance from her reach. It may have been a pleasurable sensation if it hadn't been such a startling, extraordinary experience. She absorbed some kind of strange, otherworldly knowledge that she was leaving her earthly concerns behind her. She had not experienced that unexplained type of knowledge since childhood and had almost forgotten about those unrevealed impressions. The new awareness ushered in some kind of speechless peace inside her.

All the questions she would normally be asking seemed to be slipping from her head. It didn't matter how she was still breathing in this atmosphere...or where she was going...or how she'd get back. She closed her eyes again and simply let the sensations silently wash over her as she slid through the velvet black night skies.

*Thump*. She had come to a stop. The sensation of darkness suddenly disappeared, and she felt unusually rested. She could feel her lungs fill with the sweetest, cleanest air she had ever breathed. It was scented with lilacs and inexplicably tasted like apples.

When she opened her eyes, *everything* was different.

# CHAPTER FOUR

## Familiar and Foreign

Before Cotton lay a valley of fields and flowers and trees for as far as she could see. Cedar wafted in the air. Behind her was a gentle mountain that sloped into the clouds, and all about her were colors that she couldn't describe. Some were familiar, but far more were foreign. They exuded light and movement. To sort of quote Dorothy, she wasn't in South Carolina any more—where Spanish moss draped upon most things that stood still and humidity draped upon the rest.

The really odd thing about the landscape, however, was that it was peppered with rocks, some large, some small, all of various shapes and colors.

Cotton could always figure things out. She just needed to try a little harder—to put on her thinking cap and employ her acutely honed skills. She looked down and realized she was in the most hideous of clothing. How did that happen? At least it was some odd shade of red, her signature color, but the long dress, if you will, felt like a sack, long sleeves and hanging about her ankles. In it, she had no discernable figure. *Yuck.* And her feet were bare.

She took a few steps, stopped and gazed all about her. Standing under a tremendous live oak tree, like the one in her backyard when she was a child, she sensed that she was…connected to it somehow...belonged to it...or it belonged to her. As she looked beyond the shimmering green leaves on the grand branches, there were three paths that spread out in divergent directions. The paths, however, seemed to somehow be...alive...moving slightly and then returning to their original positions.

One path led to the gentle mountain behind her. The mountain was apparently alive with light—and almost breathing. One path led toward—what she could only describe as multi-colored fields. And one path led toward a forest. But something was beyond that forest, and it pulsed like a dark, colorless heart. Terror struck her chest, and she quickly turned her attention from that direction.

Under the tree was a huge boulder, and in the lower portion was a fissure, large enough to fit all sorts of objects. It was all too strange.

Concern crept up in Cotton for the first time since she'd left the confines of the church yard. What had happened to her? Where was she? How was she going to get home now?

She felt unusually light, and when she stepped, she moved with a nimbleness in her gait like she hadn't had since she was seven. She even felt a child-like sense of wonder mixed in with the reticence, and then she saw a single, tiny little light that buzzed in the limbs above her. It wasn't a star, like she'd thought at the church. She sensed…fear in the little light, as well. All those old unaccountable, mysterious sensations she was so familiar with as a child were inexplicably returning to her since the accident. It had taken an elaborate education and arduous training to rid herself of those peculiar feelings and a simple accident to bring them all back.

Confusion overtook her, and she suddenly felt…incapable of figuring things out for the first time in her adult life. Her ability to put together a story to explain what had happened to her was gone, and she knew it. This was going to take a whole different set of skills.

Cotton inhaled a fragrance she hadn't encountered since her grandparents had died. In her grandparents' yard was an unusual type of magnolia tree that her Mimi had called a banana tree…because it smelled just like what you'd think a banana flower would smell like. Cotton missed climbing that old tree. But Cotton had given up climbing long ago when she had embraced her fear of heights.

During those early childhood years, after she would climb down from that old gnarled magnolia-banana tree, she would go inside her grandparents' house. Mimi would be standing in her warm kitchen in her old apron and would have sweet tea and apple pie waiting for Cotton. She looked around her present circumstances, and just beyond the oak tree that she belonged to was a grove of those gnarled banana tree-scented magnolias.

Suddenly, she smelled buttermilk biscuits and cane syrup and a hint of apple pie spices. The scents imparted an overwhelming sense of love for some reason.

"Well, there you are." The voice came from the direction of the mountain, and she knew exactly who it was before she even turned around. It was her grandmother. Mimi had died so long ago, but Cotton would recognize her soft voice anywhere. Anywhere? But where was that?

She turned toward the voice. "Mimi?" she asked, tears filling her eyes. She heard her own voice tremble.

Though Mimi sounded the same, she was different. Her hair was still white, but her face had no wrinkles. In fact, it was beautifully smooth and colored in a translucent golden color. Mimi held out her arms. "I've been waiting for you."

"Mimi, you look so…young," Cotton said as she stared into a face that almost looked like hers.

"It was that acorn I kept in my pocket for all those years. My own grandmother told me to keep it there because it would keep me young. Who knows if it truly worked, but it sure did keep my own dear, sweet grandmother alive for me…in my pocket…and in my heart." Mimi giggled.

Throughout Cotton's childhood, Mimi had often told her of her own grandmother's old wives' tales. The funny stories had been fanciful and entertaining when Cotton was small, but she had grown to doubt them all. As education and knowledge had filled Cotton's head, all her grandmother's old folk tales lost their rustic charms and credibility. Cotton had a world of real information at her fingertips on her smart phone, on her computer and at her job to refute nearly all of them—and all of the magic they had once held.

Cotton somehow folded herself into Mimi's arms and

couldn't speak for the longest time. The knot in her throat grew larger as each moment passed. Ever-growing emotions overtook her. Oh, how soft and fragrant those arms were. Time regressed for a while, and magic filled her heart again.

But Cotton decidedly knew what this meant for herself. Her grandmother had died. Cotton wasn't going back for her car…for her phone…for her life. She absorbed the once-familiar scents from her grandmother. The warm apple pie spices seemed to impart love and waft into Cotton and become a part of her again. She was then completely overwhelmed by the aroma of sweet sugarcane syrup and tangy buttermilk biscuits drifting from her grandmother's arms. She could stay there forever, soaking in her childhood, reveling in her scented memories and feelings of being cherished.

Mimi eventually halted the hug and held Cotton at arms' length. Her grandmother had on a lovely white garment that was loosely tied with a thick khaki apron. "I've been waiting a long time to hug you again. You were my only grandchild." She smiled. "You are my forever grandchild." Mimi had always had a way with words and old Southern sayings that were just the right salve for a sore, as her Mimi used to say. Mimi was the right salve for Cotton's sores in many ways right now.

Something like sadness spilled out Cotton's eyes, and something like guilt filled her heart. She'd never even thought about hugging her grandmother again. Mimi had died, and that had been the end of her in Cotton's mind—just a few scattered memories would pop up now and then, but Cotton always tamped them down. She couldn't even find the time to clear off a few Virginia creeper vines and dead twigs from Mimi's grave, much less be considerate enough to plant a few flowers on it.

How awful Cotton was. "Mimi, I'm so sorry." They were not just words. It was the same regret she felt in the churchyard before she left.

"Whoa. You have no need to apologize to me. All with us has been forgiven, child," she said.

Cotton didn't exactly feel forgiven—not in the parts of her that mattered. Then she caught another glimpse of one of those strange little lights that had been hovering near her since her accident, and then it was gone again. She looked all about her to get her bearings—the limbs of the huge, old oak kissed the soft, fragrant earth below them. Beyond them, the landscapes luminesced. The banana-magnolia trees bloomed, and everything everywhere…radiated.

"Mimi, what is this place?" She could hear the awe in her own voice as she drank in the visions before her.

The colors of the tall pine trees glowed. The grasses in the fields shimmered. The sky twinkled a shade of white and baby blue that was illusory.

Her grandmother joined Cotton in glancing around, as if to embrace what Cotton was newly seeing.

Mimi looked back at Cotton. "Oh, sweetie, you'll sort it all out. That's what we're all here for. To figure things out," Mimi said. "Let's take a walk, and you can see for yourself."

As they strolled, Mimi pointed out some of the seasons of beauty around them. Wheat fields swayed and danced with living shades of green. A rose garden, filled with every color rose imaginable and unimaginable stretched out before them in a triangle that began at a point with them and then angled out to the broadest horizon. Rocks of various sizes and kaleidoscope-like colors punctuated the beauty.

"Stunning," Cotton said, mesmerized at the movement of the colors. But how can the tones move and change?

"Abundance is the word that I think of when I look at the rose fields. I sometimes come here to gaze at the triumph of the colors," Mimi said.

Triumph of the colors? That was an odd way to refer to the roses. "They remind me of your rose garden," Cotton said.

"Oh, that old thing. I hadn't thought about that in…" Mimi smiled. "Oh, I'm supposed to show you something else."

Mimi grabbed Cotton's hand and gazed into her eyes. She paused. "I sense you still have it," she said.

"Come, let's go," Mimi said, pulling on Cotton's arm.

But for some reason, she couldn't really *feel* the touch or the tugging. Instead, she *sensed* it. They walked for a while as Cotton marveled at the perfected landscape around her. No words needed to be spoken. As baffling as it was, it seemed that their spirits were becoming reacquainted in some undefinable way.

Mimi eventually stopped and gazed ahead.

In the distance, Cotton saw a great tree, a willow oak, grander than any she'd ever seen before, and it cast refreshing shade over the ground below it. From their vantage point, there were people milling all about, under the tree and in the fields and gardens all around. Though all the people were in clothing of various kinds, the colors were all white and khaki, some fine, some not, all of a quality of thickness, though. Cotton felt no personal connection to the scene, but, nevertheless, was drawn to it. Something was oddly there for her.

"Come," Mimi said. "Let's get a bit closer." She grabbed Cotton's hand again and led the way.

When they arrived at the edge of the shade cast by the tree, she watched as a long banquet table, made of rock, was being set. Fruit fragrances spilled over her, and the earthy, yeasty scent of bread filled her lungs. She imagined foods being in the bowls and platters, but in truth, she couldn't exactly make out what was actually in them. They glowed of…goodness.

A man in the finest clothing, adorned with gold braids, called out to the helpers, "Go and ask my good neighbors to come to feast."

Slowly, the helpers spread out into the surrounding areas. Trees of various sizes appeared and dotted the landscapes, like houses. As each servant found the neighbors under the branches of their respective trees, they asked them to come to their master's home. Somehow, Cotton intuitively knew what the discussions were about—even though she was too far away to actually physically hear. She watched as the dutiful servants held conversations under all the trees about them…then each helper returned. Alone.

The man in fine clothes lowered his head as if he were sad, and after a while lifted his head high and said with great confidence. "Now, you must travel beyond the fields and the trees, to the gullies and caves and rocks, and ask all who dwell there to come to my feast."

The helpers looked at one another, uncertain about what they were being asked to do. But one by one, each headed out.

Cotton couldn't believe she could see as far as she was seeing. For some crazy reason, distance didn't seem to matter here. It had been transformed, too.

"Mimi, why are we watching these people?" she asked.

"It is the way," she said, not taking her eyes off the scene before her.

Was Cotton supposed to know what that meant?

They stood there for what seemed only a moment longer, and the helpers started showing up on the small trails that led to the road that she and Mimi were standing on, and behind each helper were people. People who were still dressed in the same colors as the owners of the grand trees, but some of them were dirty; some were bandaged; some had patched their tan and white clothing.

As each entered the protection of the master's grand tree, it illumined, more and more, until it glowed like a fire.

Mimi nodded, like she knew what was happening, but she never took her eyes off the people.

But Cotton didn't understand.

She turned to Mimi. "Are we going to eat with them," she asked.

Mimi turned to her and looked surprised at the question. "Why, heavens no."

Cotton really didn't comprehend why they were still there, but then she turned back to the feast under the tree, and the strangers were gone. Instead, it was the same as it was when they had first arrived. The helpers were preparing the platters for the stone banquet table once again, like they had before.

She could feel her mouth open, but didn't know what to ask. She had a brain—a journalist's brain at that. She could figure out the meaning. Right? So…she thought. The wealthy man under the tree invited people to dine with him, and few responded.

*And…I'm supposed to learn—*

Cotton reasoned that if she had ever invited people to dinner and they had not come, she would never invite them again; however, she also realized that she would have never invited them in the first place with her busy life.

*Maybe I'm supposed to invite people to dinner?*

Mimi broke her trance and said, "That is enough. Come, child, it's time we headed back."

As they walked back, Cotton had seen nothing that she had seen before. Where was the beautiful rose garden? The grains in the field were there, but they grew more and more yellow as they passed the section of farm land. She thought of the word *harvest*. Boulders, large and small, lay next to the road they traveled.

Cotton kept thinking about the feast under the tree, though. Surely, the man who held the banquet should have a house, if not a castle. "Are there no buildings here?" she asked. Maybe the man's home was the tree. Did it symbolize something? And what about the boulder that was a table? Should the table or the man be associated with the *harvest*? And why did Cotton land under a tree, as well?

Mimi cast a confused look her way. "Did you not see? Did you not learn?"

"See what? Learn what? How am I to understand? None of this makes sense to me."

Mimi touched Cotton's chest, though Cotton did not feel it. "When you were a child, you used to use the inside," Mimi said and turned her attention toward the sky. "It's getting late. I'm going to have to go as soon as we get you back to your tree." A smile spread over her soft face. "I don't want to miss anything."

"My tree?" Cotton said, not understanding all of the particulars about how the tree was hers—even though she sensed it was. "May I go with you? I don't know what I'm supposed to do here. I have no clothes…or a place to sleep…or food."

Mimi giggled. "I'd fix you a big pot of my chicken soup with dumplings, if I could. That would make you feel better. But there are no chickens here to…sacrifice." Mimi gazed at her curiously. "You aren't hungry, are you?"

Cotton hadn't even thought about it. She hadn't eaten since the day before yesterday, she thought. "No. Not really. I'm not." How odd. In fact, there was a warmth in her tummy in the exact spot she had felt the paramedic touch after she fell. Cotton was full. And not in need of anything.

Still, she wished she could have some of her grandmother's chicken soup because it had always made her feel better—someplace deep inside. It was the one old wives' tale in which Cotton truly believed, no matter how old she grew. When she was sick, it made her well. When she was down, it lifted her up. When she was confused, it calmed her.

In the next turn in the road, they came upon a circle of stacked stones about waist high, a large weeping willow grew a few feet away, its branches, dangling all about the circle. Cotton moved the tendrils of leaves aside and startled when a woman popped up from the short stone wall opposite her. Mimi smiled at the woman, but the woman didn't seem to see her. In fact, the woman looked troubled. Cotton's grandmother kept walking, like the woman wasn't even there.

Cotton had never known her grandmother to not assist someone in need. The woman was noticeably upset as she lowered her bucket into what Cotton sensed was a newly-sprung well. Because it had not been there when they had passed earlier. When they had walked down the path far enough for the woman to not hear, Cotton asked, "Do you know her?"

Mimi stopped and stared at Cotton. "Why, child, we all do. But you are obviously not ready for the well, yet."

Cotton wanted to stamp her foot like she had when she had been a child, spoiled and frustrated. So, she did. "I don't understand, Mimi. Just tell me what I need to know!"

Mimi smiled. "We will return here one day. It is the way of things. There is order, and you will not be shown some things until you are ready—until you are ready to see it and possess it…and strong enough to bear the…weight of it. Does that make sense?"

No. But nothing here seemed to make sense. In fact, nothing in the last twelve hours seemed to make sense. Some journalist Cotton was. If she were her station boss, she'd even fire herself right now. Cotton suddenly remembered something Hamilton had once told her when she had approached him about the anchor position she wanted. He had said, "That's going to happen when you figure out how to enlighten our audience beyond the facts."

That had never made sense to her. In fact, in all her journalism textbooks, college courses, internships and everything she'd ever learned about a free press came from the principles and rules in her journalism textbooks. In fact, those textbooks were the reason she won the Excellence in Journalism Award while at Clemson. She had always planned to go back to Hamilton to ask him exactly what he had meant by those words. But now, even that didn't matter.

A worried look spread over Mimi's face. "I'm so sorry, but I may have shown you the feast under the tree a little too soon. You did once have the dispensation, so I figured it would come quickly again. I just got so excited, and I wanted to get my chore done. It was on my list." She shook her head. "No worries, though. The truths always repeat themselves. I can always take you back to see it again." Mimi looked behind her and then ahead, toward the mountain that seemed to glow even more. "Hurry. We've got to go."

Cotton was further confused. She was a chore? This place was like some kind of dream. Only it wasn't. It was like no place she'd ever even imagined before. In fact—in some way—this place seemed even more real than home did.

Still intrigued by her grandmother's insistence that they leave immediately, Cotton turned back to look far away in the direction of the woman under the weeping willow tree and saw a man, dressed in colors she'd never seen before, standing beside her. He walked to the well, and he talked to her. Then they both looked into the well together, like they were looking for a gold coin or something she'd tossed over and now regretted.

"We must hurry," Cotton's grandmother said with urgency.

But why? Where could they go? Was something going to happen?

Cotton looked back again. The woman had dropped to her knees, her beige skirts curled under her, and her head touching the man's feet in a kind of…worship.

What had he shown her in that well? Her coin? Her foolishness for dropping it in? Or emptiness? Cotton was leaning toward emptiness because that was how she was feeling.

Mimi walked ahead, and Cotton hurriedly ran to catch up with her. Eventually, Cotton saw the large, amazing tree in the distance where her grandmother had found her. But now the leaves had begun to turn color and fall. She hadn't noticed before, but it was surprisingly like the one in her parents' backyard when she was a child. When she arrived, she saw a little light darting around, amongst the lower branches and leaves. It had a faint reddish glow. Cotton stopped and stared at it, but then it threw itself down and into the fissure in the great rock under the tree. Suddenly, she saw five others of different sizes but in the same faint crimson-red hue, hiding in the leaves. Then, three more descended, but they had a yellowish, golden glow about them.

Her grandmother looked toward the mountain longingly. "We must go…but you'll be fine here."

We? Who was her grandmother referring to as *we*? No one was even there. "Mimi, please don't leave me," she pleaded as she looked at all the little gold and crimson lights floating and darting about.

Her grandmother paused, pushed her gray curls from her face and looked confused again. "Are you afraid, dear?"

Cotton thought for a moment and searched her heart as leaves fell all about her. She didn't think so. She shook her head.

But she had so many questions—about her senses after her accident, about the strange shadowless light when she experienced her fall again, about how she had even transferred to this place. She wanted to ask about her connection to the tree, all the colors and smells, about the revolving scenes she had just witnessed...and the little lights that she'd seen in the church yard and here in this most unusual place that didn't behave like anything she'd known before. How had so much happened that day, yet it seemed to pass in only moments? Why had she been robbed of all her abilities that had been bestowed to her in college?

Mimi smiled and kind of touched Cotton's face. "You'll sort some of this out tomorrow."

Cotton nodded, knowing that she was going to be unable to change her grandmother's mind.

Mimi stared deep into her eyes, and her voice became serious. "You must remain under your tree. It will be your protection. Understand?"

Cotton understood deep inside and said, "Yes." "But why is this *my* tree?" Cotton asked.

"In time, my child. I really need to go." Mimi glanced toward the mountain that seemed to be increasing its pull on her.

Why did Mimi seem so excited to get back to the mountain? Cotton looked at it, and it seemed to breathe and glow in a faster tempo in the fading light.

Mimi turned, waved to the little lights to come to her, and held out her apron for them to gather. She smiled at Cotton and started walking away…with the little lights gathered together in the khaki cloth. So, Mimi thought of the little lights as *we*? Apparently so. As they traveled down the road a piece, her grandmother let go the edges of her apron.

Cotton watched as the nine little lights flew up and frolicked and played about her grandmother. As her grandmother strolled, she seemed to glow…golden. Cotton noted the similar sort of luminosity in three of the little yellowish ones. Six, though, glowed that pinkish-reddish color. As Mimi walked toward the mountain that seemed to almost burn in the waning light, her grandmother lovingly touched each little radiance as they strolled, her steps seeming to grow lighter the farther she moved away from the valley where Cotton and her tree remained in the growing darkness.

As the daylight around Cotton continued to fade, and the trees and bushes and flowers turned into shadows, she didn't know why, but she was not afraid, just like her grandmother had suspected. However, she was weary and tired. She had no idea how long she'd been away with Mimi, but the soft earth below her seemed to pull her down to the fallen leaves. She gave way to the mystifying tugging, and when she rested upon the warm earth under the tree, she sank into it like she did into her mattress at home, only deeper and softer. The heady fragrance from the grass and leaves and ground were almost intoxicating, like some kind of sleeping potion. From the feel of the ground, she had an idea…no, more like an urging.

She leaned to one side and peculiarly pulled up the grass-covered earth below her into a pillow. It was as soft as the one she'd left behind in her bed. Then, she reached over and grabbed the folded grass, like a blanket, and drew it over her legs. She smiled at the unspoken knowledge she'd gained.

*How could I know to do such a thing?*

She'd listened to the knowledge that was inside her chest, like Mimi had told her about, like the knowledge that had inherently been inside her as a child. That inexplicable knowledge had left Cotton long ago, and it felt so unusual to have touched it again.

Her eyelids lowered like windows closing in an old house; sleep was impossible to resist, even though she knew she should be upset that she was no longer where she had once lived—was no longer able to pursue her amazing career—was no longer able to finish the charitable project she had begun—was no longer able to make amends to Caleb.

Like Mimi had said, she'd sort it all out in the morning.

62

# CHAPTER FIVE

## The Revelation of Light

Cotton woke up in her dorm room at Clemson University. Was she eighteen again?

*The light was brighter than it had ever been. And shadow-less like it had been when she'd re-lived her fall. Is this some kind of piecemeal life review? Or is it just a dream?*

She remembered this room. Orange and purple were everywhere. The stuffed tiger her mother had left with Cotton after she'd decorated the dorm room stared knowingly at Cotton.

The leaves on the willow tree were falling outside her window. She'd only been in school for a few weeks and still felt the newness of it all. She should be studying, but something more important was on her mind. Journalism 101 would have to wait.

She dashed to the restroom that co-joined the suite beside her.

Everything that she'd eaten earlier in McAlister Hall had come up. Tucker, her boyfriend from high school, had not bothered himself to visit this weekend. Her problem materialized when she had said goodbye to him before leaving for Clemson. He'd promised that he'd wait for her. But he didn't.

She hadn't really made any friends that she could count on at the university yet, though her mother had constantly urged her to try to rush a sorority. She glanced at the imposing stuffed tiger on her bed that her mother had positioned in her stead. There was only one thing to do. Call her mother.

"Mom," she said, barely able to bring out the words that she needed to. "You were right about Tucker." The words had clawed their way out her throat and had left scrapes and raw patches in their escapes.

After a long silence, her mom said in a flat tone, "Cotton, are you in trouble?"

Cotton stroked the soft, stuffed tiger she'd placed upon her chest. She didn't want to say it, but she had to admit to her mother that she was right. "Yes." The word had barely squeezed out.

Her mother cleared her throat. "Girl trouble?"

Cotton took a deep breath. "Yes."

*She could almost feel the unusual light in the room in the re-living of it all.*

There was a long pause on the other end of the phone. "Well, I can take care of this. I'll be up on Tuesday after I make all the necessary arrangements. Your father has a huge faculty party this weekend, so that's the earliest I can come."

Cotton wanted to cry. Things her grandmother had told her came rushing into her spirit. Things she'd learned in Sunday school kept echoing in some chamber in her heart. "Aren't we even going to talk about it? Like about the alternatives."

Her mother snorted. "Alternatives?" Her voice was tight. "There are no alternatives when it comes to girl trouble. How could you possibly care for someone else when you can't even care for yourself?" Her mother breathed in deeply over the phone. "I am not about to be a granny and give up my life. This was your mistake, and you are going to amend it. You are not going to waste that scholarship. You're going to be a broadcast journalist."

The weird light made the tiger's eyes shine more brightly as she caressed it. "But shouldn't I talk to Tucker?" She questioned out loud, even though she couldn't reach him on the phone any longer.

Her mother laughed in a way that made Cotton even more nauseous. "Tucker Boyd? I told you how worthless his family was before he ever took you to that stupid homecoming dance your junior year. For the life of me, I cannot understand why you'd date someone like him. I know his family. He was a loser before he was born."

*Thump.* Did that mean what was growing inside Cotton was a loser, too?

"Sweetheart, we've got big plans. Now, study for that test you told me about last week, and I'll see you on Tuesday. I've got to get my mani-pedi for the big party this weekend."

Cotton looked into the eyes of the lifeless tiger, unable or unwilling to think for herself. "Yes, ma'am."

Charlotte Rivers texted Cotton when she hit the road at six a.m. on Tuesday. But there had not been any need really. Cotton had lost the small piece of…trouble inside her, slowly, drop by drop over the weekend. The details were sketchy in the continuing strange light. She had told her mother on Monday not to come, but she did anyway—probably out of some sense of duty.

Later that day, her mom burst through the door of Cotton's dorm room with two large shopping bags from Macy's. "Okay, we're going out to lunch. FATZ, your favorite. However, for the life of me I cannot think why." She stared at Cotton for a moment, unable to see her sadness. "Well, get up and get dressed."

She did as her mother demanded. As usual.

Her mother drove her in silence, occasionally glancing Cotton's way, as if to say, "I told you so." Cotton was so relieved when they pulled into the almost empty parking lot. Most of the students were in class and not having to deal with Charlotte Rivers.

*In that familiar restaurant, the lights were low, as they always had been, but Cotton could see better in that dining room than she'd ever seen before. In the new shadowless light that plagued her thoughts as she reviewed this devastating part of her life.*

They got a booth in the back. Cotton slipped into the oversized brown leather-looking bench and ordered the marinated steak, like she usually did.

After they got their soft rolls and sweet tea, her mother reached for a piece of bread, her diamond tennis bracelets dripping from her arm. She began. "What have I always told you about…prevention? It is absolutely necessary."

As Cotton reached for a roll, she tuned out her mother's redundant speech and recoiled at some of the words her mother used, words like a friend would use. But her mother was not her friend.

Why couldn't she just be Cotton's mother? But sometimes she thought her mother acted like she was talking to herself, like she was grooming herself for life, to accomplish the things that she hadn't when she was young.

She knew her mother had her best interests at heart, but her mother's best interests sometimes bruised Cotton's heart. It reminded her of something her father had once written in a poem for *The Shako*, the Citadel's literary magazine. One line read, "Her heart had not been broken, but merely bruised, making it tender when anyone tried to touch it." Cotton had always remembered that line. She absolutely loved her father's poetry. It had always spoken to her heart, until she'd stopped listening to it.

She had seen herself in that particular musing. Her own heart ached and felt sore from all the times she'd been hurt.

Her mother took a second soft roll from Cotton's hand and motioned for the waitress to come take the basket from their table, and she continued with her diatribe when the young woman left. "You mustn't allow anything like this to happen again. Do you understand?"

"Yes, Mother," she said. "I won't."

Charlotte Rivers continued. "I've made an appointment for you when you come home for Fall Break. Until then, I put some…protection in one of the bags I brought."

Why wasn't her mother like some of her friends' mothers—like her loving grandmother? Why didn't her mother give her any advice about morality or abstinence or some kind of guidance like that? It was as if she didn't really even have a mother—just a friend who wanted Cotton to do all the things she hadn't been able to do when she was young.

Cotton desperately needed a mother right now, not a friend.

When they arrived back at her dorm room, her mother brought in a few more bags, new outfits and some more orange and purple decorations. Cotton sat on her bed, cuddling her tiger against her hollow belly as she watched Charlotte Rivers hang a few more banners and signs in the strange light. She was beautiful and thin, her auburn hair bounced as she hopped from the chair.

"Oh, and here are a few more binders. You have become so good at organizing things in them, like I taught you," her mother said.

Charlotte Rivers had taught Cotton how to organize and schedule everything from laundry to linguistics in notebooks and binders. And they had helped Cotton accomplish all that she had so far. Her mother had convinced her that they would be the trick that would propel her to the success that she knew would be hers one day.

When her mother finished putting away the binders on Cotton's neatly arranged desk, Charlotte straightened the blue and gold plaid infinity scarf at her neck and tucked in her mustard-colored blouse into her size-four skinny jeans and asked, "Are you going to need anything else?"

Cotton simply shook her head. How could she tell Charlotte Rivers that she needed a mother? How does one even say such a thing? One can't. But her heart could still long for that.

The beautiful, pulled-together woman looked at her watch. "Well, if I leave now, I can make my women's club meeting tonight." She said a few other things about the slightly unsanitary state of the co-joined bathroom, kissed Cotton on the forehead and then left.

Despite the decorations, Cotton's room felt empty. She felt empty inside. She *was* empty inside. She wanted enlightenment as she stared into the eyes of the tiger. Nothing came from the still, orange beast.

*So, she steeled herself in the eerie purple and orange un-shadowed light of that room. Toughness was what it was going to take to survive.*

※

Morning came, and Cotton was lying prone on the ground under her live oak tree at the apex of the three rustic roads. Without her earthen pillow. Without her grassy blanket. The leaves that had fallen last evening had somehow disappeared, and the leaves on the branches above were green again.

Her head buzzed with the vision she'd had during the night. Only it wasn't a vision. It was a memory. A vivid memory. An enlightened memory. More than that. She was a witness. Impartial and uninvolved, a student of sorts. But why? Why would she even think about that incident? Especially now when she had so many other things to consider? Cotton had long ago come to terms with the sadness of that incident that had plagued her for years. It was gone. Buried. She didn't *need* to think about it.

When she looked toward the mountain for Mimi, the brightness nearly blinded her, like the white paint did on the church Mimi had taken her to as a child—the one she had been painting prior to her fall. What was she to do while she was waiting in this strange place?

Something caught her eye in the branches, and she turned her head upward. There were those little lights again. This time there were more. Maybe ten or twelve. And two were much larger than the others, one, about the size of a navel orange, and one the size of a very small…grapefruit. Still, they all had a similar crimson hue.

Those two floated high above the others, and she sensed…a great anxiety in them. And they seemed to…split…no, tear. Parts of the two larger little lights tore apart inside their aura and then rejoined themselves, almost like they were showing her something.

The smaller ones, the sizes of grapes and berries, and a much smaller apple-sized one, were darting about—almost playing—in the lower branches. Maybe she could touch one like Mimi had. She reached up, and they all whizzed away toward the larger orange-sized one and the small grapefruit-sized one. And then she saw the tiniest lights of all, almost specks, like the duckweed berries on the ponds where she and her grandfather used to fish. Duckweed, too, was a fruit, but not one that was prized or cultivated like grapes and berries and apples. Duckweed was unwanted. These little duckweed lights came closer and closer to her, seemingly unafraid, but they still kept an arms-length away from her. How was she even seeing them? Seeing lights in the brightness of day. Light behaved differently here, like it did after she'd fallen. Like it did in her…remembrances.

Suddenly from behind her, she heard someone walking down the trail, the one that hooked a hard right. A man was talking to himself. He had on khaki pants and a flowing white shirt. Over his shoulder, was a satchel, like a messenger bag. He reached inside the bag, again and again, grabbing fistfuls of something and scattered the contents along both sides of the road, some falling upon the hardened path. It had reminded her of a tale she had learned about Johnny Appleseed when she was young. As the man passed, behind him, some plants grew with rapidity and some with slowness on either side of the trail. Time was not an absolute thing in this place. It didn't behave like it did where she had studied and worked her entire life. As the plants grew, so did the ground underneath them, or rather, it transformed, some into rocks, some into thistle and vines, and some into good, dark earth that had a ripe scent. Behind him, birds plucked up the seeds that had mistakenly fallen upon the hardened path. When the man approached her tree, she walked to the path. "What are you doing?" she asked.

The man replied in a soft voice, "Whoever has ears to hear, let them hear."

If he wanted people to hear him, he'd better speak up. "But I don't understand," she said, glancing back at the differing areas beside the road, the barren plots, the strangling weeds and the plants that thrived and spread like they'd been fertilized and watered.

He continued walking, talking in undertones, oblivious to her and her concerns.

This was a place like no other with people like no other. Even her own grandmother was confounding her, almost frustrating her. No one seemed to want to give her any answers. What was she supposed to do? Figure things out for herself?

*Thump. Yes.* The word came to her like she'd heard it. But she hadn't. And she knew then and there. She *was* supposed to figure things out for herself. She *had* to figure things out for herself.

Well, if she were to make some sort of a meaningful discovery, she'd need to investigate what was going on…what was growing…or not. As she meandered down one side of the sandy path, she touched the plants struggling beside it. An urging took hold of her, and she pulled away some of the weeds and vines, and saw what she instinctively knew to be wheat. Suddenly, some of the wheat unrumpled, now that it had no longer been held down by the vines, and it began to grow, very slowly. Beside it was additional plants that looked healthy, but all of a sudden, the stalks began to die. She parted the plants and saw that they had grown amongst the rocks where the soil was shallow. Pieces of something she'd heard as a child darted through her head, but she couldn't make any sense of it all. She walked to the other side of the road where the wheat grew tall and strong and spread out in every direction. *Think, Cotton, think.*

She knew she could figure this out if she could remember some of the old stories she hadn't heard in years. It had simply been so long...and she hadn't had need for the lessons they had once taught. Unfortunately, they had gotten mixed in with all of Mimi's old wives' tales and Cotton had discarded them all.

She walked back under her tree and leaned against the rock and tried to recall what she knew to be just under the surface of her mind. Miss Tree had taught her something about seeds being planted in different soils.

*Harvest.* That's it. It was the same word that had come to her yesterday. Then she knew what she was supposed to understand from the day before, too. She'd heard similar words in the little church she'd attended with her grandparents—words from the pulpit, words from Bible school, and words from Sunday School—all proclaiming the same thing.

Suddenly, the rock against which she was leaning felt...different. She stepped back to see a small portion of it...transform, swirl with dark light in one little spot. Letters appeared that she didn't recognize...but somehow, she understood the meaning.

*"Though many hear the call, few prepare themselves to be His chosen."*

Cotton looked out over the field of green-hued wheat. She knew immediately the meaning of the banquet yesterday. Instinctively, she also knew that the words she'd heard so many years ago had not grown and spread in her own heart like some of the wheat before her. The strange words on the rock disappeared.

She turned to look at the other side of the path. There were three examples of harvest. On her right, was the wheat that had been covered over by the vines and choked out by the weeds…to her left, the grains that had never taken hold in the dry, rocky soil…in front of her were the bountiful fields of quickly growing wheat. *Thump*. She knew she was one of those examples. But which one?

The question pierced her heart, and she swallowed hard and looked at the sandy soil beneath her bare feet. She slowly inched away from the rock, toward the trunk of the tree.

She sat under the protective branches of the old oak, seemingly her new home—if—at least—only temporarily and looked upward. The various-sized lights still twinkled and darted about the branches. Did they belong to Mimi? Why had they come without her? Cotton studied them for a while. Though they were of differing sizes, they all seemed to belong together, and then an illumination came. The ones in the tree all glowed the same. Their colors were the same, as if glowing on the same…vibration or…temperature. And when they gathered together, Cotton thought they emitted a fragrance like…warm apple pie.

Another noise startled her, and she watched as a woman walked down the same path the man before her had, but she was walking in the opposite direction, toward the mountain, like her grandmother had the evening before. She, too, was dressed in white and tan. She stepped like springs were on her shoes. In her hands was a wooden box, new and smooth, like it had just been made. When she got closer, Cotton noticed that four lights, the size of large grapes, danced around her heart. And they glowed the color of the woman's aura, a sort of purple color, but not quite purple. Cotton walked toward the woman and met her in the road.

"Do you live here?" Cotton asked.

"I live," the woman said and smiled. She seemed so preoccupied with the little lights that she hardly counted Cotton's presence notable. A small sparkle landed upon the woman's cheek. She kissed her own finger and touched the little light, which glowed even brighter at the touch. The three other little twinkles nestled under her chin, and the woman seemed to glow brighter. An aroma of sweet grapes emanated from them. The scene was tender, but what did it mean? The lights were definitely connected to her, and there was certainly something, some strong emotion, amongst them.

Cotton stared as they made their ways down the road.

*Thump. A shock drove a spike through her. Love.*

It came to her just like that. The woman loved her little lights, and they loved her.

# CHAPTER SIX

## The Journey of Knowledge

Cotton left the path and returned to her tree. The import of what she'd seen seemed great. But why? *Why* did the woman love her little lights? They were just lights. And what about the box? Was that to store the small twinkles?

She looked into the branches above. The little reddish luminosities had floated down a couple of twigs, like they were curious. Well, so was she. But there was not love or any other emotion that she could discern between her and them. They were just…glows, in extremely light shades of…crimson.

Her head instinctively lowered in an awareness of a…a coming. She suddenly smelled…leather—leather laced with love.

"I was told you were here," a man's voice boomed behind her. Her father's voice.

She tiptoed, turned and twirled, all in the same instance. Joy rose up in her as she leapt to hug his neck.

"My baby girl. Oh, how I've looked forward to our meeting," he said, blue eyes illumined and twinkling. Let's sit a spell. He, too, was dressed in fine clothes of khaki and white, a style that had no era upon it, just like the others. Thick, quality cloth in only those two shades. She looked down, and noted that her own clothes were of a different quality. And the red color appeared earthly, unlike the luminous colors around her.

"Daddy, I had no idea about all of this," she said, looking all around her. "I can't understand most of it. Can you?"

He chuckled, his blue eyes growing lighter. "You will. Give it time. It all takes some adjusting."

Her insides felt like they were smiling. "I saw Mimi yesterday. Where's Momma and Poppy?"

He breathed in deeply. "You will see. Your grandmother believes that it will happen soon for you because you once had the favor. The understanding takes a while. You must have patience." He straightened. "Time is but a cloud that drifts and changes," he said in the same tone as when he read one of his musings. He brushed his hand over the greenest grass upon which they sat.

"Favor?" she asked.

"I, too, had the blessing when I was young, and I understand how the world can take that away if you don't guard it," he said.

She looked up into the tree above her. The green swayed, and she only caught small specks of the little glows. "I'm not so sure about that, Daddy. I didn't know that I had anything to guard. I've just been busy with my career." She stared at her father. "I never even visited the graveyard to clean off your grave. I'm so sorry."

He chuckled. "Oh, my. I haven't been to that place in so long. You have no need for any apology to *me*."

She squinted and shook her head. "I am just so filled with regrets."

He nodded as if he understood. "How did you arrive so soon, Princess?"

She hadn't been called that in a long time. "Sort of a painting accident. My ladder fell. At our old church—the one Mimi and Poppy used to take me to when I was small."

A look of relief, of all things, came over his face. "Oh, I'm so glad you went back there. I had been worried about that since I arrived here. That church and all those people were very special."

She didn't have the heart to tell him she was also doing a promo story about her connection to the community. She cocked her head, remembering something. "Didn't you start attending there after Momma died? Before your heart attack? When I was at the Greenville station."

"I did. And it's a good thing I did," he said, staring forward, looking at the miles that stretched before them down different paths.

"Why was it a good thing?" Her heart earnestly wanted to know everything. Maybe something she could learn from him would help her figure things out.

"Because what was important in my life for far too long was in my literature books back then. That and my poetry and musings. I had forgotten about the favor I had had as a child." He paused and stared out like he was looking into the past. "While I was married to your mother, the world—my world—was always with me too much. I thought of little else. Eventually, after your mother died, I was able to sort some things out there. In that little church. About myself. About your mother. I had grown hard, like that soil back there, and…deaf." He pointed far beyond the tree.

"Deaf?"

He nodded. "Like the guests that had been invited to that grand feast yesterday. I needed to understand things with my heart, you know, deep inside." He patted her hand. "I had been covered by too much of the earthly cloth. It happens all too easily. The yoke of the cloth got heavy."

She was beginning to get the import of the surface of words and phrases. Deaf and cloth had meaning beyond their denotation. She glanced up and saw the little glows had—once again—left their hiding places.

"Let's walk," her father said.

They stood, and she brushed herself off. Her father didn't. She realized that she really hadn't needed to either. The world she'd left was still too much with her, too. Somehow, she was still tied to the habits she had developed there. She understood that she would have to let them go in order to learn the meanings of things here.

Looking back at the little crimson lights, she wondered if they'd be there when she and her father got back. But why? She didn't own them. But somehow, they were lovely to look at, and besides, they were her only amusement under that tree.

"They are to remain." It was as if her father had heard her wonder.

She strolled with him, silently for a while, not passing anything she'd passed with her grandmother the day before, though they were on the same path. The trees were different; the flowers were different; the rocks were different and in totally different places. That was strange. How could she walk down the same road and pass different scenery? There had been a transformation of sorts.

"Where are we going, Daddy?" Her insides were filled with joy, being with her father again, something she'd never imagined.

"Where help is needed," he said, appearing to be saddened.

The joy that had filled her leaked out upon her father's words.

After walking for what seemed to be another mile in silence and through barren land, two men and a woman joined them and walked a space behind them. It appeared that they had been traveling a long time. They looked frail and gaunt. Then another and another traveler joined them. And elegant women, too, many dressed in finery, and some on carts, pulled by donkeys, so they looked refreshed, not hungry and tired, like the first three. Many looked as if their journeys had just begun. When they all arrived at a small village of trees, the men and women walked up to the villagers who had gathered in the dusty street.

Cotton and her father lagged behind and waited at a cluster of small boulders at the edge of the makeshift town. Somehow, she thought of the rocks as sentinels, marking the beginning of the small village.

"Look," her father said and pointed.

She knew she was to learn something, but she'd had difficulty the day before with Mimi, so she didn't have much hope for immediate success. Still, she looked.

Powdery dirt hung about the road in the town as the villagers milled around. As they were approached by the travelers, the townspeople stopped and listened. One by one, the villagers invited in the strangers in fine clothes, until each had been escorted by a resident toward his or her large tree, which Cotton knew to represent their homes. In their exchanges, coins passed from the travelers to their hosts. Under the hosts' trees, wine was poured and cheeses and meats were laid out on long tables with silver trays.

After a while, all that were left were the three people in dirty rags who had first joined Cotton and her father—the two men and the weary woman. They looked exceedingly sad and tired. One man had a bandage on his head, and the other was so thin, he looked like a skeleton. The woman had a nagging cough and a slight limp.

At the end of the lane was a small, gnarled tree with many broken limbs. It looked like it had weathered many storms. A man walked from under the tree and toward the road. He looked surprised to see the three exhausted travelers. Joy overtook his face. He shook the men's hands and nodded and smiled at the woman. Again, like the day before, Cotton's ability to hear was magnified.

"My wife is preparing a simple meal of bread and olives, but we would be honored to have you eat and stay," he said.

The two men and the woman looked at each other, concern covering their faces. The extraordinarily thin man spoke. "But we have no money."

"That is of no concern to us," the man who lived under the old gnarled tree said.

The man's wife came to the edge of the road. "Come in! You must be tired. We have water, and you may wash. I will prepare beds with the blankets I have made. You may rest after you eat."

The three smiled and were ushered under their tree by the man and woman. No exchange of coins took place under that tree.

*Thump.* Cotton looked up at her father. "I remember a verse from church when I was small. Something about accepting the call and doing something for the least of these. Is that it, Daddy?"

He closed his eyes. "I wish I had done more." His shoulders slumped. "I thought I had more time."

So did Cotton. Something pinched her heart. Guilt. "I haven't done anything to help anyone, unless I had something to gain." The image of the rocks and brambles and the dead seeds of wheat came to her. She knew that all the seeds that had been thrown at her had landed in unfertile soil and upon the hardness and shallowness that she was. "Is there anything that can be done now?"

He cocked his head and looked toward the mountain. It had begun to glow and breathe in the weakening light. "We must go," he said.

Her heart fell again. All about her lately was a sense of falling…and it seemed to be attached to a sense of…sinning…like the fall of man. Was her physical fall on that perfect fall day connected to the fall of her own soul? It was all too many falls to sort out, and her head ached, like it was trapped in a vice.

They turned and walked toward her home—er, tree, passing new scenery as they traveled. Cypress trees dotted the sides of the path and emitted a verdant fragrance, far more powerful than the bald cypress trees that grew out of the swamps near where she grew up and attended church. As they walked, she remained deep in thought about how the poorest travelers had been helped. It didn't matter that they had no coins because what is money, really? If she had some here, she couldn't use it. Heck, it couldn't even be used to burn for warmth because there was no need even for that.

They walked in silence, and in what seemed a tenth of the distance, they had arrived at her tree. They both sat on the soft ground without speaking as the leaves floated down all about them. Cotton had been so immersed in trying to unravel what she'd been shown about the least of the travelers that she hadn't paid much attention to anything she'd passed beyond the cypress trees. She closed her eyes.

Her father broke the silence. "We are all here to help—while we are needed." His voice changed and a serious tone colored his words. "It needs to be known. Who have you willingly helped without compensation, Cotton? Monetary or otherwise."

Had she ever helped anyone she'd ever encountered? She

thought. She hadn't helped any person she'd ever interviewed. She certainly hadn't been a good friend to Caleb, even though he'd had such a good heart. And she was even using the church to further her own goals. Certainly, she had to have helped someone unselfishly in all those years. She closed her eyes, the years of people she'd met passed through some kind of visual memory screen she didn't know she possessed.

She opened her eyes and felt her own disappointment in what she was about to say. "I helped paint the church."

Her father lifted his brows.

"Well, I did, didn't I?" That was something, wasn't it? Her heart hoped that would count, even though she was getting as much out of the work as they would. Or maybe more.

"I don't make the decisions here, Cotton. I am present to show you things. It is my…chore—the least that I can do. It is you who have to do the hard work—to see, to feel, to understand." She saw a sternness in his eyes that she'd never seen before.

Her heart sank. Things were not looking good for her in this place. "Will I get a chance to go back home since I helped with the church?"

Her father inhaled. "Things don't work that way. Some things still need to be sorted out and decided. It's very complicated" His forehead wrinkled where there had been none.

"You mean I can't fix this?" She felt impatience at the same kind of ambiguous answer her grandmother had given her.

Her father breathed deeply and looked up. "I have to take them back with me."

She looked up, too. The little lights twinkled in the tree between the falling leaves. "Okay, but why? I don't understand them. I think they're afraid of me." She shook her head. "I saw some small ones of a different color earlier today, and they loved the woman they were with, and she loved them, I think."

He nodded. "You will know them. When it is time."

The ground *clunked* and softened. He stood, and the lights, big and small, buzzed about his head. "We must go. Oh, and don't leave your tree."

Of course she wouldn't. Somehow, it was her home. Cotton stood and watched her father walk away, and as the scent of leather disappeared, so did the feeling of love she had felt. Sparkles of crimson light flitted all about him as he made his way toward the living, breathing mountain glowing in the distance. She watched until she could no longer see the little glimmerings and her father appeared to be a speck.

She'd seen a lot today. It all had to have more profound implications than she has deciphered. She instinctively knew it was all set before her to give her knowledge, but not knowledge like she'd received in college. It was different.

*It is spirit knowledge.*

She felt the pull of the ground like she had the night before. Where had all the time gone? Was that even the correct word for the passing of moments and lessons here? As she lay down, she gathered her earthen pillow and covered herself with the blanket of folded grass. As her eyes began to close, another dream settled before them. Only this was not a dream. It was a nightmare. And she had lived it.

Cotton was back in Greenville, South Carolina. She could tell by the rolling hills and fiery-colored trees she'd passed in her car. She had been working at WCLM in Greenville from the month after she'd graduated with her communications degree in broadcasting from Clemson. She loved living at the foot of the mountains, where the fall was more brilliant and the landscape and air changed more quickly and fervently than it did in the Lowcountry.

*Thump. This…vision was not going to be pleasant. Again with that same light—the one that casts no shadows.*

Her mother had passed, so she had no one to call to tell that she was…worried about where she was going…by herself.

It was her goal to get to the point where she could film more human-interest stories—things that were interesting and mattered and not the cub reporting that she was used to, like the school board meetings, store openings and parades. If she could show her expertise, she could work more conventional hours. But tonight, she found herself over her head in an unassigned story.

It was the only way she could prove herself—to be a self-starter—to get what she wanted. This time she'd self-started herself into what would be danger.

*Cotton didn't want to see this. It had been enough to experience it the first time. God, no.*

Greenville County had seen an uptick in gang-related activity. Her idea was to tie in the news of the criminal activity to how the neighborhood residents felt about the gangs in the area—news and the human side of the news. Her ultimate grand plan was to eventually establish some sort of neighborhood watch program and scare away the gangs. If she could do something like that, it would look awesome on her resume. And it would help the community.

She'd reported in numerous areas and knew exactly where to knock on doors. This was a preliminary, expeditionary search for people who might want to go on record, which she knew would be difficult. Who would want to slam a gang in his own apartment complex?

But she could promise anonymity. Film from behind. Disguise the voice. She could quell any fears a person may have about being on camera. She was armed with an agile mind and enough college Spanish that she knew she could handle almost anything that arose. Right?

She pulled up to the apartment buildings that looked like an abandoned military base, all serious and no landscaping, save the one huge tree behind the complex whose limbs spread out in every direction and toward the large harvest moon that night. It had surely been there for more than 100 years, long before some entity had decided to erect the barrack-like red brick buildings before her. Everything important in Cotton's life seemed to be connected to trees—the peaceful, the dangerous, even her heart.

Pieces of trash blew across the pot-holed parking lot that had only a few cars parked in it. Home of West-G, one of the most dangerous gangs in the area—and many elderly people who had no choice but to live there. She turned off her car and sat in the eerie light and silence for a moment.

She inhaled and closed her eyes for a few seconds. The

remnants of what had once been strong in her as a child told her that she shouldn't be there. Unfortunately, everything else in her education and life had replaced all those impressions of feelings and pieces of spirit knowledge away. She gathered up her extensive training and education and pushed away the last remaining remnants of the whispering in her soul—the whispering that told her to leave. Now.

It would have been a good idea if she had been able to take a camera man with her, but her star had not yet risen that high yet. She had to get the story on paper first. Show it to her producer, and then get permission to procure a cameraman and equipment. Something sank in her. This was investigative news, and she was over her head. Though she'd lighten up the story with some human interest, she knew that this was the most dangerous type of journalism. The station's viewers would most definitely be interested in the way the gangs were changing the neighborhoods in Greenville County. This move was brilliant for her career. And stupid for her person.

Standing on the corner was a man with auburn hair, dressed in dark clothes. His back was turned to her and he was staring at what had to be his phone. This was looking to her to be a bad idea for her safety—a good idea for her career, maybe. She wondered how her mother would have felt about where she was and what she was doing.

With all the strength that her intellect could muster, she stepped out the car with her reporter's pad and pencil and hit the button to lock her car. The loud beep caused the man on the corner to look her way.

She started toward an apartment that appeared to have a light on behind some old lace curtains. Surely, an elderly woman lived there. Who else would sport old curtains like that? A cold November gust blew around her legs and skirted up her dress. She had already been branding her signature look, red shoes with everything and fitted, professional clothes that coordinated. Tonight, she'd worn her favorite red dress, a decision that she now regretted. The frock wasn't sexy at all, but the color caught everyone's eye everywhere she went. How out of place she must have looked with her shiny blond hair, crimson lips, red dress and matching high heels.

Well, she was here now, so what was she to do?

She knocked on the door of the little old lady's apartment. *Rap. Rap. Rap.* She noticed a light on in the window across the way, as well. But it was sterile with no curtains or blinds.

*The odd light around her illumined things she hadn't noticed the first time she'd lived this nightmare.*

She hadn't really thought this through and couldn't really count on who would answer, even though she was hoping for an older lady who needed some assistance with her neighborhood in her retirement. Perhaps, it may even be a young mother with small children. Either would work. What she hadn't considered was what she got.

A young man in a larger than normal hoodie answered the door. Emblazoned across the front was some kind of bizarre character that looked like a dragon or a demon, something she'd never seen before now. He didn't say a word.

"Hi, I'm Lawton Rivers, from WCLM. I was hoping you would talk to me about—"

Suddenly, she realized how foolish she was. Could this man actually be one of the members of West G? If he was, was she about to ask him how he felt about his own gang? Oh, no. What had she done?

She could think fast. Couldn't she? "If you could talk to me about a proposed park for this area."

He stood there with his arms crossed, staring a hole through her red dress at about chest high and didn't say a word.

She was in trouble. "I think I have the wrong apartment," she said as she took a step back.

He took a step forward. "Get a load of this stupid woman," he yelled toward the street. He was not happy that she was there, invading his…territory.

She looked behind her, and the auburn-haired guy that was on the corner turned and started walking toward them. Her heel turned on the stoop, and she nearly fell.

It hit her. Flee or freeze.

She chose to flee, but her red high heels wouldn't cooperate. She tried to sprint and lost the one that had twisted on the stoop. Her notebook and pencil fell from her right hand and she held on to those keys with all her might. They were the only things that could possibly save her at this point.

*She wished this horrendous vision would stop—this vision that still haunted her so many years later.*

Fear froze her voice for the moment. She thought she could scream. She wanted to scream. But she couldn't scream.

Both men sprinted after her in their clothing that blended in with the night. The pound of footsteps and the odd sound of jeans rapidly rubbing against its own cloth were the only things she heard. The scent of old, soured garbage cans plagued the air.

She valiantly tried to reach her car, keys in hand, ready to open the door, but she was yanked down, her head snapping back and her blond locks swirling in front of her face. Suddenly, she regained her voice and screamed the loudest, most blood-curdling scream she'd ever heard.

In the distance, she heard a lone dog bark.

The light across the way in the window immediately went out, and from somewhere in the dark shadows of the building, a third man in black clothing emerged, like a dark shark, sensing blood, her blood.

The first two men grabbed her flailing arms, and she struggled as she threw the weight of herself into their clasp, trying to break the hold. Nothing worked. The self-defense lesson she'd taken when she was first hired was useless. All her education was useless. The only thing that seemed that it may have been of use was that small remnant of heart knowledge that she so stupidly pushed away. But it was useless now, too.

The third man grabbed one of her legs and made easy the carrying of her light frame toward the large water oak tree behind the building. They threw her to the ground, and the two men at her arms pressed her shoulders into the dirt. Her heart was pounding so hard in her throat that it swelled, making her attempted screams sound like a rabbit's cry. She continued struggling fruitlessly, only to increase the massive brutal strength of the three men, determined with dark intent.

*There was nothing she could do in the odd light that only illuminated her red dress and one red shoe.*

To save herself, she eventually stopped struggling and screaming and hoped that they'd stop punching her face and would uncover her mouth so that she could breathe.

She gazed at the glowing harvest moon through the crooked branches of the arthritic tree and tried to take herself to a time when she was a child, napping under the old oak tree in her own, safe backyard on the cool, solid ground with her wooden menagerie.

Tears leaked out her eyes as she focused on the round radiance above her.

# CHAPTER SEVEN

## The Weight of Knowledge

Cotton sat up, breathing heavily after the vision ended. The darkness that lay opposite the mountain seemed to engulf her and sent a shiver over her entire body. For many years, she had worked really hard to put that experience out of her head. She even denied it in her heart. Why, here, does she have no control over its coming and going?

She turned from the unending darkness behind her and stared off toward the distant mountain horizon the rest of the night, if you could even call it night. The living lights that blew over the mountain never dimmed, and they illuminated everything in front of her in some kind of liquid glow that played unearthly music. The nearest comparison would be that of the Arora Borealis, which she had never seen, except in a documentary. A light breeze blew from the mountain, and in it was the scent of honeysuckle and love. She stared at the breathing mountain. Her grandmother and father were there. Probably her grandfather and mother, too. And those little lights were there. She wished she could be there, too.

She had a lot of questions for her grandmother. As much as she could tell, Mimi would be in the best position to answer them. Maybe Cotton wasn't asking the questions correctly. Instead of asking broad questions like, "What's going on?" perhaps, she should state what she thinks and ask for confirmation? She didn't know. What she did know was confusing.

Eventually, as the darkness receded a bit in deference to the coming morning, she saw a figure walking down the road. Before she could see his face, she smelled cedar wood and knew it to be her grandfather. Love wafted upon the scent. Leave it to her grandfather to be up this early, like he used to be when she was a child. He used to get up early to build a fire in the fireplace for her and her grandmother, and then he'd take to carving while Mimi would cook their breakfast. Cotton had spent many mornings with him in front of that fireplace. He would have his coffee, and Cotton would sip on the cocoa her grandmother had made for her. He would tell her stories, and she would sit at his feet, enthralled with them. It was then that she'd decided that she wanted to tell stories like him when she grew up. Those stories her grandfather had told her turned into the bulb that grew like a vine and knotted into her love of journalism.

But even at the height of her broadcasting career, she knew that her grandfather's rudimentary, fanciful stories contained something that hers lacked. Maybe it was that thing her station manager referred to when she asked him to consider her for a promotion.

She watched as the little crimson lights trailed behind her grandfather. They were all there, all twelve. The ones the sizes of fruits, the ones the sizes of various berries, and the ones the size of duckweed.

The little lights drifted up into the green leaves in the tree above as they arrived. She felt like she should have known them…or at least what they were or why they were there.

*Thump.*

Something hit her. Hard.

*You haven't wanted to know them.*

Knowledge. But what kind of knowledge was that? She thought for a moment. It was born of her mantra for getting out of trouble…out of responsibility: *Ignorance can be its own reward.*

Though she had thought many times that her credo had served her, here, it was making her sick in her heart. Here, there were no rewards for ignorance. She needed to know things in order to sort them. How foolish she had been.

When her grandfather finally arrived, she stepped toward him. "Poppy, I'm so glad to see you."

He opened his arms wide, and she fell into them in some otherworldly way. Love engulfed her, along with the scent of cedar. Touching was so different here. He hugged her for the longest time. "Let's sit for a while, like we used to."

Each found a place in the grass under her big tree, away from the large stone. Not even one of the fallen leaves from the evening before was on the ground. How peculiar that was. How peculiar everything was in this place.

She noted nearly the same appearance in her grandfather as she'd noted in her grandmother. Though he still had gray hair, his skin was as smooth as a man at thirty. But something was the same about his eyes. They were still gray and clouded like they had been when she remembered him last. "You look worried, Puddin'," he said.

She lowered her head. "I'm so confused. I'm having dreams, and visions, and nightmares. I know too little to put this all together." She felt like she wanted to cry, but there were no tears to drop or well in her eyes, just the feeling that they should.

"There, there, Puddin'." He put one arm around her, and she placed her head upon his shoulder. But it didn't have the same substance as when she had touched him as a child.

"Oh, Poppy, I'm so sorry I didn't spend more time with you in the end—like you did with me when I was a child."

"That is the way of things. There is no requirement. We had love, and that was enough."

Cotton absorbed those words into her head. But they wouldn't penetrate her heart, though she tried so hard to break it open.

They sat together in silence for a very long time as she breathed in the familiar woody fragrance.

"Hey, I have a new lion joke," he said.

Cotton smiled, even though her head was buried under her grandfather's arm. It was merely days ago that she was reminded of his corny old lion joke by Mr. Earnest. And she'd promised herself that if she ever got that chance again that she wouldn't roll her eyes. Well, this was her chance. She sat up straight and looked into his cloudy eyes. "Tell me, Poppy." Her emotions welled in her heart for her good fortune.

"What do you call a lion with the best wardrobe?"

This was the way of it. Of course she wouldn't know the answer, but her grandfather would want her to try to answer. "Ummm…aaaaaaaa…a tailor?"

Her grandfather straightened up and leaned back to see her response. "No, silly, a dande-lion."

Laughter burst out from her innermost child. Her eyes did not roll, like she'd promised herself. Her laughter did not burst forth because of his corny joke. It was also from her joy at being able to experience him and his unique sense of humor again. "That's really funny, Poppy. So, you learned that here?"

He nodded. "Yep. We learn things here, too. We have fun and laugh. Whatever we need is supplied. We do the work during the day, and at night, we rejoice."

Staring into his face, she recognized his joy at making her laugh once again. It was just like her grandfather to make jokes in a situation like this.

"I brought a lot of my old jokes with me here, but I had to register them before I was allowed on the mountain with them," said Poppy.

"Register them?" What a curious idea.

Her grandfather nodded and looked around like somebody might hear him. He whispered, "I had one about St. Peter getting *a head* in line of St. John, but they wouldn't let me register that one." Poppy giggled and put his bottom lip over his top one, making the same silly face he used to make at her when she was a child.

She giggled. "I'm not surprised. That one is awful."

After the laughing subsided, they sat together in silence for a few moments, then, a serious expression grew upon his face. "So, what do you need?"

Shaking her head, she said, "I don't know. I don't even know why I'm here. I'm just so confused by everything. Everything is different, the properties of things, the importance of things, the purpose of things."

He nodded as she spoke. "It will all become clear in the light."

She wished that to be so, but this was the strangest light, in the strangest land, that was governed by the strangest principles. Why couldn't someone simply tell her what she needed to know or do?

A bit of brightness returned to his clouded eyes. "How would you like to go for a little stroll, like we used to," he asked.

They stood and walked together past her tree, away from the little lights. She looked back to see them whizzing amongst the leaves. She somehow knew they'd be okay there, darting and dashing around the branches. Hmmm. That was an odd thought. She had some kind of new concern for those little illuminations.

As she and her grandfather walked, she noticed that her grandfather had lost the limp he'd developed in his last years. Arthritis had set up home in his joints. But now, it was gone.

"I have something to show you," he said.

She nodded. Daylight turned its temperature up slowly as they walked. The leaves on the trees around them glowed a thousand shades of green. The path upon which they walked was soft, and though dust rose up with each step, their bare feet didn't get dirty. The largest boulders they passed swirled in places, like they were living.

The entire time they strolled, her grandfather had a gentle smile upon his lips. "Hey, remember when I used to give you my lunchbox at the end of the day when I was working?"

"Of course, I do. You always saved me something from your lunch. Sometimes it was an egg. Sometimes, chips. Sometimes a mint. It wasn't the thing as much as the thought."

He chuckled at the memory of it. "Yep. That's right. You got it. Those are the things that are of the insides."

She did get it, even back then—when she was full of favor.

"Do you remember our little secret? I hope you never told your grandmother, or she would have killed me back then?" Again, he covered his top lip with his bottom.

"Absolutely, I remember. You always saved me a few sips of your sweet, creamy coffee in your thermos. I never told Mimi. Or Mother." Cotton could almost taste the sugary dark liquid that she loved.

"Good thing, or they would have had my hide." He chuckled. "I knew you liked it because you used to put down your cocoa when your grandmother wasn't looking, and you'd grab my coffee off the coffee table in the morning, and you'd take a sip."

She smiled at the memory. What a wonderful childhood she'd

had, especially the parts with her grandparents.

They continued walking and soon enough they arrived at a hill dotted with boulders. Her grandfather suddenly stopped.

"This is the place," her grandfather said.

Okay. She supposed that this was one of those situations from which she needed to glean something—some meaning or knowledge.

One boulder looked like a large sofa, with a low part and a higher part. One looked like a teardrop, and one looked like a human heart, completely unlike a valentine. It was as if she'd seen them all before, but that couldn't be. Boulders as large as these cannot be moved. They seemed to be everywhere, even in places they should not be. Though the rest of the landscapes looked like her beloved Lowcountry, all the rocks were atypical of her familiar home.

She perched herself against the one that reminded her of a human heart. She was so very worried about her own. From her vantage point, she looked out over a great city. But what was unusual about it was that it had no buildings. It was a city of trees. All the inhabitants were in the streets or under the branches or sitting upon low branches. A city of trees? Maybe that didn't matter. Maybe that was a question that was only intended for an earthly mind.

In the center of the city was a grand tree, taller than anything around it. From its center arose a staff with a large colorful flag, embroidered and bordered in gold threads. In its center was a golden crown, a king's symbol.

Many smaller, less impressive trees grew near it. There was

much activity on the streets, children running, old men talking, wives carrying goods. The air was filled with the scent of freshly baked bread and olives.

Though there was buying and selling everywhere, Cotton's attention turned to the grand tree that reminded her of a castle. A great king in fine white robes, made of flowing silk and gold thread stood on some kind of platform, like in a treehouse, looking over all that he commanded. A servant poured wine in a challis and handed it to him. As he surveyed the streets, his attention settled upon a particularly stately tree. A beautiful young woman was bathing behind flowing drapes under the branches. Atop her tree was a flagpole, and attached to it was a white flag with a purple crown. Cotton knew it to show an alliance to the king, though no one told her. That knowledge inside her could still work—if she tried hard enough.

After a while, the young woman's servants came with white and beige cloths and wrapped her in them. Another came with a simple white dress and placed it over her head. She reclined on a lounge chair as one of her servants braided her long, dark hair. After some time, a handsome man with a sword on his side arrived and kissed her.

Cotton watched as all this took place. Her earthly heart wanted to look toward her grandfather, but she knew that was not where the knowledge was. It was in front of her.

The king finished his third glass of wine and called for more. He lifted his hand to summon another servant. The servant hurried away and in moments was under the tree with the handsome soldier and the beautiful woman.

As the servant talked, the woman sat up and began to cry. The servant left, and the soldier kissed the woman goodbye.

"I think I vaguely remember this story from bible school," Cotton said to her grandfather.

The scene before her began to wave in slow undulations, and enigmatically she knew it to be the passage of time. Nothing behaved properly, like it did back home.

When the ripples in the air stilled, Cotton saw a black flag flying atop the woman's tree. Was that for the woman's husband? Cotton remembered a piece of that story, but she didn't want to look at the aftermath of the King's sin.

The rock she was leaning on was warming and pulsing. She moved back to stare at the rock, to understand it...or to comprehend what it was supposed to symbolize. She concentrated and willed herself knowledge...discernment...insight.

Letters formed in the rock like liquid clouds, but she didn't recognize the language they formed, like yesterday.

*Thump. The shock weakened her knees.*

Then, like she'd realized before, the strange words formed from the rock made sense to her.

*"In the final days, peril will reign. People will love themselves, will covet, will boast, will be proud, will blaspheme and be ungrateful and disobedient to their parents, and will live unholy."*

*Thump.* Those were *her* words. Not words that she'd spoken, but words that belonged to her. She reached out to gather them so that she would never forget them ever again, but as soon as she did, they melted into the rock, like dark, mysterious clouds dispersing in the skies.

She had been all those things written in the rock. Shame flushed her cheeks red, her signature color. Guilt welled up in her heart. She was embarrassed that her beloved grandfather was witnessing her acceptance of her guilt.

Still staring at the rock, she asked, "Poppy, I once had God's favor, too. How can I make up for what I've done?" She looked up.

He closed his gray eyes, contemplating what she had said, and hung his head. "It is yours to sort."

She inhaled his words and placed them beside the knowledge from the rock. *Thump*. The Rock. Suddenly, she understood so many more names for that huge, immovable boulder—The Everlasting Rock, Rock of My Strength, The Tested Stone…and more. She could sense her eyes widen with the knowledge.

Poppy nodded. "See, it will be illuminated. When you are ready. We must continue," he said. "I have more chores before tonight."

She followed her grandfather. After some distance, as she trailed behind, she sensed she was walking with more weight down the path. Her head was swirling with her new knowledge and how she'd acquired it. "Poppy, what were those words? I mean, they were foreign to me but I understood."

"They were the original words—the old Hebrew and Greek words—the ones The Stone spoke first. In them are more meaning and less of the…ummm…contamination than the words we use. How can I explain? Ummm. They are purer with more depth." He continued to walk and stare straight ahead as he clarified.

She got that. She'd studied Spanish in college, and some words in the English and Spanish languages just didn't translate, and when someone tried to approximate the meaning, they had to use additional explanations. She liked the way Poppy explained the words. *Pure and uncontaminated.*

Along the path was every sort of tree and bush imaginable and unimaginable, in every shade of green imaginable and unimaginable. The white skies swirled with light blue iridescent circles and moved across the landscapes. They walked along in silence for at least an hour, the strange words she'd claimed further embedding themselves into her heart, like seeds into the earth. Was she going to get a second chance? To go home? To be a better person? To repair all the damage she had caused?

Somewhere in her inner heart, she'd always thought she'd go back to her beginnings, her Sunday school days…after she'd accomplished what she and her mother had planned for her career. Who knew she'd never reach that point in her life?

She had clearly made some poor decisions. Certainly, there had to be a way to resolve this conundrum—this place—this mess she'd made.

When they finally rounded a corner in the path they were walking on, a tranquil lake came into view. "Have you been fishing lately?" Poppy asked, smiling like he knew the answer. He used to take her fishing all the time when she was a little girl. In his little boat, she'd listen to his stories and laugh at his jokes while she had played with the little wooden animals he'd carved.

They walked to the huge rocks that were beside the aqua lake that swirled like the skies. Again, the fact that she wasn't in the Lowcountry of South Carolina was glaringly evident—even though this place had some familiar traits. She lived and played and worked on flat lands without rocks, surrounded by wet lands with marsh grasses and swamps with scrub palmettos. This was different. Poppy stood like a sentinel beside her as she leaned against another rock that reminded her of a shallow bowl or some vessel that could hold water.

"Poppy, is this a new rock, or has it somehow moved?" she asked. "So many look familiar."

He thought for a while. "There is no place without the Rock," he said. He picked up a stick at his feet and eyed it like he used to when he was looking for a piece of wood to carve. He leaned against the tree like he knew they'd be there a while.

The lake spread out to the horizon, and as far as she could see, it was clear as it eddied, the surface sparkling like billions of diamonds, every color imaginable and not. She could see the depths of the water, and she could also see the churning waters were teaming with all manner of fishes. A boat somewhat larger than her grandfather's contained four men and a large net. Each stood at the four corners of the roped mesh, knelt with it in their hands and prayed. In concert they threw over the net, and she watched it sink to the bottom of the deep waters. In the next moment, they pulled on the ropes they retained in their hands. Shore birds hovered behind them on the blue wind that whirred a song that sounded unearthly. The fresh air was scented with the sea. When the net was at the surface, the men lifted the huge hall of fishes into the boat with what seemed like super human strength. They let go the ropes, and the fishes spilled into the boat, filling it with all manner of species of fish.

She looked at her grandfather who was smiling. "Look," he said and pointed.

The men lowered their heads once again and prayed. From the skies came a column of crystal light and halted to rest upon the little boat. Then the men began to toss out some of the fish. She thought she heard the fish crying, but that couldn't be. Every once in a while, a man would lift up a fish toward the light and pray. Sometimes he would throw a thrashing fish behind the boat, and sometimes he would return the contented ones to the boat. The shore birds behind the skiff were diving and grabbing the fish that were thrown back and would fly away with their catches.

*What are they doing?* She thought. She knew she was supposed to figure this all out for herself. She tried hard, like she did before.

Her grandfather said, "Their job, child." He had a shiny knife in one hand and the stick he'd found in the other.

He had heard her thoughts—even though she had not said a word.

Cotton turned back to the scene, and the boat was empty again, and the men were kneeling like they had at first.

*Where are the fish? The men couldn't have possibly thrown over all the fish so quickly. What is she supposed to know from this?*

"They are fishing all over again, aren't they?"

Poppy nodded. "They are *living* it."

Cotton searched her head. Yes, that's what it was. They were a living…lesson. As they all had been. And she was supposed to learn it as if by osmosis. How unfair! She was getting so frustrated by all the vague answers and rhetorical statements.

*Couldn't someone just write it all down in a book and just hand it to her?*

Her grandfather said, "He did."

He'd heard her again. Something inside her sank. She'd been given a book before, in church, an important one, that she'd set upon a shelf and allowed the dust to cover.

In Sunday school, she had learned some of the stories in that book. But this wasn't one of those. The knowledge inside her told her this living lesson was symbolic.

She realized how blessed she had been that her grandparents had taken her to church—that her little mind had learned about Jesus. Her little soul had been cared for without her even understanding. Over the years, she missed those days in church as she'd depended upon outsiders more and more for her dim education and dull enlightenment. She missed those simple days with their simple stories, concepts and principles.

Sadly, she turned back to watch as the men in the boat again divided the fish prayerfully. They threw away certain fish and they kept other fish. She squinted her eyes and concentrated really hard.

*And thump. The shock of it shot through her heart.*

*There it was. The knowing.*

And another word became clear to her. Discernment. She'd

learned something about it in church.

The truth rose up in her like a tide.

*The good from the bad.* The fishermen were sorting out the good fish species from the bad or inedible ones.

*This place is The Sorting Place.*

She understood. She slumped back upon the rock.

She looked at her grandfather, and fear rose up cold in her face.

He continued to stare at the scene before them.

"I am being judged, Poppy." She knew. The hairs on her arms prickled and tickled. And stung.

She looked at her grandfather and felt his affirmation again.

Underneath her, the massive gray rock warmed. She slid off it and turned to face it. Strange letters formed again, like dark, tumultuous clouds, swirling in stone. She could not read them or call them out because they were the pure words she'd seen before, but the growing spirit knowledge in her instinctively knew what they meant.

*"God will judge all deeds—every good action, every evil work, and every secret thought."*

She knew the words had come from that book she didn't read, but there were no references to the numbers she used to worry about so—the numbers about the chapters and verses that Miss Tree made such a big deal about.

And then the stone words melted like butter, swirling back

into the hot rock.

She looked toward the area where the fishermen had been, but they were gone.

"That is enough," said Poppy.

Was it? She had a million questions. About her earthly life. About her fate. About the lights. But she knew no one was going to answer them. She had to figure them out—sort it all out for herself. It seemed that anything that dealt with *her* life, *she* had to figure out—to weigh—to discern.

"We must go back now." He held up the stick he had picked up earlier and examined it with his cloudy eyes. After his consideration, he tossed it. "This is not the one."

She wanted to go back, all right. She wanted to go back to the day she was painting the church. No, she wanted to go back to the beginning of her career. Better yet, she wanted to go back to her childhood and make every decision she'd ever made over again. The feeling weighed on her like the weight of the fish in that net.

They walked in silence down the path that would lead her to her tree. She knew there to be beautiful gardens on both sides of the road, but they didn't demand her attention. Her soul unsettled itself inside her as they walked. She had made some really bad decisions in her life. And here she was being judged for them. In The Sorting Place.

Her Poppy had always been her protector, but she sensed he could not protect her here. She sensed his sadness about that as he walked.

Ahead in the road, they came to an impasse. Their way was blocked by animals. The shepherd was very quickly trying to get his flock out of the road. He pulled at one, and he pushed at another, until their path was clear. She and her grandfather began to pass. It was odd that she hadn't noticed how the shepherd had accomplished it, but he had somehow divided his flock, his sheep on one side of the road and his goats on the other. She realized she hadn't been looking. At anything. Her entire life. And all the while, the dividing was being accomplished as she was living by her ridiculous mantra. *Ignorance is its own reward.*

This sorting out thing was not going to go well for her. She could tell.

When they arrived at her tree, she asked Poppy to sit with her for a while. After some time, the leaves began to fall all about her once again.

They both sat, she with the heaviness of what she'd been shown. The people, the fish, the sheep, the events, the rocks and the trees—all seemed to have more import than she had—at first—assessed. Though she had been given knowledge, for her, there seemed to have been more questions after the knowledge. All the questions ran through her head.

"Poppy, why do I live under a tree? Why do we all live under trees in this place?"

Poppy looked troubled. "Puddin', what need have you for a house?"

Cotton thought. None. In this place, it did not rain under her tree, nor did it get cold. But there should be meaning beyond that, she thought.

Knowledge settled upon her heart again. "These are like living houses," she said. "All that is lived underneath the canopies is not in secret." She had convinced herself that she had kept secrets from people on Earth—secrets even from God.

Trees had always had more draw for her than houses. Each significant tree in her life imparted meaning that she felt in the depths of her heart. God knew their meanings…and her secrets.

Her grandfather continued. "Sometimes, when we don't figure out the important stuff in The Choosing Place, we must figure it out in The Sorting Place. You'll understand even more if you try."

She reached for Poppy's hand under her tree and silently held it in some sense. She turned her head toward the sky. She watched as the spirited lights darted high amongst the branches near the top. They seemed to be playing a game of avoiding the falling leaves as they flitted about.

Poppy looked up, too. "They are delightful, aren't they?"

She didn't know what to say. Maybe they delighted in confusing her. Still, she seemed…mesmerized by them…somehow…strangely connected to them in a strange way. But why? How was this new discernment going to help with that?

A strong sense of wood and love emanated from Poppy, and she breathed it in, wanting to hold him inside her lungs for as long as she could.

"You haven't settled with them yet, have you?" he asked.

She took her eyes off them and looked at Poppy. "Settled what? I'm trying to settle with myself. Why am I here? Why do I keep visiting the visions of the worst days of my life? Will I get to go back and stay there. And make something more out of my life?"

"What? Go back to The Choosing Place?" He stared into the tree with his clouded eyes and did not answer her.

He didn't need to speak. She tiredly said, "I already know. It's to be decided, but what will that decision be, and who will be making that determination? Don't I get a say about what is decided about me?"

Poppy cleared his throat. "We all made mistakes. I did. There were times I could have helped my neighbors, and I didn't. There were times I could have loved your grandmother more, but I worked instead. Yeah, I made my share of mistakes, too." He closed his cloudy eyes.

She thought on that for a moment. Made mistakes? That's most definitely past tense. Maybe there's not going to be any going back for her. But Poppy had made mistakes, and he was here, living on the mountain. "I don't understand any of this."

Poppy nodded. "You will discern when you dream or He deems."

Her head was jumbled. "Am I asking the wrong questions? In the wrong way? Should they be—I don't know—like *Jeopardy* questions?"

Poppy laughed. "The answer is…you're going to have to answer the questions from the set of answers to the questions that have already been answered for us all." He pulled his bottom lip over his top lip again.

"Oh, Poppy." She wanted to giggle, but something inside her knew that there was real seriousness in what he'd said.

Poppy and her grandmother used to watch *Jeopardy* with Cotton when she had been a child, but she'd never heard such a convoluted answer, such as his.

He looked at her sideways. "You know, a lot of your questions and statements have the word I in them."

She thought. Yes, they did. Caleb was right again. She was selfish. He aptly pointed out that she was always using the word I, as well.

Looking intently at her grandfather, deep into his eyes, she cleared her throat. "Well, what if I asked a question that dealt with you? Would you answer that?"

"Hmmm. If I could. I have limits in my chores." Once again, he drew his bottom lip up over his top to make a silly face. "Go ahead. Ask."

"Why are your eyes still dim? I mean, they're still covered by the cataracts. It almost looks like you can't see, but your body otherwise seems healed."

His silly face disappeared. "Oh, I am proud to tell you why. I chose that. On purpose." Her grandfather had a knack for silliness, but choosing that was just crazy.

"Aaaaand why?" She moved from her comfortable spot on the ground to stare straight into his face.

"You see, when you grow old, in The Choosing Place, you

tend to turn your vision back, inward. And you think of the interior things, and you are not bothered by the distractions of the outside—the silliness of nothingness. I like the way the gray helps to keep me focused upon what's important. In the heart. I see well enough."

"Well, at least that's some kind of explanation." Though she didn't exactly agree with it.

"And I'm confused about your age. I mean, you and Mimi and Daddy look so young, like you are all the same age."

"Ah, that. We are the sum of all the ages we have been."

That made no sense whatsoever. Just like this place with the swirling skies and word-filled rocks.

He glanced at her from the corner of his eye. "Numbers and math behave differently here."

She huffed. "Well, that's fine. I was never any good at numbers when they behaved normally."

Poppy punched her lightly on her arm, which she didn't really feel, but sensed, and they chuckled together. Humor ran in the family, she guessed.

She took in a deep breath and looked up at the lights. In their play, the orange-sized one and the grapefruit one continued to occasionally split, dim, and re-join themselves. "Why do the larger lights do that?"

He stood, tugged at a branch and broke it from the tree, a loud splitting sound startled her. "This is the one." He handed the branch to her. "Many things that God intended to be whole are torn apart by man."

She looked at the piece of limb and passed it back to him. Well, that was the second closest thing she'd gotten to an answer in this place—if you could call either real answers. Because she was just as befuddled as ever.

He pulled the mirrored knife from his pocket and sat back down. He eyed the round, crooked stick. First, up one side, and down to the end. He began carving into it, whistling an old song she'd heard many times in church, "Just as I Am."

Every once in a while, he would blow at the stick to remove the shavings. Poppy always liked working with wood and whittling, carving things into it or things out of it.

She sat, listening to him whistle the old song and whittling the crooked stick for quite a while under her tree. She wanted to absorb every second deep into her heart. She had missed the old man so. Occasionally, she glanced up through the limbs at her small lights. *Thump.* Yes, she knew they were actually her lights—just like the tree. But why?

Though she understood some of what she'd seen today, she tried desperately to understand the big picture, the whole of it, the import of it to her.

The day began to fade, though. She knew that she'd be alone soon. That seemed to be the way of it all. Here. In The Sorting Place.

At the top of the stick the canopy of an oak tree was emerging, limbs and leaves beginning to form. It was going to be beautiful, as all Poppy's work was.

"Hey, Poppy, how did you get that knife in here?"

"Hmmmph. I had to get special permission. But when I promised I'd use it for the lessons, they told me I could bring it in if I kept it in my pocket." He chuckled.

Cotton embraced the moments with her grandfather. He had always been a source of wisdom and entertainment to her. She breathed in his aromatic scent again. How much longer would she be able to absorb him? "Poppy, how long have I been here?"

He laughed, "Oh, Puddin', as long as it has taken for you to understand what is yours."

That was not an answer. "Well, how much longer will I be here?"

He stopped carving for a moment and thought. "For as long as it will take. Your situation is complicated."

Complicated? What does that even mean?

Maybe what she was experiencing as days could be weeks or months. Maybe time and space in The Sorting Place were unorthodox, bending to suit their own requirements, and maybe she'd never understand them. Maybe they didn't even matter here.

Finally, Poppy came to a stopping point and folded up the reflective knife. He looked up at the glows that darted through the branches. "I must take them back now." Her grandfather stood with the stick and brushed away the wood chips on his khaki-colored pants. "And, remember, don't leave the protection of your tree at night."

"I won't," she said, almost wanting to roll her eyes, but she'd promised herself to never roll her eyes ever again in her grandfather's presence. She stood and hugged her Poppy with a hug that really wasn't a hug. "When will I see you again?"

He gazed into her face with his cloudy eyes. "It has already been decided."

Another anti-answer. It's complicated, but it's already been decided? How can that be? All the words swirled around in her head, along with the messages she'd gathered from the rocks.

She watched as her grandfather walked away, occasionally pointing the stick toward the mountain that seemed to be alive, the little burning lights in tow, following him like he was the Pied Piper. Something inside her wished they didn't have to go.

If only she had real explanations and not all this vague rhetoric—the stories, the living lessons, the parables, the allegories. What? Was this a literature lesson, filled with metaphors and symbolism? She sat and thought about all that had happened, all that she'd seen. The broadcaster in her wanted to turn it all into a neatly constructed factual story that could be told in a three-minute segment, but nothing added up. Piled up, maybe. Bad decision after bad decision that she had made in The Choosing Place.

The skies around her began to fade as more and more leaves fell. She didn't want to give in to the pull of the soft earth below her, so she resisted. Maybe she could think her way out of all this. Maybe if she prayed. Maybe He would give her an answer.

Bowing her head and pausing, the words felt rusty in her head. Eventually, she began.

*Jesus, I am so sorry I've neglected You in my life after I stopped going to church with Mimi and Poppy. I'm sorry that I stopped talking to You. I wish I hadn't done many of the things I've done, but I didn't know any better.*

A thunderous *boom* came from deep within the ground. She stood up. Was that Jesus? Or God? Was He angry? What had she said? She just wanted to say that she was sorry. Fear sprung up in her. If she had angered God, there really was no way to fix any of this here…now. She walked to the tree's trunk, sat and leaned against it. But the tree had hardened in the waning light, and she found no comfort in it like she had before. None of this was going her way, like her life had.

# CHAPTER EIGHT

## Welcoming the Unwelcome

Cotton hadn't remembered falling asleep. Not even how she'd made it to the ground. Maybe she wasn't asleep, but what she knew was that she was sinking into another of those troubling visions—revelations in the unusual light. This one, months after the last one—after her assault. *Thump.*

*The light was the same incandescent, brilliant light as in her other visions. No shadows. Every little thing was illuminated. Even things she hadn't noticed before.*

This day was the one that she'd tried her hardest to put out of her mind. And had successfully accomplished that to a great degree. Necessarily so. Until recently. More than anything, she did not want to see that day in this light—in the light of discernment.

She was all alone. That was why she'd put off the procedure

for so long. There was no one to call. There wasn't any decision to make. She was about to go from cub reporter on assignment to a real personality in front of the camera, if she got the Charleston job that she'd interviewed for last week. All indications were that the job was hers. She'd even given them her direct deposit information. The only thing that remained to be done was for her to agree to the numbers on the contract. And for her to sign. She couldn't take that job and make that move, though, unless she was…unencumbered.

An old Beatles album played softly in the background in the exam room. She'd liked them well enough. *At least, at this point in her life*. Her mother and father used to listen to oldies all the time. "Strawberry Fields" was playing, and it had been one of her favorites. Until this day.

She groaned under her tree and tried to bring herself out of the awful vision because she'd experienced the hell of it once before. When it had been real. But something was very different this time around. Her tummy tumbled, and she became nauseous.

*There was so much light. And no shadows. Every little thing was illuminated.*

Someone must have turned up the music this time. She could hear the song, "Something." Glancing at the clock above the door again, she noticed that an hour and a half had already passed. She'd been told the procedure would only take about thirty minutes.

The doctor who was hovering at the end of the table made a couple of grunting sounds. "Hey, Renee, hand me another speculum. A size up. Oh, and get me the largest uterine curette, while you're at it. They are in the top drawer over there."

The nurse at her side got up and retrieved the requested instruments. She paused briefly beside the doctor to see the activity at Cotton's feet. This time around, Cotton noticed that the nurse looked troubled. She glanced at Cotton and quickly returned her eyes to the doctor's hands.

"Um, I'm going to need you to call Ms. Flowers and Dr. Ashburn," he said. "Oh, and when you've finished, give her another dose of the sedative and an additional dose of antibiotics. This is taking longer than I'd planned." He used his forearm to wipe the considerable sweat from his brow.

"Yes, doctor," the nurse said. She took off her sterile gloves and threw them in the trashcan beside Cotton's head. The nurses' shoes had brown stains all over them, and Cotton watched them as the nurse walked toward the intercom phone on the wall.

Cotton had never had a procedure like this before, but calling for extra assistance had not been a part of the expected process.

At least that was what she'd been led to believe when she'd come in for her consultation. That consultation was so cut and dry. Words like procedure, evacuate, medication, dilation, medical waste and normal were used. It sounded nearly like it did when she was seven and had her tonsils out. Only she got ice cream and a sucker back then. There was no reward this time.

The nurse called as she'd been instructed. Her voice broke in the middle and she glanced back at Cotton and then toward the doctor. "Ms. Flowers will be here shortly, but Dr. Ashburn is tied up at the moment.

"That's fine," he said, continuing to struggle and sweat.

Cotton was really worried. If she could, she would stop

everything right now—get more information—clarification. But that wasn't an option. In the middle of things. Why didn't she ask more questions on the day of her consultation? She was a journalist, right? She was supposed to ask questions. But, no. Cotton did absolutely no research, like she would have done on any other kind of investigation. She simply acted on auto-pilot, the one her mom had put her on, the one society had tried to normalize.

What was inside her was a secret. What was happening to her inside secret was a secret. What the doctor was doing was a secret—all covered by the dark veil of her uterus, white-washed terminology and in a building that was most definitely misnamed.

The nurse returned to her side with water in her eyes. She blinked several times, held up a syringe and emptied it into the port in her arm. She tossed the needle into one of those red biohazard containers, and then she grabbed a second syringe and did the same with it.

"May I get you some water," the nurse asked, some kind of compassion was carried in her words.

Cotton nodded. The cold in the room seemed to intensify. She tried as hard as she could to not shake.

The nurse opened a small bottle of water, inserted a straw and held it to Cotton's lips. "Ms. Flowers will be here in a minute."

Why did they even need Ms. Flowers? Cotton was confused. Ms. Flowers, by virtue of her very moniker, was not a doctor. Why would she be needed?

Ms. Flowers was the woman she'd spoken to last week and

was the director of the misnamed clinic. When she walked through the door with all her great importance, a second nurse followed closely behind.

The three conferred in whispers at the bottom of the table, and though Cotton tried desperately to make out the words, she couldn't because "Help!" was playing too loudly through the audio speaker above her.

Shouldn't they tell her what was going on? After all, it was her body. And isn't that what Ms. Flowers kept insisting at the evaluation appointment—that it was Cotton's body, and she could do anything with it that she wished.

Cotton felt her body being pushed against by the physician's hands. Inside her felt…uncomfortable. She was filled with…apprehension about what she was doing—what she had to do. None of this felt like a choice. She didn't choose her assault. She didn't choose to be pushed and pinched and probed and prodded like she was by the doctor. She didn't choose to be cold and alone and scared. This hadn't been the "choice" that they all pushed for her to make, by telling her that it was so easy. Instead, it felt like this "choice" had been the only option offered to her. And now that "choice" felt more like a punishment.

"Wait," Ms. Flowers said. She retrieved something out the cabinet in the corner. She tried to keep it out of Cotton's view, but she saw the stainless instrument shine when Ms. Flowers turned and handed it to the doctor.

Oh, no. The device looked like Mimi's poultry shears. Oh, that can't be. She didn't sign up for any of this. Fear rose up in her.

"Try the upper left quadrant, where the fundus meets the fallopian tube," Ms. Flowers said. Her head was level with the doctor's shoulders, intently involved in this "procedure" that should have only taken one quarter of the time it was taking.

Why was this director giving advice to a physician?

*The words swirled throughout the room and finally arranged themselves before her: No expertise is needed when the outcome is extermination.*

*Thump.*

After a few more pushes and tugs, Ms. Flowers stood up. "There. I thought that might do it." She left the room as the doctor tossed his crimson-stained instruments upon the stainless tray on the table—only now the tray was not stainless. Cotton's blood stained everything.

Cotton looked at the nurse at her side, red faced and avoiding eye contact.

The second nurse took a shallow steel pan to a table against the wall and stared into it, occasionally looking back at the physician. She left, but moments later, a few other nurses buzzed in and out of the room with her, coming to look inside the pan.

*The light in the room seemed to grow brighter.*

The doctor finally said, "That's enough. Tell Dr. Ashburn that I'd like to consult with him for a moment.

The nurses left, looking like they'd been reprimanded.

A second doctor in his sterile white coat came in.

"Ah, Dr. Dawson, how may I help you?" he said looking past

the man who'd performed her procedure.

They turned from her, like she didn't matter, so she couldn't hear much of what they were saying. Dr. Ashburn grabbed one of the instruments from the tray and returned to the shallow pan. He and Dr. Dawson spoke, exchanging terms that she didn't understand and communicated in mumbles as the speaker above her blared "Hey, Jude."

Somehow, she knew this was not over for her because they kept glancing back at her. Dr. Ashburn made a second call, and in a few minutes, in walked Ms. Flowers, right past Cotton, ignoring her very existence.

They conferenced in hushed tones as "While My Guitar Gently Weeps" wafted through the room.

She left and the two doctors conferenced some more, glancing at Cotton and then back again at the stainless-steel pan.

Eventually, the first doctor came to her side, blood and substance all over his white coat, and said, "There's been a complication, and I'm afraid the complication may affect your future fertility. You need to know this now in case you don't make a follow-up appointment with us."

Cotton's heart sunk. "What? I thought these things were simple and safe," she said. "Ms. Flowers didn't say anything about anything like this. That wasn't a part of the "choice" I'd been given. I didn't choose this."

"Usually, this process is very efficient. But this is—after all—a medical procedure, and each patient is different and complications can arise."

Oh, heck, no. He wasn't going to get away with an explanation like that. She was almost an investigative reporter. "I'm sorry, but I need facts and information about this." After all it was her body.

The doctor inhaled. "The size was advanced beyond what we'd first thought. And it complicated things."

"I told you exactly when I was assaulted." She drew in a ragged breath, causing her entire body to shudder. "Am I still…"

"Oh, no. No. The pregnancy is terminated," he said in a matter-of-fact way.

The word hit her like a lead ball in her stomach. Terminated. What a word. Was the "termination" in that bowl? It was a precise word for a disordered job. Terminated. When she was working on a story, she'd once looked up the word in her favorite resource book, a Thesaurus. It meant ended. Finished. Completed. Sacked. Closed. Dissolved. Concluded. Dismissed. All synonyms for terminated.

All the world had said it was her "choice." Her judgement. Her prerogative. Her ruling. Her verdict. Her conclusion. Her pronouncement. Her resolution. Her decision.

Her right.

*The lights in the room brightened to a degree that was almost blinding.*

*Was it her right?*

Dr. Ashburn glanced into the container one last time and left the room. The nurse who'd been at her side during the confusion and the doctor who'd performed her "procedure" finished up whatever it was they needed to do at her feet. "I Want to Hold Your Hand" rang out of the speaker above her.

As they worked, she was drawn to the lonely, stainless pan on the table. This time, it was more illuminated than she had remembered. Shinier. More important, somehow. Her efforts to decipher its importance made her nauseous. She stared at it until something seemed to…to…to move.

She startled and shook the table she was on.

The doctor looked up and said, "Are you okay?"

She nodded. But she wasn't.

What had she just seen in that pan? It couldn't be. She thought she'd seen a tiny, translucent hand stretch out.

"Uh-eek," she gasped. But that was impossible. Tears formed in her eyes.

The doctor stopped. "Are you sure there's nothing wrong?"

Everything was wrong. But she didn't know what to say. He couldn't know that she was…hallucinating. Only crazy people did that. And she was anything but crazy. She was a reporter, and she dealt in facts. That…hallucination in that pan could never fit in with her set of facts about the procedure. She'd heard the pro-choice pieces on the major news networks and gathered the brochures in the lobby of the clinic. Her mother had preached the information to her as she grew and became a woman.

Maybe her hallucination was because of the medication. She couldn't tell him that either, that she was taking a taxi home to be by herself because she had no one.

Dr. Dawson finished and stood. "When you've recovered sufficiently, in a few weeks, we'll do some tests, unless you have your own primary care physician. You could always follow-up with her."

She'd heard him, but her eyes were trained on that sterile pan on that sterile counter. To prove herself wrong. To align the facts. She definitely needed more facts.

"Renee, help her get dressed and see that she'll have the proper help when she gets home." He walked over to the pan with a towel, placed it on top and carried it out with him.

Cotton got dressed, but she still felt naked. Naked and hollow. Naked and hollow. And dead.

⚘

Cotton awoke to the smell of buttermilk biscuits, cane syrup, and love. Maybe this was all a dream. Maybe she was back at her grandmother's house. Maybe she was back at church and Miss Tree had taken her homemade biscuits out of the oven.

Maybe. But no. She had awakened under that same live oak tree in The Sorting Place, but she knew Mimi was close.

"There you are," her grandmother said, letting go her apron.

Cotton sat up and looked skyward. The green leaves on the old oak were not focused. She felt something like tears blur her eyes, but they would not fall.

All about Mimi were the little lights that seemed to belong on the mountain. Together, they all glowed an iridescent sort of ruby color, not like the shimmery yellowish color her grandmother glowed.

Cotton looked down through the blur in her eyes at her own body. Maybe she glowed and didn't know it. She strained to see it, really strained. Wait.

Was that a trick? She thought she saw a dull crimson…flicker. If it was, it was the same hue as the little lights that were floating toward the branches. Maybe it was just her rustic red dress, and her eyes were playing tricks on her because of her dream or vision or whatever she'd just experienced. Maybe the tears that had formed in her eyes in her vision had remained. She couldn't tell.

She jerked her head in the direction of her Mimi. "Am I supposed to be glowing?"

"If you are, you should see the color," said Mimi. "I told you that you should have eaten more of those carrots I used to cook for you for your vision."

Cotton looked back at the crimson lights and then again at herself. Even though it was faint, she did have some kind of soft glow. The colors were similar, but the little lights were absolutely dazzling, and her own light barely emitted a crimson stain.

Cotton glanced back and forth between the glows in the tree and herself, comparing the reddish undertones. "Wait. Like, do I need to learn something from them?"

Mimi smiled, but didn't answer. "Child, we have something very important to see today."

Cotton stood and hugged her grandmother as hard as she could, but it still felt like air. And that air encompassed Cotton in a sense of overwhelming love.

In some way it seemed important to spend time with Mimi, but Cotton felt the grander pull to come to terms with all that she didn't understand. Maybe Mimi could help with that.

Cotton was so tired of the visions and the riddles and the parables. Why couldn't someone simply tell her what she needed to know, like she did for her viewers? She inhaled, let go of her grandmother's ethereal form and gave in to Mimi's directions because she had to.

Cotton turned and checked on the vermillion glows in the tree, knowing that they would be there when she returned, knowing that they would be fine. She puzzled as to why she would even care about them.

The two women began to make their way down the road. Flowers decorated the left side, and bushes with blooms decorated the right. She saw the gardenias, the azaleas and the camellias.

As they walked, Cotton thought of many questions. Things just didn't make sense, like why Mimi was wearing an apron. Since her question was about Mimi and not her, she might get an answer. It had worked with her grandfather. So, she asked. "Mimi, why do you need an apron here?"

"Oh, child, I don't need it. It is just the way you saw me as a child. It is a comfort to you."

Cotton was thankful that she actually got an answer to her question. Still, the answer made no sense. The apron may have been a comfort to her as a child, but it had no bearing upon her comfort now. Not really.

They walked down the path for a while longer, and soon they

were in a forest. Everything looked the same, tree after tree, acre after acre. Then they arrived at the end of the forest. Three huge boulders marked the completion of the path. The huge rocks seemed to have been everywhere.

"We will go no farther," Mimi said. "You must finish this now."

Before them was the town she'd seen earlier—the one with the great tree castle and king—the one that she'd not wanted to view in the aftermath of the King's sin. But she had to look now, and from the looks of things, great tragedy had befallen the once thriving town.

This was the way of things now. Maybe Cotton was getting the hang of it. She leaned against the largest rock and waited to learn.

The beautiful woman who bathed under her tree was there. Her clothes were muddied and she emitted a faint, dark—almost green—otherworldly glow. She was alone and sad.

Cotton blinked several times, tears like she'd had earlier were still forming, clouding her vision, but none would fall. A dark, lonely light, about the size of a small melon descended from the tree. The woman cried as she struggled to catch it. When she did, she cradled it in her arms, like a baby. But the dark round light writhed to be free.

Cotton remembered the black flag atop the woman's tree. Cotton had thought that it had been waving for the woman's deceased soldier husband. But it was not.

Now, Cotton remembered the rest of that Bible story.

God had not smiled upon the sinfulness of the union between David and the beautiful woman; therefore, the king's baby died. Yes, the beautiful woman's baby had fallen away from her.

That dark round ball with the greenish black glow was her baby.

*Thump.* A great shock rattled Cotton to her core.

*The crimson glows are my babies!*

She slid off the rock with the knowledge.

"Oh, Mimi! No, no, no. How can that be?"

Mimi walked over to the rock and lightly rubbed her hand over it. The rock seemed to move, and upon it, words were formed in the pure language Cotton had seen on the rocks previously. Cotton interpreted those words into thoughts that she could understand.

*"You saw the unformed substance that would eventually become who I am, and you saw every day that I would live. My life had already been ordained and written down, even before I was completely formed."*

"Oh, Mimi. That's impossible. I know of the possibility of only two lights. There are twelve of the crimson ones. They cannot be mine. No all. They absolutely cannot."

Mimi said, "Long ago, I, too, lost three little lights, lights that I had wanted very much."

"The yellow ones?"

The answer was in Mimi's sad eyes.

Cotton glanced back at the rock. All the words had disappeared save two. "Unformed substance." Her heart became sick.

She placed her hands upon that rock to receive this unwelcomed knowledge.

She breathed in the knowledge. All of those little crimson lights *were* hers. She stepped back from the large stone. *Thump*. Then came the knowledge of the rest.

That awful doctor had told her that she'd never bear children. So, she'd never seen the need for any birth control as she'd lived her life in willful ignorance, relying upon her smart phone for information and philosophy, listening to others' takes on cultural morality, which changed with the seasons. The practices they encouraged were never the same, always changing with their whims of a cold culture.

After her assault, she'd only had two relationships—Mason, the man she'd dated after her nightmare…and Calab. Guilt about those relationships pierced her heart. She had thought her recurrent lateness, skipped cycles and heavy times as peculiarities of her infertility.

*Thump*. Instead, something else entirely had been occurring. The little red illuminations that visited the tree every day were hers, not yet fully formed, not yet fully planted, but hers. The little raspberry, strawberry, and small apple one, and the duckweed-sized lights were her babies—babies that had fallen away from her because of all the damage that had been done on her day of "choice." She had been completely unaware!

And the two larger lights that kept tearing apart in front of her. *Ummph.* She knew when they were—who they were. Oh, she wanted to vomit.

They all had souls. Each one. Little, illumined souls.

# CHAPTER NINE

## In the Settling

As Cotton trailed behind Mimi through the forest, the light in it was different, the tall pine trees greener. Cotton carried with her the weight of twelve little souls, and they were heavier than anything she had ever carried.

They walked until Cotton was sure she would collapse under the weight of what she'd learned. Ahead on the straw-covered path were three little golden lights. Waiting. When Mimi got close, she reached out to them. They danced up her right arm and lay upon her chest, all glowing golden, together.

Though it had been buried somewhere deep inside her, she remembered her Mimi telling of three little angels that would be waiting for her one day. They had been. In this place. And now on this path. Waiting.

Mimi turned to her and held out the smallest of the three. "I had always wanted a large family, but it was difficult for us. I lost this one the second year your Poppy and I were married." The middle-sized light landed upon her hand. "This one fell away only the week after I had learned of her. It took five years after that before your father was born." Her face lit up. "Poppy and I were so happy when your father started going back to church. We knew then we'd see him again, too."

Cotton's attention darted from light to light. "What about the largest light?"

"Oh." Mimi's face saddened. "She is the Stone of My Heart. About twelve years after your father was born, we were blessed again. Accidently blessed. At least we thought we were." She cradled the larger light. "We called her Hope. I lost her in the eighth month. She was perfectly formed. Perfectly beautiful. But her little soul never breathed in the air outside me."

"I'm so sorry, Mimi. I think you may have told me about them once." How shallow of Cotton not to have marked it as important, life altering. But she didn't understand all of these things. Gracious, she was just a child for much of that time.

Mimi nodded. "I thought about each of them almost every day, but Hope got caught in my heart and her death turned into something hard, like a stone. I didn't forgive God for taking her for a long time. It was the thing my deepest soul longed for but could not have."

How insensitive of Cotton. She'd been thoughtless concerning Mimi and concerning the little souls, her own little souls, that never got to breathe the air she did. No wonder they were afraid of her. She'd seen to it herself that one of them never got that chance, and by her doing so, damaged the chances of the others surviving. Her body had been inhospitable to the little things. And it was her fault. No wonder they feared her.

Cotton's heart was heavy with the new knowledge, but she knew it was weighted with even more portend than she understood. "There is more tragedy in the little illuminations, isn't there?"

Mimi nodded. "You are finally using the gift God had bestowed upon you as a child. Such endowments are sometimes lost on little ones. But I had seen a spark in you—the favor—the blessing. I just knew you were going to use the gift of discernment that you possessed. I heard your words of understanding when it came to things of the spirit. You were my spirit child...spirit grandchild, rather. Your mother thought it was your imagination, but I knew better."

"I remember now. I felt things, lying under that big ol' oak tree in my backyard. I knew when my friends needed my friendship. I knew that I had much to learn from Ms. Tree at church, so I worked so hard at getting myself ready to go with you and Poppy." She inhaled. But I turned it all off, one course at a time when I got to college."

Mimi brushed at her apron. "And your mother didn't help."

Cotton nodded. "But that is neither here nor there now. Those baby lights are what's important now. And I know I have failed them. I know I have hurt them. I know they are damaged."

"In a way. Yes. They never got to experience the happiness of life, the joy of salvation, the gift of love. Though they never experienced the pain of life either. It's a sad trade. When we celebrate at night in The Rejoicing Place upon the Great Rock of

Ages, after all our daily work is done, they rejoice with glowing, but they haven't the voices and the arms to lift toward Him. There is a sort of incompleteness in it." She lowered her head.

Cotton's choices and actions had been…eternal. "Oh, Mimi, is there anything that I can do now? My little lights won't come near me." Her heart beat with a slow, heavy thump.

"You will know what to do. When the time comes to do it." She looked toward the sky. "And speaking of time, we have one more stop, so we must go."

They continued to walk, silently this time, by trees that glowed a thousand verdant shades alongside the road. The weight of what Cotton had done to her own little illuminations pulled down on her heart like lead weights. Sorrow filled each step she took.

At the edge of the other side of the patch of piney woods, they came upon another village of trees. Two large boulders stood sentinel at either side of the path. One was the shape of a log and one was almost a challis. She would watch what was before her, but she would keep her eye on the Rock for a message because that was the way of things here—if she truly wanted to know. She comprehended that now.

She had no idea how she understood, but she knew it to come from her desire to know and from the Rock's mercy in allowing her to have the knowledge. And strangely enough, from that little gift she'd been given in childhood. The favor.

A very young, pretty woman came to the dogwood tree in the forest village in front of her. The scene faced directly across from Cotton. Under the pretty woman's dress was a small bump, almost indiscernible. Another woman, heavy with child, came to the edge of the shade and welcomed her. They both looked down at the older woman's belly. They both laughed, and touched the bump like it needed to be held down. Then the two walked under the shade, hugging one another's shoulder. Cotton knew this to be the story of Mary's visitation to Elizabeth when she was six months pregnant with John the Baptist.

On the Rock, appeared words in the language she now knew to be Hebrew. She read the unadulterated language and interpreted the words in her own head in real time. It was discernment. It was knowledge.

*"Just as Elizabeth heard Mary call out to her, the baby inside her turned over in excitement, and the Holy Spirit filled her soul. She then called out to Mary, 'You are blessed above all women because your baby will be holy!"*

Cotton remembered the story from Sunday school. Inside Mary, the baby, just formed weeks before, was Jesus.

Those two babies, preborn, one a few weeks inside his mother and one, a few months inside his mother, knew each other. And their mothers knew their babies' true worth. They weren't cells or blobs. They were Jesus and John the Baptist.

They had a future. They had a purpose. And now they had a history.

Obviously, God knew Mary to be a holy woman, worthy of being Jesus's mother. But what did He think of Cotton? Most probably, he knew Cotton to be worthless, unworthy to bear her own children. And didn't.

Cotton had seen to her babies' futures...to their purposes...and to their histories. She found it hard to breathe. But her little ones had never breathed at all.

*Thump. Except for one.*

But that couldn't be. That knowledge would be too difficult to bear, if it were true. That was why Cotton had shoved it out of her mind and had closed the door on any thoughts that were related to it.

How selfish and stupid she was. It was her willful ignorance. Her practice of her stupid mantra: *Ignorance is its own reward.* She was wrong. Oh, so wrong. So very, very wrong.

"Oh, Mimi, I think I'm going to be sick." She bent over in anticipation of throwing up her knowledge.

Mimi seemed unmoved. At my old house, I'd have pinched your nose and would have given you some ginger. But there is no physical sickness here. What you're feeling is a heart sickness—the sorting sickness. And there's nothing I can do to help, my child."

Why hadn't Cotton sorted all this out when she had the chance to do something about it? In The Choosing Place? She had thought she had been so smart with all her degrees and facts. In reality, she'd been the most stupid woman alive. The knowledge about the lights was so obvious here.

"There, there, child. It will pass." Mimi reached out to Cotton, but she didn't grab Mimi's hand. Cotton was even unworthy of that. "We will go," said her grandmother, her eyes fixed on the path ahead.

As they wandered down the winding, sandy path that led to

Cotton's tree, they passed all the beautiful fields of golden, glowing flowers and bending trees. They passed the rose garden that seemed to spread out toward eternity. And the rocks.

Cotton was reminded of all the living parables she'd seen before and the lessons she'd received from them. Deep lessons—far deeper than they had seemed in Sunday school.

On one side of the path were the brambles and the seeds; on the other, the great rock table under the tree that had been prepared for people who'd accepted the invitation. As they walked farther, the little boat floated solitary upon the water where the fishes had been caught. A lone sheep grazed on one side of the path, and a goat bleated on the other side.

She passed the forest village where the great king once ruled. The trees there still had barren branches, and all the people in the village looked lean and hungry.

Cotton lagged behind Mimi, contemplating all that she'd seen in The Sorting Place.

And then there were her visions. How do they all fit together? Her mantra was of no use to her in The Sorting Place, and now she hated it—abhorred it—despised it.

When she finally saw her tree, with its branches spreading downward, nearly to the ground, she stopped. Her little lights would be amongst the branches. She stared as some of the leaves floated down.

How could she face them now? Knowing that she'd—

Mimi, with her three yellow glows, stood motionless in front of Cotton. Mimi didn't turn around to look at Cotton. Standing in the middle of the trail, she simply said, "Do you know what you must do?"

*Thump.* The knowledge hit her. Tears returned to Cotton's eyes, never spilling, but clouding all that she saw. "I must apologize to them, reconcile with them." But was she up to the task of reconciliation? Where would she even begin? She couldn't take anything back now.

She felt her heart wanting to vomit again.

"Yes, you must settle with them," Mimi said. She let out a great sigh.

That was the perfect word. Settle. How could she have done what she'd done? How could she ever…settle things with them? What she'd done was unforgiveable.

*Unforgiveable.*

When they arrived at the tree, Mimi hugged her hard, though Cotton only felt it in her spirit. "Today has been difficult, but the deeds have been presented. They are yours, and you will settle with them tonight."

Cotton hung on to her grandmother's ethereal arm. "But I don't know what to do. What do I say? Will they even understand?" A thousand things swirled around in her head in a fog.

Mimi smiled a sad little smile. "They understand the language, child." She touched Cotton on the chest with her hand. "Use that which God gave you a long time ago to guide your words."

Cotton nodded, and words choked out her mouth. "I will."

Mimi huffed, and with that, she said, "We must hurry or we'll miss some of it." She and her three little golden illuminations glowed toward the mountain alone, leaving behind the little crimson lights in the approaching night for the first time.

Cotton felt like someone had just dropped off twelve baby orphans at her door. And she wasn't prepared to take care of one. She wouldn't need bottles and diapers, but wouldn't she need something. How could she possibly take care of them all by herself?

Cotton had never felt uncomfortable in her own skin. She had sported her red dresses and red shoes with red soles and had been full of confidence and herself. All in front of a camera, no less.

But now, she felt great discomfort in her own skin. Guilt overtook her. She didn't really know herself at all. It had all been a façade.  How could she have done such a thing? To ones so innocent. They were as guiltless as Jesus but were still passively and unintentionally sacrificed. For nothing. All but one. The one that she chose to sacrifice.

She looked up into the grand, heavy oak tree, the branches crooking downward, the leaves drifting about her. Were the little lights even still here? Or were they hiding? Craning her neck around to see from various angles, she became dizzy, the memory of falling out of that tree in her backyard rushed into her brain, but she replaced it with the steely resolve that she'd mastered under that tree after she'd recovered. She had lived through that and worse. She will live through this, though much, much more difficult—because it involved spiritual matters that were eternal.

She kept looking for her little lights. They were nowhere to be found.

Then, something caught her attention from the corner of her eye. In the fissure of the rock, she saw a twinkle. They were in there—hiding, like they had been punished and were afraid of being punished again.

Cotton hung her head and began sobbing. She'd been told that no tears would fall in this place, but there they were. They had come from her sick heart and her mourning soul and had to escape. Oh, how awful this thing was that she'd done.

Her remorse and regret formed words in that strange language in her heart. *"Oh, God. What have I done?"* She experienced the weight of the question in her body.

She'd said many prayers in her childhood, rote ones, earnest ones, but this was different. She needed this prayer to come from some place deeper.

Facing the fissured Rock, she dropped to her knees with a *thud,* the shock of it shuddering through her. She lowered her head and held out her hands. "Dear Jesus, I wouldn't blame You if You cannot forgive me, and I will never forgive myself. I have committed the most heinous of sins. Against the most innocent. My own innocents. I foolishly altered a plan that was not mine, what You had marvelously and secretly formed inside me before I even knew. They were…Yours, Yours to delight in, Yours to watch grow, not mine to…terminate. They had…" It was hard for her to continue as the words knotted in chains in her throat. "Little baby souls. That were Yours, only Yours. Please, God." She turned and reached toward the glowing mountain, keeping her unworthy head pointed toward the earth below her.

*Tsur.* Suddenly she knew. Tsur was the name of the enormous, glowing mountain. "Tsur, please help me to settle with them. Oh, how I wish I had known what it really meant to do what I did."

A slow rumbling came from deep inside the earth under her.

She was afraid. The sadness and sickness in her heart poured out in tears for what seemed to be hours. Until there were no more. But still, somewhere deep inside her, her prayer seemed incompetent and incomplete. An unnamed stone remained deep inside her.

She sniffled and left her face on the ground. When she grew so tired that she could no longer kneel, she collapsed onto her earthen bed and closed her eyes.

Time was an unmanageable entity under the tree, so she wasn't sure how long she'd been there when she sensed a presence. She opened her eyes. About two feet in front of her was one of the tiniest, rosiest glowing lights. She bent upwards slowly, bowed her head and held out her hand. Moments later, she felt a tingle on her fingertip. She sluggishly lifted her head to see the little light atop her ring finger.

"Hi, you," she said and started crying again. Though her vision was blurred by the tears, she could see the little thing dart away, toward the fissure in the Rock. She shook her head. "I won't hurt you—"

*Thump.* She had already.

Discernment formed like a fog and roiled in her soul. She shook with tears because she knew the words that she needed to say. She looked toward the little light in the lowest branch and then toward the others that had come out of their hiding place in the Rock. *Sela'*. It was the name of the Fissured Rock, the Hiding Place, the Place that Gave Shelter. "I am eternally sorry, and I won't hurt you—any of you—ever again." She inhaled a deep breath and gathered what remained of her heart. "Because—" Something deep inside her released. A swoosh swept through her. "I love you. I love you all."

She felt her own glow inside and looked down to actually see it come over her, only lightly at first. A faint, red glow was surrounding her. She looked into the fissure, and the little lights seemed to broaden their rosy, scarlet glows. Rays shot out from the split rock.

She and her little lights matched. Perfectly matched.

Like the woman who'd walked down the road with her little purple lights. Like the woman in the King's city with her dark green glow. Like Mimi had with her golden illuminations.

Ever so slightly, each additional little light began emerging at different paces from their safe shelter, first the little duckweed glows, then the little raspberry ones, then the little strawberry lights. She counted them as they revealed themselves. There were ten, all of differing sizes, all of the same reddish, crimson glow. Under the tree burned in a beautiful crimson radiance. She'd never been so filled with happiness in her entire life, not when she'd graduated Clemson, not when she'd won the Associated Press's Broadcaster's Award, not when she'd gotten the job at the Charleston NBC affiliate station. Those were all brick-and-mortar pleasures. This was a pleasure of the soul.

But two were missing. The larger two, the orange-sized one and the grapefruit-sized one. All of a sudden, the orange-sized one shot out of the rock and flew to the top of the tree, knocking the dark leaves off their twigs.

She lifted her hand. "Wait." But there was nothing she could do to stop it.

As any mother would, she had to attend to her brood of lights that were around her, so she continued to rejoice in her reunion with her little radiances, she touched each little glow and felt their tingles as she intermittently glanced upwards. She saw one of the lights, the orange-sized one, timidly peering from behind a limb, but she could not see the little grapefruit soul. Where had it gone? Was it still hiding in the Rock, or did it find an opportunity when she wasn't looking to ascend to the top of the tree?

As she stood, ten of the little lights lifted up with her, seemingly dancing all about her. She lightly twirled amongst them and tingled as they touched her, the scent of apple pie swirling in the air. She held out her hand and three settled upon it. She crooked her neck and two found hiding in spots at the base of her hairline, one nearly the size of a plum. She reached out and gathered the others and brought them close to her heart. She had never heard her heart beat outside her, but she did when they were on her chest.

*This is love.*

She'd felt others love *her*, but she'd never experienced this level of love for anyone—even as much as she thought she'd loved her own family.

These were *her* little baby souls, colored the same as her, glowing the same as her, scented the same as her. They were a part of her.

But she had two other parts. The orange-sized soul, and the little grapefruit soul. She checked the split in the rock. It was still empty.

She held out her baby souls and spoke tenderly, like a mommy to her babies. "I have to go get your brothers." *How'd she know that?* She glanced over the gaggle of lights and knew each baby boy soul and each baby girl soul.

*Discernment.*

She drew her hands down and outward and they all hung in the air. Giggling, she pulled the two from her neck. You little ones cannot go with me. I must do this alone. I must settle with them."

Walking to the tree, she felt her old fear of heights rear its ugly head, but this was not a time for fear, but for bravery and action. All her bravery and strength had been steeled under that childhood tree she'd once fallen out of, and it was a solid grounding because she'd promised herself that she could face anything, overcome anything. She had accessed that bravery the afternoon she had to save Buddy. But tonight, she would need more strength than that. She would gather the strength from her heart, where it was the strongest, where her love for these little ones had formed.

Those two atop the tree were the most important things ever in her life now, and should have been from their forming, no matter how they had gotten formed.

*She knew now. God had been at each forming.*

Even in chaos. Even in sin. He had been at each forming.

Her heart told her exactly what she had to do. Climb that tree. To the very top if she needed to. No earthly memory or fear would stop her. She was going to go to the very pinnacle to tell them what she knew. Suddenly what had happened under that dark tree that dark night with the men in the dark clothing had no more hold on her. Even the fear of that night vanished. God had even been there with her.

With new determination that she hadn't gained *under* that childhood tree, she put her foot on the first branch and suddenly lifted herself up into the tree. It was easier than she'd thought, and she was lighter than she'd imagined being. Somehow, she could see each and every branch that she'd have to master to get to them. The knowledge of her intended path upwards filled her full. The fears fell away.

One by one she traversed those branches to the top. She maneuvered until she was seated about four feet away from the faint glows that seemed to be trying to hide their luminosity—to disappear.

Watching for a few moments, she saw the little lights shiver. How frightened they must have been. Their little souls knowing so little when they were taken. Just that she—the person who should have protected them—destroyed them in different ways—by her rejection and by her…choice.

She stared at them and tried to find the words in her heart to say to the innocent lights. In that moment, she felt so much affection for them that she could hardly hold it in. Her heart wanted to burst red rays towards them.

"I have come for you. You needn't fear me any longer. I will love you and will repent of my ignorance of your souls for all eternity."

The orange-sized one let her see it and radiated a faint red light.

"You are mine. You are my glow. I want to protect and love you with all that I am and all that I have."

The orange-sized one glowed a deeper crimson, like herself. The more she poured out her love, the deeper the color became, and the more they matched. He was the little soul that her mother had planned to help her be rid of—before it left on its own over that weekend at Clemson.

The larger one peaked from behind its limb, trying to hide its ruddiness. He had been the one that she'd chosen to be rid of herself.

*Thump.*

She felt something reverberate through her to her very core.

"You were gloriously and beautifully made, and I didn't recognize that then. But I do now. Look at you. I desire to hold and kiss you and shower your beautiful little souls with love all the days to come."

The orange-sized one came closer to her, and the little grapefruit one showed half of himself.

To the little grapefruit one, she said, "I thought I may have seen you in that pan, but it was too painful for me to believe that it was you. I pushed away that possibility and believed what I had been told, the numbers of it, the sanitized social correctness of it. What manufactured facts they gave me. I would change all that, if only I could."

It moved from the branch, turning up its glow ever so slightly.

She reached out. "Come down with me, and I shall prove my love to you both."

The little orange-shaped one came closer, and Cotton reached out farther to touch him. He allowed Cotton to caress him. You shall be called Preston. Little Preston glowed at her touch.

*Thump.* In a pump to her chest, she felt inspiration. "And you," turning her attention to the larger boy light, "You will be called Max, because you are so very strong. You were strong in that room with me, and you are strong now. You are my tough, tough boy, and I will wait for you to forgive me all my life if that is what it takes." If only he could see her heart.

She lowered her head. "But I will love you as much as I love your brothers and sisters, and I will regret every minute that we are not settled."

As she continued to cuddle with Preston and wait for Max to change his mind, she became uncertain about how long she'd been in the tree because the concept of time was broken here—or…maybe, it had been fixed. She knew instinctively that she needed to get to her other little babes.

"Come with me," she said to Preston. "Max, please come when you're ready. I must attend to the others," her mother's heart told him.

Preston followed closely as she climbed down the tree.

Preston and the other lights danced about Cotton in celebration of their reunion. She began naming the other little lights as the inspirations settled upon her. Harper and Hunter.

Clarabelle and Annabelle were twins and shaped themselves into one little bell at times. She'd heard twins ran in her family. Willow, because she was filmy, like a weeping willow tree. To the smaller apple-sized girl light, she said, "You will be called Honey, like my favorite honey crisp apples."

Cotton gazed at her little charges, her little souls. Two of the duckweed lights came to her for names. "Sissy and River," she said as she touched each. Of course, she had to name one of her little ones with her maiden name. All Southern belles did that.

Finally, she saw the last two, the smallest of all, hiding behind their brothers and sisters. "Ah, Georgia and Skyler. Look at how precious you are! You glow more sweetly than all the rest!"

Love flowed from her like she never knew existed. Long into the night, she rejoiced with her babes as their scents of apple, vanilla, flour and sweet cream filled the air with fragrances that caused the air to smell like apple pie. Until they all grew tired and their glows dimmed and they settled upon the earthen bed. Her practice of pulling up a cover of grass had gone because there was really no need. The temperature did not require it. It had just been an earthly habit.

Sleep settled upon them all, and they slumbered as one low, slow, burning, crimson glow.

When she awoke much later, she was the first to begin to glow brighter under that big tree with the leaves all green once again. All about her were her little souls. Eleven of them. She looked over to the edge of the tree on the low limb and saw Max. The twelfth. Alone.

It will take him time. She was willing to give him all the time he needed, as long as she had.

A shimmering came to her…that she didn't know how much time she had. She sensed that The Sorting Place was only temporary—a place to accomplish a task.

She smelled leather. Her father was coming today. Though she was excited to see him, something in her was just a little disappointed because she had hoped—at some point—to be reunited with her mother—to smell her expensive perfume again. Humph. Maybe tomorrow.

She slowly got up, careful not to awaken her babes, and she walked down the sandy path between the tall loblolly pines to greet her father. The Rejoicing Place on the mountain behind him seemed quiet in the early morning light.

"Well, hi, Princess'," he said, hugging her with his spirit and smiling. Love was engulfing her in his ethereal embrace.

He held her away from his body, and she returned the smile. She could tell that he sensed her joy.

He looked over her face. "I can tell that you are settling."

"Yes, Daddy, I am. I am so sorry, and I am filled with so much regret. I am also filled with shame over my ignorance."

"Each of us is when we go through the sorting." He became really serious and put his hands beside her temples without touching them. "But be careful of your early discoveries. All may not be completely revealed." He gazed over her face.

She inhaled. "I was afraid of that," she said.

He lowered his hands to his sides. "Yes, it's a complicated thing to put together. Our earthly eyes and ways try to take shortcuts to make mortal sense of things that are actually complicated and spiritual. Eternal." He opened his eyes wide and nodded. "But the way things worked in The Choosing Place is vastly different from the way things work in The Sorting Place."

She nodded in agreement. "I understand. I'll try to be careful with what I am learning. But everything is so convoluted."

His big blue eyes widened. "You ready for today?"

She nodded, looking over her shoulder, not wanting to leave her new charges. She walked to the tree and told them to stay under the branches. "I love you all so very, very much." She looked up. "Max, did you hear that I love you?" There was unfinished business with baby Max, and she would give anything to finish it. Maybe something she might learn today could help.

Her father smiled a huge smile.

They began to stroll together, slowly, not going very far.

"Yes, things are complex here—especially for you," he said.

She squinted her eyes. "That's what I'd like to talk to you about. I know I need to reconcile some of my visions with some of the living parables I've seen."

"I know. That's a part of the sorting," he said, somehow grabbing her hand as they walked.

"Some things just come without me trying, like I learned Tsur's name last night."

Her father nodded. "The Great Mountain Rock. Breathing. Unmovable. Eternal."

She smiled. "And He gave me the name of the place in the Rock to hide in Him when we are fearful."

"Sela'," her father said.

She nodded, proud of her gifts. "But some knowledge is so intricate, dense and hard."

"Yes, that is because certain things about you have not been decided." He stopped and stood silent for a moment. "We shall go to the cliffs today." Sadness covered his face and his luminous blue glow dimmed.

"The cliffs?" Something in her heart sank, but she had instinctively known where they were. They were the dark pulses beyond the green forest that she had become aware of on the day that she arrived at The Sorting Place.

"Yes, and beyond the cliffs is The Regretting Place."

*Thump.*

Cotton didn't want to go there for fear she'd discover something even darker about herself.

She had once been the most central matter in the world. To herself. But no more. She had more important concerns now. Her heart worried. "Will my darlings be okay?"

"They will always be well. They always have been." He turned and gazed at them under the tree from a distance, some beginning to move and glow more radiantly.

She halted. *Yes.* Because when they left her, they immediately had the protection of the Rock of Ages. It felt good to her, however, to possess that mother's love and that instinct of protection toward her baby lights. If she'd only known the fulfillment and joy of it in The Choosing Place.

Her father took her hand again and led her in the direction she'd never wanted to go, down the trail to the left—toward the cliffs—toward The Regretting Place.

The initial landscapes reminded her of her beloved Lowcountry of South Carolina. This whole place was filled with a mix of the familiar with the unfamiliar—the known with the unknown. The super tall Loblolly pine trees along the edges of the sandy path gave way to hardwoods, sweet gum trees, willow oaks, live oaks and the occasional sycamore. And rocks everywhere—where they didn't belong. The sandy path turned darker as earth mixed with the grainy soil. Eventually, the hardwoods became fewer, and cypress trees dotted the landscape. The path became wet and then muddy, and they entered a swampy area, littered with cypress trees and palmetto scrubs, all still familiar to her Lowcountry world. And still the rocks so seemingly out of place.

She wondered if each sorter saw his or her own homeland. Like the way she saw Mimi with her apron. The familiarity was comforting in the landscapes where all else was so strange. But why so many rocks?

As they walked, Cotton grew aware of a sort of thrumming or beat—far in the distance. The beat grew more and more distinct until it sounded like a drum. But she'd never heard such an ominous drum beat before. Finally, they came upon an area that made the hairs on her arms stand at attention. Icy fear crept up her spine.

Something faintly putrid hung in the stagnant air.

The long gray strands of Spanish moss hung all about her and formed a kind of room of moss—a waiting room, it seemed. The room obscured her vision beyond it. She moved a tendril aside at the back of the area to reveal what she could only describe as a veil or some kind of weird curtain across the room at the opposite end. But she'd never seen such a veil as this. It was a living cover, intended to obscure. Red and pink colors swirled together to appear like some kind of breathing red-colored galaxy. It pulsed like blood ran through its veins, and it dripped. Blood. She sensed that this was some kind of momentous secret—some kind of ethereal end.

"So, what now? This…thing is not to be penetrated," she said to her father.

He nodded. "Not by most. Definitely not by me. But it is here for you to see." He looked away. "Put your hand through it and behold."

Cotton glanced back at the dripping veil. She cringed at the thought of touching it—this wet, living curtain made of who knows what? But did she even have a choice? She shook her head. No. She didn't. She inhaled a deep breath and thrust her arm through the living veil. The fleshy material tore apart in a small section so that she could see what was behind it.

Rocks formed an odd shape before her as they made a large throne. She leaned forward to see more clearly. Upon that throne, emerged a figure that appeared out of the multitudinous stones that shaped it. What? It had the features of an over-sized man's body, but the head was of a different figure. Was it a bull? Or an ox? Or a creature? She couldn't tell as the stones seemed to be moving, forming and reforming themselves into the fearful, writhing figure. She glanced beyond the throne and could tell that the veil encircled that throne. From the fearful figure's direction, she heard a guttural groan. Her attention snapped back from the encircling veil. A puff of an acrid, putrid smell wafted out its mouth. Icy wisps ran up her spine and impeded her ability to move.

She looked to her father for help, but he was pushing aside the tendrils of Spanish moss around him, trying to escape the entire scene before her.

This was only hers to see—hers to understand.

She broke open the veil even more. There was a dark magnificence around the throne, for it was flanked by great gold pillars and harrowing bronze statues that guarded the stone creature. The grandeur of the surroundings was alluring and glittered with small stones that sparkled and shone. But the enthroned beast was solitary and unadorned.

Cotton vibrated inside from an ominous echo that shook her very core. The eerie drum-like beat continued, as well.

In an ever-increasing crescendo, music that sounded almost alluring played. It was unlike any other she'd ever heard before. Then, from behind the curtain of pulsating pink and red, four of the most gorgeous women she'd ever seen walked out and stood, like sentries in twos on the sides of the throne. Cotton was mesmerized by the beautiful women. Their dresses were bejeweled and custom fitted. Their makeup had been applied thickly and perfectly. Two had platinum hair, and two had inky, black hair, and not a strand was out of place. Their heels were higher than any Cotton had ever worn, and the women appeared to have had no trouble gliding over the ground beneath them with perfection.

Cotton knew she had perfected her own image, but these women really had it all pulled together in a way she had never seen before. Cotton's innermost being realized these women were symbolic, iconic figures that somehow she had been trying to emulate.

*So why is she afraid?*

Then the stone creature on the throne moved and groaned again, the rocks making low, grinding sounds. At that moment, the two beautiful women closest to the throne dropped to their shapely knees in their blood-colored dresses. The other two bowed their heads and pressed their hands together as if in prayer to the figure.

All the while, the thudding continued in the distance.

The rock monster shifted on the massive stone chair, creaking and moaning and causing something in her to be disturbed by the tremors. The belly of the figure appeared to transform into a glow. Did all beings here have their own glow?

He reached out his hardened arthritic arms as if to welcome the worshipers to him.

Only, the obedient women, did not approach him. Instead, they all stepped away, through the veil and toward the moss-draped waiting room in which she'd just passed through to stand at the living wall. Cotton pulled her gaze from behind the veil, as well, and glanced toward her father and saw that he still had his back turned to the thick patch of Spanish moss that created the waiting room.

There was no need to ask her father anything, though she was extremely confused and didn't understand any of what she was seeing. Obviously, she was here to learn something, but this was not going to be easy because this was so foreign. She had no framework or paradigm for any of it. None of this was in any Sunday school lesson she ever learned.

She reached way down inside herself for discernment, for the favor that God had once given her.

*Earthly and evil.*

Cotton turned her attention back to the beautiful women she was so drawn to and had unknowingly emulated in The Choosing Place. They walked toward the path, pushing aside strings and clumps of the grand moss.

To Cotton's surprise many women were standing patiently. The beautiful sentinels moved apart the moss to allow the patient ladies into the makeshift antechamber. Each woman stood, clothed in dark brown, rough-woven cloth with babies of various sizes in their arms.

The beautiful, scarlet women were whispering charming sounds to the brown-clothed women who nodded at the utterances. The first young mother was ushered to the veil by her beautiful escort. The common woman was not allowed to step beyond it—to see beyond it.

Cotton could hear something going on behind the veil, so she spread the living wall again and watched.

On the stone platform upon which the throne sat, emerged that strange writing Cotton had seen on so many rocks. She watched as the swirling stone formed deeply carved letters into words. She had gotten better at reading and understanding the ancient scribblings. A larger word appeared above a phrase. The moniker for the stone figure read MOLOCH, and underneath that two additional words emerged:  Melech Boshet. Cotton understood immediately the names and their depth of symbolism because it pertained to so many, even her.

*MOLOCH, King of Shame.*

The throbbing continued to pulse inside Cotton.

The lady that had been ushered out of the waiting room line bowed her head and handed over her baby to the beautiful sentry.

The platinum-haired woman divided the curtain with her left arm and stepped through with the baby cradled in her right.

Cotton immediately parted the veil, as well. She was obliged to watch and learn from the scene before her. She knew that deep inside.

The undulating figure before his gorgeous attendant stretched out his arms. She placed the squirming, innocent baby in them.

Cotton wanted to vomit.

If only the mother could see beyond that fleshy, red veil, she would have never handed over her precious baby! But she couldn't see the reality of what was behind that living veil.

Cotton wondered what the stunning assistant had whispered in the woman's ear.

A malodorous hot breeze blew around the throne. Cotton could see the scene clearly from her vantage point. The belly of the beast glowed brighter and took on the appearance of a bronze receptacle—almost a furnace. The beast folded the silent, squirming baby into it, and it glowed even brighter, white smoke escaped from behind the stone throne, and the monster belched a rotting stench. The discordant music hummed louder and the drumming vibrated even more.

Cotton heaved, wanting to pitch out everything inside her. But nothing happened. Closing the curtain by removing her hand, she looked back at the young mother.

The brown-clothed woman, now without her baby, was ushered by the sinisterly beautiful scarlet-clothed woman to the thick flanking of moss that enclosed the antechamber. The hostess parted the moss, and the woman walked into the darkness.

Where did she go? How could she just walk away like that, leaving her baby to the unknown?

Cotton stepped back. The rock beside her twisted with words.

*"God gave you freedom to choose, but do not use that allowance for the flesh..."*

Freedom. God has given his sons and daughters an allowance of freedom. That's why the mothers chose what they chose. Freedom. No rules, no laws, no edicts had the power to change hearts. Because God gave them the same freedoms He had given her. The world sold that allowance as "choice."

The din of music that emanated from behind the red curtain morphed even more and even louder and became even more discordant. For a moment, Cotton thought she heard some kind of moaning in all the dissonance, but she couldn't be sure. Maybe it was just another beat of the drum that was striking terror into her soul. Then the eerily beautiful woman walked back to the antechamber line to stand guard and wait until it was her turn to be an usher again.

This process repeated itself again and again as the moss-draped waiting room line became shorter and shorter. Each sinister hostess whispered her soft, siren-like noises in an ear of each new prodigy. One by one, each innocent baby seemingly sensed something and began to fidget and squirm.

There was nothing Cotton could do but watch and be appalled.

None of the young mothers were aware of what was truly going on behind the enflamed veiled circle where the enthroned creature sat.

For a while Cotton looked back and forth between the line of women and behind the living, fleshy curtain at the unimaginable scenes taking place at the alter as each baby silently disappeared.

*They have no voices. Thump.*

Cotton had the sudden revelation.

Make it stop, God! Make it all stop! Why was He showing her this? This...this...tragedy. Cotton knew it was happening everywhere...locally...nationally...globally. Oh, the untold numbers of them all. All the silent babies. Of different ages. Of different ethnicities. Of different potentials.

Cotton nearly collapsed from the weight of all the silent

deaths and leaned upon the large rock that nested behind her. It warmed. God was giving her another message or phrase or word.

She didn't want any more—any more words—any more knowledge—any more guilt.

The words emerged in that pure language that she hadn't learned to master in The Choosing Place.

*"They are My Quiescent Children."*

The letters *QC* appeared below the sentence. These words were not in the Bible. They were written for Cotton to personally understand.

The babies were God's *potential children*, His QCs. Cotton had given God twelve quiescent children—ten of whom had been mysteries—even to her.

Cotton prayed with all she was for the scene before her to be over, but she knew it to be never ending. It had started at the beginning of time and will continue until the end of time. She felt like a Prometheus, bound to her rock, to watch this repeating nightmare again and again.

Unlike many of the other scenes, this was no parable she'd heard about in Sunday School—no bible verse either. Why wouldn't this troubling scene before her stop? She got it. She got it! Stop! Stop! Stop!

But Cotton couldn't stop the discordant music or the thudding, or the occasional distant screams of the women through the final covering of moss and into the abyss, or the whispers of the scarlet women. Her glances darted around the scene before her to find some kind of relief. There was none. The stone monster that consumed the tiny infants seemed to grow more and more red with each innocent baby.

She walked to her father who was standing outside the moss-draped antechamber. He had closed his eyes. She didn't blame him. She didn't want to see it either.

She cried out again for it all to stop. Or at least she thought she had, but through the din of music, she was not sure.

*God, why won't you reveal to these women what's truly going on behind the red veiled wall? God, stop this awful holocaust of silent, innocent infants!*

Where was God? And how many babies would it take to satisfy this insatiable monster, this King of Shame?

The line of women had seemed never ending for quite a long time, and then, thankfully, Cotton saw the completion. When the last woman was escorted to the obscure veil, instead of placing her child into her beautiful attendant's arms, her escort pulled open the curtain and allowed the mother to step inside and place her small child upon the stone alter—at the feet of the monster. The child that was a little older than the rest turned toward Cotton. He was maybe just under a year old. His angelic face was perfectly formed, with rosy cheeks, eyes the color of robin's eggs and dimples. In all his innocence, he reached for a stone to play with and struggled to grab it because it was just beyond its reach. He had no idea of his own danger.

Cotton wanted to run to him—to grab him and run away from the alter. She wanted to scream at the ignorant woman who placed her angelic child there in the first place. But Cotton was paralyzed and without a voice.

The rock rumbled in an unearthly tone to the baby. "So, you wish to be entertained, do you?" He reached inside his belly of molten fire. He pulled out something that was ablaze. He chuckled a most evil sound. "So do I." And he threw the white liquid fire at the child's angelic face.

There are no words for what Cotton saw.

"Oh, God, no!" Cotton turned and screamed, but she couldn't hear her own scream or the baby's scream because the din of discordant music drowned out all else and rose up to the leaden sky above them. "Get me out of here!" she yelled. Everything turned and knotted inside her. She was in the presence of pure evil. She had to get out of there. But there was no escaping the nightmare before her. She closed her eyes to stop the scene before her and backed up until the rock with the ancient words stopped her.

When she opened her eyes, the baby was gone, and the mother walked through the final veil. The earth beneath Cotton's feet began to shake, and the horrible, grand throne began to vibrate and crumble. The discordant music grew louder and louder.

The wanton creature began to growl and laugh from someplace murky and malevolent inside him. The beautiful, pulled-together women who had guided the new mothers with babies crouched before the cracking throne.

Suddenly, the scent of sulfur filled the air as the discordant music with its fearful beat subsided. The monster and his hostesses were absorbed into the large stone throne upon which he had sat. As the throne and grand rock surroundings continued to crumble, Cotton saw what was behind them.

The abyss. The place of eternal regrets. The Regretting Place.

Cotton could more clearly hear the thrumming over the edge. She'd never heard such a terrifying sound before. Her ears pierced with pain, and she put her hands over them to quell the noise.

The remainder of the throne and its surroundings fell off the edge of the cliff upon which they were perched.

Cotton's heart was beating so hard and so fast. She wanted what she'd seen to disappear from her memory forever, but it had been burned there by that insatiable, molten fire and the rocks that were its fuel.

She looked down to where the throne of evil had been. The ground had turned red and was soaked with an earthy smell—the blood of innocence.

"Daddy?" She heard the shaking in the word.

Her father had his back turned to the abyss. "I know," he said with a tense voice that was restricted by a tight throat. He was crying. "It is the world's greatest tragedy."

*Oh, God. Oh, God. Oh, God.*

To her horror, Cotton fully realized that she had—during her time in The Choosing Place—unknowingly sacrificed innocence, as well. Her vision darkened, her knees became weak, and she slumped down to the ground amongst the rocks, barely aware that she was alive.

*Oh, God.*

⁂

Cotton didn't know how long she'd been collapsed amongst the rubble crying, but she finally felt like there were no more tears inside her. The Sorting Place wasn't supposed to be a place of grief, but the grief next to the abyss of The Regretting Place was so enormous, there was nothing else to be done.

Cotton inhaled and looked up through the tears still puddling in her eyes. "I understand so much more, now, but what were the whispers about? What were the beautiful women telling the mothers, Daddy."

"What they wanted to hear. Each one a different lie. Anything to accomplish the Darkness's secret agenda. Some were promised success; some, freedom. Some were told lies about science—that those babies were merely cells or matter—matter that didn't matter. All were told they had a choice. In reality, they did. Each could choose her own path."

Cotton, too, had listened to the whispers of beautiful and learned women who'd advocated for her "choices," which, in reality, had turned out to be sacrifices—to her career and image...and convenience. It was all veiled behind an illusion—obscured—hidden behind the womb—hidden in the womb. But God had seen behind that veil—inside each womb—inside Cotton's womb.

There was nothing worthwhile or redeeming about the entire affair of choice. There really was not a choice. There was life. And there was death. She glanced up, sick with her new knowledge.

"And where did those mothers go. After they had dropped off their precious babies?"

Her father nodded. "I can tell you this, too. They went back to live their lives in The Choosing Place."

Cotton swallowed the lump in her throat. "So, they'll have to reconcile with their babies one day, too—just like I'm having to do?"

He nodded. "Yes. Either in The Choosing Place or in The Sorting Place." He gave her a little time with her unwanted knowledge.

She closed her eyes. She thought she'd had all the information needed to make her decisions, but she hadn't. Spiritual things were happening behind the physical things. How could she have known?

"We have a little farther to go," her father said, staring out over the cliffs.

She opened her eyes and stared at the waiting room that had been secreted by the Spanish moss. "I need to get as far away from this place as I can," Cotton said as she got up. She realized she had shared in the bloody guilt of this ground, and she wanted to claw it out of her memory. But knew she could not. Ever.

They walked together for a while, both silent. At the end of the path, a rock that appeared to be step-shaped marked the end. Infinite darkness lay beyond it. The last of the cliffs. The larger abyss. A different lesson.

She didn't want to climb the rock. She'd seen enough darkness for a lifetime, so she stepped back. Her father was close behind her. There to her right was another human heart-shaped boulder of a grander size. She knew what this meant, as well. So, she found a place to lean against, avoiding looking at the dark cliffs that pulsed so near. It was almost as if there was a deep throb, too low to physically hear. Though the beat throbbed trepidation in her, she preferred it to the horrible sounds from earlier. And, moreover, she preferred it to the silence of the sacrificed innocents.

Her father took a pace closer to the step-shaped rock that overlooked the cliff. He climbed it and huffed out a profound breath. There was no glowing in him any longer; his blue light had disappeared altogether. She feared for him as he stared out into the vast blackness.

She looked down. Her low crimson glow had gone away, as well. The principles in The Sorting Place did not work as well so close to The Regretting Place.

Uneasiness grew inside her as she waited for her father to begin. Instead, he continued looking over the edge of the cavernous gorge and at the rolling, midnight fog for what seemed like hours, though she knew it not to be because time was merely an illusion here.

As she watched him, it was as if he were communing with the dread over the edge.

The low, monotonous throb beat a foreboding rhythm into her soul.

After so very long, he turned to her. "This is the place for your questions." He stepped down. "I am limited by the chore I have been given to answer them, but I can sometimes lead you to discover what you need to know. As I did at our last stop."

Inhaling enough nerve, she said, "I have so many of them. I have been trying to figure them all out, but I don't even know where to begin with some. A few of the answers have been coming slowly, but now that I'm settling, I feel an urgency of some sort."

He nodded. "It is to be expected. The Sorting Place is not a forever place."

She lifted her head. "And now I have a new question. Why did you really bring me here?"

"To talk about the Stone of Stumbling." The words seemed to match the expression on his face.

Was that some kind of riddle or did it import more? "What stone of stumbling?"

A louder, discordant sound waned in the distance.

"It is different for each of us. I know yours is *becoming* now, though you must figure that out in the sorting."

She looked down. If she could only live her life over again. She'd never make the same mistakes again. What kind of woman would do what she'd done? But she didn't have a clue back then.

He gave her a sad smile. "Would you like to know mine? It may help."

She smelled a pungent scent in the air, like vinegar. She didn't know if she wanted to know or not, but she knew she was going to know. She nodded.

He straightened his chest. "You must place your hand near my heart and close your eyes and truly desire to know."

Like she desired the knowledge from before. She slid away from the rock, took a step toward him, toward the cliff. She closed her eyes, placed her hand close to but not on his chest and felt a *swoosh*.

For a moment she couldn't breathe. It was like when she'd felt when that paramedic had been hovering over her.

*Thump.*

She saw her young mother and her father at her old home, watching TV on a Sunday morning in the spring. She could tell by the news show that was being broadcast. Each had a bloody Mary in hand. Her mother was looking through a fashion magazine.

But where was Cotton?

By some way of involuntary movement, she backed away from the scene through the open window and into the tree where she'd climbed to a precarious height, at least it seemed like a precarious height through her five-year-old eyes. Just above her head she became distracted by a small, pink light and tried to touch it.

A loud bell chimed a low bong in her head, and at the same time the window on the house slammed. She had fallen, and something inside her little body had loosened.

Cotton struggled with her heart to divine the meaning. Nothing came at first. So, she accessed the depths of her heart to pull up something. And then it hit her.

His Stone of Stumbling came to her through discernment, her blessing, her favor. Her father had abdicated his role as leader of and protector of his family and had lost them—her mother and her. Her father had slammed the window on God when he'd needed to lead his family to Him. *Oh, no.* The dark knowledge rose up in her. Her mother was connected to the dark fog, and her father felt responsible.

Cotton's eyes opened wide, and she jerked her hand from him, suddenly able to breathe again. "Oh, Daddy."

"I am sorry, Princess. Had I been a better husband and father, I could have saved our family so much heartache. I have lost your mother forever." He glanced over his shoulder and into the shadows of fog.

Could her father really be to blame? How much of this whole thing was her fault, too? She didn't like his Stumbling Stone, his feeling responsible for her mother's entrapment in the murky fog and her bad choices. *It wasn't fair.*

"Fairness is a mortal concept," he said, like he'd heard her. "In The Choosing Place, I chose to work, and I practically lived at the Citadel, leaving your mother and you alone in Summerbrook during the weekdays for years, and your mother found her own entertainment. With my friend, Randall Pratt. Going out to lunch in his McLaren, in his bed, on his yacht. In many ways, it was my fault she'd taken that path. And though I may have been able to have stopped her if I had been the husband I should have, she was ultimately the one responsible for her decisions, and she is the one who has to answer for them in The Regretting Place. For forever."

She shook her head. "Dad, you just didn't know. Just as I hadn't had an idea about what I was doing and whom I affected. How could I have known? Everyone said I had rights and choices, and I listened."

He stared at her shrewdly, his steely blue eyes piercing through her like a saber.

She didn't want to take the scrutiny of the glare from her father, so she looked out over the cliffs at the dusky, rolling fog over the low, quaking drum. It was as if someone had stirred it because it roiled even more.

A deep rumbling vibrated through her soul. She tried to shut it down.

She turned her attention back upon her father. Sadness cut lines in his face as he stood on the precipice of the cliff.

Her father made a furrow on his forehead. "I ran from all understanding when your mother was alive. I suspected what she was doing, but I hid the knowledge somewhere deep inside me, so that I didn't have to account for my shortcomings. I sought to make myself happy—to pursue my career goals—until she had passed. And now it is too late. I could have led her to the Rock of Salvation."

Oh, her poor, poor mother. And her poor father for feeling responsible for the weight of it.

"Though I had nearly hidden it from myself, deep in the bottom of my heart because it hurt so much, it was my Stone of Stumbling, and it kept me from the Rock of Eternity. We all have a Stone of Stumbling, a heart-stone, if you will—something that is so dear to us, and when the heart is burdened by the stone, it causes us to stumble. We wallow in grief or guilt or regret, and sometimes from an inability to forgive others—or even ourselves."

"What is mine, Daddy—my Stone of Stumbling?"

He closed his eyes. "I cannot say. We each must figure it out and settle with it here in The Sorting Place, if we get that chance. Not everyone does."

Cotton searched her heart. So much lay hidden in it. Her life-long mantra, Ignorance is its own reward, was her enemy here. But she'd used that refrain masterfully to accomplish all that she had. Cotton slumped down to the pebbled ground beside the great Rock.

Her father sat beside her in silence.

After turning over her father's Stone of Stumbling in her heart, she said, "So, our mistakes can cause others to make mistakes, and those mistakes have eternal consequences that others must pay."

Her father didn't respond, and her words simply hung in the air, like the thick humidity in her beloved Lowcountry. *Thump*. And he also felt responsible for her falling from the tree. But she couldn't figure out the deeper meaning of his guilt about that. She inhaled the incompleteness of it all.

Maybe this is the place to figure out what her own Stone of Stumbling was. So many things ran through her head. Her mother, her career, her pregnancies, Caleb, her abandonment of her friends and of the little church that had still awaited her with open arms. She'd made a real mess of things with all the secrets and hardness she kept in her heart.

After sitting without words for a long period of time, her father said, "There is more that you must learn at the cliffs. I think you are going to have a problem with the implications of this knowledge."

Cotton didn't want to hear that. She'd just learned that her mother was in the great fog; her father lived with the guilt of it, and that she now needed to figure out some kind of stumbling stone thing that was in her own heart. She'd actually had quite enough for one day. But that wasn't the way of things here.

That indescribable sense that her time was running out pulsed inside her with the throbbing over that dark edge.

Her father stood, lowered his head and walked to the rock at the cliff. He stepped upon it and held out his hand.

She didn't want to, but she stood and took it. It was necessarily the way of things.

The dark brown mist parted in places as she looked out over the abyss, and through the clearings, she saw something that she could only describe as unclean, murky glows. But, somehow, the glows—if she could call them that—were not emitting light. They were absorbing light.

The drum beat echoed ominously. The waft of a sweet perfume hit her, but underneath that note was something sour and rancid. She strained even harder to see the sources of the mysterious, sucking glows. And as each section of film parted, she saw boxes—the televisions, the computers, the smart phones, the tablets, the video games, the movie screens. After each revelation, the miasma rolled back together to hide the causes of the shadowy, slurping boxes.

*Thump. The boxes. It is how the Liar transforms and hides the truth in this age of culture.*

She shook away the knowledge. That couldn't be true. The implications of it would be enormous.

"Let the knowledge come, sweetie," her father said.

*Thump.* No, she didn't want to understand this.

But it was the way of things, so she allowed the understanding to roll over her, and she absorbed the awareness.

In her life, the boxes had subversively and systematically indoctrinated her. They dismissed the parables she'd learned in Sunday school. She'd let the boxes preach their principles instead, in their cartoons, in their sitcoms, in their ongoing programming of her brain and heart.

She shook her head. "I had always thought that the boxes had brought information and enlightenment to people. I thought I had done that, too."

Her father hung his head. "I can tell you what I learned—that too many times, the boxes brought me a false truth—the Liar's idea of his truth. It was a contrary truth, and it was obscured by the fog. The boxes were used by the enemy for programming and indoctrination. The boxes are dark enlightenment."

An oxymoron. "Daddy, this is so confusing and complicated."

Had she contributed to the falsehoods from the boxes, excusing herself and proclaiming that people should do what makes them happy—without regard to the Great Book or to whom they hurt?

She looked out over the boundless, roiling fog. "If only I had known."

"I should have taken you and your mother to church that Sunday morning." Her father breathed in a jagged breath. "I had been susceptible to the lies and the haze of the boxes, too. They had led me away from Jesus, away from my responsibilities as a husband and father." He exhaled a serrated sigh.

She recognized the truth of it now for her, as well, and slowly nodded, allowing the certainty of it upon her. "I was used by the enemy and was a part of the boxes. The station manager expected me to keep their creed. I had to promote philosophies that were not God's. I said things that were contrary to what I had learned at church. But I wanted so much, and I could get it all if I followed the requirement of the boxes." She felt tricked.

She thought of some of the tenets that came from the rectangular containers—lifestyles that had been admonished in the Great Book. Sundays were not for church. Anyone could sleep with anyone at any time. Or leave without consequence. Education was revered above personal substance. Finances and friends lived in the boxes and people were addicted to them. Words were taken and given by the cases made of metal and chips and were called good or bad. Merry Christmas had been replaced by random holiday greetings. Everyone had the right to choose anything she wanted for her life. And others' lives. Life was expendable for convenience's sake.

The boxes were filled with politics and cultural practices that had never been written on the Rock, and if anyone disagreed with them, she was shamed. Choice had become a religion to some because people were without any other kind of faith. They could not lean on God, so they insisted they have the "choice" to direct their own lives, playing God themselves.

*Thump.* Through the boxes of shame, she, too, had led others astray with all the sanitized philosophies of social compliance and personal choices.

Her father nodded. "It is the way now, more than ever. I finally had to turn off the boxes and open the Great Book again. The boxes are not inherently bad, and much good could actually be done with them, but in the hands of inattentive people, they have been misused."

She watched as the brown fog swirled and covered itself. "The boxes had helped me develop a selfish, mortal plan." Burrowing deep inside, she said, "I allowed Mom to help me with it, but, truthfully, it had been mine alone. I wouldn't let anything interfere with that plan. And after she died, I somehow felt like I was keeping Mother alive if I accomplished that plan, and I had little concern for the welfare of others. I had made excuses for the choices that the boxes told me were mine. Earthly excuses."

Knowledge swirled in her heart, like the dark haze below. "It was the cacophony of the boxes that had led me to destroy little Max."

If she'd only known she'd been working for the Liar all the time. Her life felt ruined and used, and her heart stained in an inky blackness—the same inky blackness of The Regretting Place.

# CHAPTER TEN

## Forward the Steps

Cotton rounded the corner to her home in The Sorting Place, hugged her father briefly and said goodbye as she stared at the great tree before her. Its leaves were falling to the ground once again as it did every evening. Her new focus was on her own heart and what she'd realized about it.

As she ran toward her little illuminations that were glowing under the tree in the waning light around her, she stopped and turned toward her father as he was walking away toward The Rejoicing Place. The realization that her time was coming to an end in The Sorting Place rose up and stung her even more than it had before. Would she ever see him again? Maybe. If the rest of the sorting and settling went a certain way. But it had not been decided. Her grandmother had told her so. Her father had told her so. Her grandfather had told her so.

She lifted her hand up at him, knowing. She watched him

walk toward the glowing mountain, his head hanging until he was far from her tree. She felt his Stone of Stumbling again for a few moments because she felt close to him in it.

Eventually, she turned back to her little ones and let go of her father's Stone of Stumbling. She lit up as kaleidoscopically scarlet as were they. Max hovered about the first limb and watched as she kissed and hugged and played with the others—all her little quiescent children, her very own QCs. How unfair of her to have created their situations—to place her responsibilities for them upon Mimi—upon Tsur. Even if it had been unknowingly.

Still Max hovered and tore his little inner glow in two. She was responsible for that, as well. But Max was strong and stubborn in so many ways, and it was going to take a miracle to break through to him—to pull him from his abeyance, like she had her others.

Cotton realized now there was additional settling to be done under her tree. Because of the boxes, and because she was a part of them, she felt responsible. But how could she express that to them? They didn't know about the boxes. Had her mistakes caused her little lights some kind of eternal suffering or sentence that she didn't completely understand? Maybe. She had definitely affected their forms. And maybe Max knew that. Somehow, Max discerned so much more than even she understood. How was she ever going to get through to him? How was she ever going to settle with him?

That knowledge of how to settle with him had to be in her heart. She would have to search it. At the right time. That was how. All of the answers to every question were inside her, if she simply accessed it. But could she? And would she have enough time because she could sense time flowing away like a stream. No one could stop a stream without flooding the landscapes around it and drowning all upon it. It was imperative that she learn what she needed to know in the time that she had been given.

She so wanted to reconcile with Max.

The little radiances darted all about her and into the tree as if playing a game. She chased them into the old oak and clumsily climbed from branch to branch, all of her fears of heights gone. She was careful, however, to give little Max the space he seemed to need. Maybe it was good for him to see her care and love for his brothers and sisters.

But he was a different soul. A deeper soul. One that had been wounded more. She watched out the corner of her eye as his light seemed to split, and dim and rejoin, almost as if he were in pain, trying to hold things together. Something was deeply damaged in him, beyond what she understood. But he wasn't going to let her get close to him. And she didn't blame him.

At last, the little ones tired and settled down all about her under the tree. She called out each of their names, Annabelle, Clarabelle, Hunter, Harper, Sissy and River. Preston, Honey, Skyler, Georgia. And Willow. She said goodnight to them all, suddenly knowing when she'd lost each of them from her. Some had been lost early, before they'd even embedded. Some had spent a few weeks trying to totally secure themselves to her damaged insides. Honey lasted longer, attaching, growing and then falling away. All those years, she had been unaware of all of them—except the two, Preston and Max.

It had been all the damage that had been inflicted at Max's termination. She sat up straight and looked around for Max. He had secreted himself in Sela' again. He was safely hidden in the fissure. "Goodnight, Max."

Though Max was her most troubling reconciliation, she knew she had others. The knowledge arose in her that she was going to see another vision tonight, one that had nothing to do with Max, one that she'd also been avoiding. So she nestled into the earth beside her little illuminations.

Caleb was a good man. She'd known that all along, but the bright glow enlightening his form in her kitchen cemented that knowledge upon her heart.

*It was that same, strange light that came with all her re-livings—all her illuminations.*

His dark hair darted over his ears, like it had been blown by the wind. His shoulders pushed against his extra-large shirt, showing the muscles he had from hitting a baseball again and again to the pint-sized guys on the little league team he'd finished coaching last month. An easy smile spread across his lips. "What would you like to drink?'

"Water."

She'd taken the day off for several reasons. It was too hot to be telling stories at the end of a Carolina summer, the heat, the humidity, the oppression.

That kind of heat was indescribable, and she'd not been feeling well because of it for days. No, weeks. She'd needed to regroup, get a mani and a pedi maybe. Pamper herself a little.

Caleb had come over to bring some food, but as soon as he entered with his handsome jaw line, his briefcase and with the garlic chicken from the China Express down the street, her stomach twisted. He hadn't even called to ask her what she wanted. He could be sort of dense like that.

*The brilliant light shimmered. She knew she shouldn't have thought that of Caleb. Now. In the new light. Without shadows. This wasn't going to be easy. Watching herself think and act the way she had. Now that she had the knowledge.*

Why had he even come over? She simply wanted to take a bath and soak in her old ball and claw foot tub in her own historic apartment. By herself. "Hey, I'm going to be a while in there, so..."

He glanced up. "That's fine. I finally got that new cell phone and number for my new office. I've got to add a few apps to it, so take your time. I've got plenty to keep me occupied here." He poured himself a glass of water, walked to the living room and turned on the television.

She stood in the doorway to the bath. "You don't have to hang around." She just wanted to be alone.

He picked up the take-out and glanced up. "Not a problem. If you don't mind, I'll just eat this, since you're not going to. Anyway, I'm going to work on my phone and watch the baseball game for a while, if that's okay with you."

It had to be. He was her boyfriend, so she couldn't tell him to get lost.

In her bathroom, she turned on the water, as hot as she could stand and dropped a bath bomb in the tub. As she was undressing, the scent of sandalwood hit her like a sewer pipe. "Ewww," she said, letting out the water and tossing the bomb into the toilet. She flushed it to get rid of the scent. Probably wasn't good for the pipes, but she'd needed to get rid of that awful odor.

She'd remembered feeling this way. Twice before. She tried to push the thoughts from her head.

She refilled the tub again, this time with no stink bomb. Who ever thought it was a good idea to sell Ode de' Sewer?

She sank into the tub and allowed the water to cover all but her face.

When she had first met Caleb, he'd had a job at a swanky downtown Charleston law firm. Broad Street lawyers were revered in Charleston and beyond. And rich. But, no. That didn't satisfy Caleb. He wanted more, or, a better way to say it would be less. He didn't want the fancy cars and swanky law cases. No. He wanted to take pro bono work from people who couldn't afford to buy soap when they needed to wash. He had taken a few cases even when he had worked for Graham and Gilliard. And he'd liked the charity cases so much, he wanted to do it full time, so he went to work for the county, thus, his new phone. Her interest in him had waned ever since. She couldn't help it, though. She kept hearing her mother whisper in her ear, saying the same things she'd said about Tucker Boyd. "He's a loser. He'll never make anything of himself now. You need to be a part of a power couple," echoed in her ear.

*In the illuminating light, she knew this was wrong.*

When she'd finished her reverie and her bath, she wrapped herself in her favorite fluffy white robe, pushed her feet into her red slippers and stared into the mirror. She couldn't believe what was happening to her after so many years. She'd thought all that had been diagnosed, decided, and behind her. She'd successfully pushed it all out of her mind. And her heart.

Shaking her head, she reached under the cabinet and grabbed another blue box. She'd test one more time. In case she was wrong, she re-read the directions again. She did as the box instructed one more time, put the strip on the counter and waited a few moments. There was that line again.

How inconvenient. If all went well with the series she was about to undertake, her career could enter hyper mode. Maybe even national hyper mode. What was she going to do? Her brain could figure this out. Couldn't it?

For a moment, she wanted to cry, to punch the mirror.

*In the shadow-less light of her vision, Cotton now wished that she could punch the once ignorant version of herself.*

But alas, punching anything would be useless. This was her fault—her fault for going to that hack clinic in Greenville, her fault for listening to the hack doctor who told her she'd never be able to have children. Her fault.

Grabbing the strip in a huff, she threw it at the trashcan. She couldn't stay in the bathroom forever. She needed to make an appearance in the living room to satisfy Caleb.

"Well, there you are," Caleb said. He walked up to her and kissed her forehead. "I was beginning to think you'd drowned."

Closing her eyes, she said, "It just felt so good." It had. The waters helped wash away the weight she felt.

His dark eyes darted over her face. "I'm sure, sweetie. May I heat up a can of chicken noodle soup for you? You need to eat something."

Why wouldn't he just go home so that she could figure this out? "No, thanks. The salt in those cans would make me look like a large marshmallow on camera."

He kissed her lips. "You'd never look like a marshmallow. A truffle, maybe, but never a marshmallow." He backed her shoulders away, flashing her that million-dollar smile of his.

A brief jolt struck her heart. "You're too good for me, Caleb Samuelson."

He eyed her carefully. "But you look like a…green truffle tonight. Do you need a trashcan or a rag? You look like you're about to heave."

"No. I'm really fine." She wasn't, but she just wanted him to go so that she could be alone. She simply didn't know how to tell him without looking ungrateful for all he had done.

*But wasn't that exactly what she was? Ungrateful?*

"Well, let me get you settled on the couch with the remote." He helped her and covered her legs with a crocheted afghan her Mimi had made her when she was eight. "There."

"Thanks," was all she could muster. The baseball game was still on, but she wanted to watch the news from her station. How could she ever learn to share her life with another? She'd been independent for so long.

"Hmmm," he said, trying to help. "You look tired. How about I get out of here and let you get some rest?"

That was the only thing that could make her happy.

*That night. In the shadow-less light.*

She reached over and took a sip of the water he'd placed on the table beside her. "I think that would be best."

He nodded and lifted his hand as if to pause the conversation. "I'll just run to the little boy's room, and then I'm outta here."

She breathed out, relieved that he'd be gone soon. She grabbed the remote from the coffee table and flipped through the channels until she found hers.

When he walked out the bathroom, he was standing in what seemed like a spotlight, completely illuminating every pained line in his face, and the light was glaring mostly on the little strip that he held in one hand and the blue box in the other.

She sat up straight.

"What's all this?" he asked. His words held the weight of betrayal.

For a moment, she thought about conjuring up some story or another. She was good at that. But she didn't. He deserved her honesty about this. All of it, even if she actually didn't know how she was going to handle it all.

"So, were you going to tell me about this? It is why you stayed home today. And why you couldn't eat the food I brought. Isn't it?"

She nodded, dropping her head for only a moment.

*The brilliance of the light dimmed slightly, but it still illuminated things in a way that exposed all that she hadn't noticed the first time. She didn't want to relive this. It was too painful. So painful that she'd isolated the knowledge of it from her thoughts for months after it had happened.*

Taking a step closer, he said, "So, this is great, right? You should be happy. I mean, you told me you couldn't get—" He stared at her for a while. He looked confused, looked out the window and then back at her. "Wait. You're not planning to—"

He couldn't bring himself to say the words.

Not only did she say those words once, she'd gone through with the procedure, and she'd never told him about it, and she didn't want to now. She was too ashamed.

Caleb's face drooped with sadness at her silence. He shook his head from side to side ever so slightly.

She would have to explain this to him. He hadn't walked in her shoes. She had, and it had scarred her. "You know that I was told many years ago that I couldn't bear children, right? That this is completely a shock, right?"

He opened his eyes wide. "That should be exactly why you should be elated. I don't understand." He collapsed into the red chair that was across from her. "And I stayed with you, even though I knew you couldn't bear children for me." He moved his head from side to side, slowly, methodically. "All my life, I'd planned to have children. But I fell in love with you, and I couldn't let you go. I came to terms with that months ago." He dropped his head. "I gave up my desire to have children to be with you!" He threw the box on the floor with one hand and let the plastic strip fall to the floor with the other.

How could she explain further without sounding so shallow? "We are not married, and I'd never want to trap you."

"Trap? Heck, Cotton, I'd have asked you to marry me a long, long time ago if I'd thought you would have accepted." He rocked ever so slightly, to and fro, ringing his hands, making the muscles on his strong forearms twitch.

Her mother's voice whispered in her ear. *You know you're up for the anchor position at the station. This could ruin everything.* And then she foolishly repeated those words to Caleb. "This could ruin everything."

*The strange shadow-less light somehow also illumined what she heard herself say.*

He stood, grabbing the back of his neck and shaking his head.

She stood, too. She'd learned long ago to stand up for herself, literally and otherwise. Remaining seated would have somehow given him the upper hand—the power. She'd learned to grab her own power and to assert it.

*Thump. Somehow that just didn't seem appropriate in the re-living of the scene in the strange light.*

He stepped toward her and placed his hands on her waist in a way that almost encircled her. "*This* could ruin everything? Do you really mean that?" he asked, his forehead knit together with sorrow between the lines. "*You* are ruining everything. This could be a miracle for us." He stepped away and grabbed the back of his neck, and shook his head, as if he could shake it enough to make her stop. "I knew there could be consequences to what we were doing, but I had always hoped to convince you to marry me if anything did happen.”

“That almost sounds like you were planning this, Caleb.”

“I love you,” he said, staring into her eyes. “I love how strong you are, how you make up your mind about something, and you go after it. I love how you try to hide the tender side of you, but I see it.” He pointed to one of the notebooks on the table. Although one sat empty. “What you’re planning to do for those orphan kids is amazing. I see how you value your grandparents. How you kept the afghan your grandmother made you. How much you love that old hall tree that your grandfather made. I love how you kept your father’s leather briefcase and take it to work every day. I love the way you keep your mother’s memory alive by pursuing your career. I love everything about you.”

How could he love her like that?

*She had been a rotten person. And now she was a confused person.*

*He was recounting all the things he loved about her, and she heard them this time. The time before, she’d simply tuned him out while wishing the knowledge inside her would just go away.*

*If only she could live this day over for real. It wouldn’t end up like this. But she couldn’t. She couldn’t change a thing, and the thoughtless words just spilled out again.*

“I’m totally confused. I have a lot to think about. What about reproductive rights and choices, Caleb.”

*She felt her insides steel, like the boxes that preached that philosophy—that lie.*

He paced. "Choices? Reproductive rights? Yes, you have the choice to use one of twenty different kinds of birth control, daily, weekly, yearly, semi-permanent, permanent." He paced more. "And women have the right to refuse to engage in activity that would cause them to reproduce. Heck, I would have used something if I knew how strongly you felt about this, but I believed what you told me—that you couldn't get pregnant." He shook his head. "And deep down, I knew we shouldn't be acting like a married couple to begin with, but I was hoping to convince you to marry me."

*Marry me?* "But I never pretended to be interested in marriage. I'm not like you."

He turned to her. "You're more like me than you think. I listened to you telling me about your childhood, that little church you attended, and how much you loved your parents and adored your grandparents." He took another step toward her. "In my experience, people are more deeply like the childhood versions of themselves than they realize. I was just waiting for you to see that." He paced again. "How did we get here, Cotton?"

"It wasn't my fault. I didn't know that I could get pregnant. That was what they told me at the clinic when they botched everything."

*There were those words of excuse again. She'd used them often. About so many things. But she knew better now.*

He stopped in his tracks and stared her straight in the eyes. "What clinic?"

She knew she was going to be in real trouble with him now. He had let her know on numerous occasions how he'd felt about abortion. That was why she'd never told him about hers. Or about the assault that had necessitated it. Of course, he wouldn't understand it for the incredibly selfish reasons she was considering it now—and especially because it was his baby that could possibly be extinguished, if she didn't lose it. Or couldn't figure out how to keep it.

"I didn't tell you because I knew you wouldn't have approved." She wanted to tell him about the assault—the gang assault, but it had been buried too deep inside, and she didn't want to share the pain of it—even with him.

He shook his head. "I don't even know you," he said.

"You wouldn't understand," she said.

He paced back and forth, like a raccoon in a trap. Then he stopped. "But that's my child, too, and I have rights, too, don't I? Why is it that the world thinks that only women have rights? And I'm not giving you permission to do this!" He nearly yelled the words.

Cotton remembered thinking that he'd made an excellent argument. Because he was a lawyer. He'd wanted his child because he was selfless. Cotton had silenced certain sensitive parts of herself years ago and couldn't yet speak about what was going on—yet. If only she could tell him that. But, instead, she remained silent because she couldn't deal with the emotions right now.

*She stared at the sweet, handsome man. He was too good for her in the strange light.*

People make romantic matches for all sorts of reasons, and some look like they don't belong together to the world—their sizes, their races, their intellectual levels, or educational levels, disparate wealth and beauty. When one doesn't parallel with the other, couples don't seem to match. But she and Caleb looked like they belonged together to all the world on many levels.

But they really didn't match at all. The only important thing that needed to be matched was the color of their souls. His was tinted pure, and hers was tainted with the selfish need to protect herself. They didn't belong together.

"Cotton, it's wrong to even consider not having it. You are listening to the wrong people, researching the wrong sources." He stared out the window by the hall tree. He put his hand on the piece of furniture, and she sensed the connection of two good men, Caleb and her grandfather, who had made it.

She had a view of Caleb's perfectly rugged and handsome profile, and the first time she had lived this, she hadn't noticed, but this time, she watched as a tear tried to find a jagged track down his face.

"I'm sorry," she said. But she wasn't really completely when she'd said the words the first time.

*However, the light illumined her this time.*

She'd been indoctrinated into the culture, a culture that had decided and had preached way before she was born that she had choices and rights. If there was anything called cultural brainwashing, she had been a victim. No, not actually. She was not a victim. She had willingly and eagerly believed because it had been convenient in her life. In this new light, and with the recognition of the knowledge that was now in her heart, Caleb's argument could have been the Rock's argument.

Cotton had made many choices to bring herself to this point again. She had privileges that she'd ignored and had trampled on as she was waving her selfish flags of choice and rights. How did she not see that? How could all those women who'd come before her ignore those truths, as well? And how dare they indoctrinate all the women who came after them that they could ignore all the choices and rights that led them to their problems, like their choices of self-control had been somehow taken away earlier. It was all lies, and they were all liars.

She saw it all so clearly in this enlightening brightness. This was not reproductive freedom. It was reproductive prison. Their choices were her chains. The rights they proclaimed were really wrongs.

He stepped up to her again, grabbed her hands and held them in his. "I say no. I'll take the child and will raise it. I'll draw up papers so that you'll never owe a dime for its welfare. Just have the child." Holding onto her hands, he got down on one knee. "Please. Please. Please. This cannot be reversed."

She closed her eyes. "I can't think right now. This will devastate my career, my chances for the promotion."

*Her heart sank in the illuminating light.*

She remembered thinking that she also didn't want to ruin her figure for the camera. How incredibly shallow of her to have even thought that.

He stood and screamed. "I don't care about your promotion or your career!"

At the time when it had first happened, she didn't like the way he'd yelled at her, and it had steeled her emotions against him in the moment. Now, in the new light, with the knowledge of loving her little lights, she loved him even more for fighting for the new life that they'd created together.

She walked to the couch and sat. He paced about the room, grabbing at the back of his neck.

*Oh, how she wished that she could go to him, to kiss him, to tell him that she was wrong. That she would have his baby. Do whatever it takes—even if she hadn't thought it through and planned it all like she did everything else.*

Though the light in the room was illuminating, it was also frozen in a way because it was a snapshot. It was the same illuminating light that she'd encountered in all her visions. She was helpless to repeat what had happened the first time. She was merely an observer that could note things that she hadn't taken in the first time she'd lived it.

The soft glow of the living room lamp revealed even deeper lines in his handsome face, lines of love. "This just isn't right."

She hadn't been affected like this the first time, but now she saw the pain in his eyes, the worried lines in his face and the wounds upon his heart, and it broke her own heart in a way that she hadn't been able to feel before.

He sat on the edge of the couch and dropped his head into his hands.

*The unstoppable scene played on.*

"I'm totally confused, but I haven't made any decisions. I have to think about what's best for me. I have to live with this for the rest of my life," she said. All the possibilities with her career flashed before her. But this time her career didn't seem as important as it had the first time she'd thought about it.

"Are you listening to yourself? I, I, I. Is that all you can think about? There are others involved here," Caleb said, his voice wounded. "When that baby kicks in a few weeks, it's not going to be your brain or muscles making it kick. If that baby decides to suck its little thumb, your brain will have had nothing to do with its little desire. Can't you see? You cannot make a choice about a life that isn't yours!"

Those were very good points and questions, but she didn't answer him.

"Cotton, you are not God, and the moral power of life and death are not yours. This is not your choice at this point." He stood up and paced. "Just like it is not a person's choice to sleep with others after they have committed themselves in marriage. It is not a person's choice to abandon his or her elderly parents because they become an inconvenience in their old age. It is not a choice to drop off one's children at an orphanage if one loses his job. You simply live with your choices and work through the issues." His lawyer voice trailed at the end, like he was about to concede his case.

So much about that evening had been hidden from her the first time, but tonight, she keenly watched him. She saw him stop his pacing and enter the nearly dark kitchen. From a corner, she saw a rosy glowing light, settle upon his shoulder as he warmed a can of soup for her. The soup she hadn't wanted.

*Thump.* The knowledge about the light came to her. It was Max. He was hers, and she'd recognize his glow anywhere now.

But Max hadn't wanted anything to do with her, even upon that night. He was more aligned with Caleb than with her on that night.

*Thump*. She knew in an instant. Caleb would have been a good father to Max—even though Max had been conceived like he had. She hadn't given little Max a chance. Or Caleb.

Caleb brought the soup to her on a tray. An act of graciousness that she didn't deserve. "I cannot bear to continue this right now. I've said all that I know to say to you." He stood motionless, just staring at her.

How could someone be so uncomfortable in her own skin? Still, she didn't say anything to him. She'd said it all. No decisions had been made, but he hadn't heard that. Just the possibility was enough to disgust him with her.

"I suppose I see how you feel about me." He rubbed the back of his neck again. "I can't be here. I just can't. If you're the kind of person who could possibly think about something like this, I don't even want to know you."

Caleb walked around the house, picking up a few of his things that he'd left over the last year as they'd spent time together, a jacket, some CD's, a few books. Finally, he grabbed the briefcase he'd brought in alongside the takeout food for her and tossed the books and CDs in the case. He took out a piece of paper and began to write upon it and placed it on the flat part of the antique hall tree that she'd rescued from her grandparents' home that was by the door. She already knew what was written on the paper because she'd never moved it from the spot he had laid it. "Call me if you change your mind" was written above his new number that she'd never call. And he'd signed it, "Love,

Caleb."

He couldn't look at her. He stood at the doorway for a few moments. She knew he'd hoped that she'd stop him, tell him something different. Not that she was confused. But she couldn't tell him anything different at that moment. She hadn't figured anything out yet. Then she watched him walk out the door, with the little light trailing behind.

Springing up from her slumbered vision under her tree, she gasped. A miasma rolled into her head. The vision was somehow incomplete. Unsettled. What had she done? What choice did she ultimately make?

For the life of her, she couldn't remember what she'd decided about Caleb's baby.

The next morning Mimi came to the tree, her three little glowing yellow lights behind her. She had her apron caught up, like she carried something in it. Somehow, Cotton knew there wouldn't be many more visits. She hugged her grandmother so tightly and inhaled her scent of sugarcane syrup, buttermilk biscuits, and love.

"I brought mine to play with yours," Mimi said.

What an odd concept, Cotton thought. Her baby lights were playing with their great aunts and uncle. All the little glows from all eternity could all play together forever.

Mimi released her apron, and two little pink lights buzzed up to the top of the tree to hide amongst the newly green leaves on the branches.

Cotton looked confused. "Where did those come from?"

"That is your half-brother and your half-sister. I thought it would be okay to bring them after all you have learned."

Cotton looked high into the tree. "Oh, Mimi. Mother never said a thing."

"You caught a glimpse of your baby sister once."

Cotton searched deep inside herself, and the heart knowledge came to her. "In that tree, just before I fell, when I was a child." The light had distracted her. It was the reason she fell.

Mimi nodded. "They remain…unacknowledged. So, they are skittish."

Cotton peered into the upper branches to try to see the pale pinkish lights, but they had hidden themselves so well that she never saw even a glow. "Poor little things."

"And your father knows about their quiescent lives. He has also never forgiven himself for your falling and the loosening."

"Loosening?" Something shot through Cotton. "How can my father feel responsible for anything that was not of his doing?"

Her grandmother looked off into the distance. "It's all very complicated, but our actions do have consequences beyond The Choosing Place. If there is guilt to be taken, one must do that himself. Sometimes it is taken when it is not deserved, and sometimes it is evaded. This is the place for understanding, but even when your mother saw her little pink lights here, in her sorting, she denied them."

"Is there anything that can be done for them?"

"I don't know. I have merely borrowed them. They are Tsur's. They do not feel recognized unless they are with Him."

Cotton understood. Somehow.

"Ready?" her grandmother asked. "We have much to accomplish."

The two women started out together on the most beautiful, temperate day.

Her Mimi took her hand as they walked. Cotton felt a sort of warmth, but not really the touch, though the love between them was palpable.

Cotton still had so many, many questions. "Mimi, why don't you ever come here with Poppy?"

She giggled. "Oh, child, if you'd only read the book, you would know. It is not a secret. Nothing in the book is a secret." After a few steps together, she said, "Marriage is a useless concept here. The book told us there would be no marriages or remarriages here." She giggled again. "There is much work to be done here. We all have chores, and who would want to complicate them with trying to figure out who was first married to whom, and a first wife died, and the husband married a second wife? And with all the divorces and remarriages these days. What a mess it would be. And, anyway, you have no use of that knowledge. It does not concern you."

"Well, what is your relationship with Poppy now?" she asked as they passed a garden of glowing gardenia bushes.

"That is a good question." She paused, seemingly trying to

think of a way to explain. "He is my favorite…neighbor, my favorite…friend." Mimi's eyes lit, "We are to love our neighbors, and I love him very much—more than any other."

Cotton liked that idea. Uncomplicated.

So much in this place was so convoluted that she didn't know how to untangle the mazes of thoughts—of interactions. Now, she had the knowledge that she had a half-brother and a half-sister. What was she to do with that knowledge? "Mimi, what does Daddy think about the pink lights?"

"Child, they are a part of his Stone of Stumbling, as well. One of them was with your mother on that yacht the night she died."

*Thump*. Cotton stopped. "Oh, Mimi. Mother didn't fall off that boat, did she?"

Her grandmother simply kept walking.

Cotton knew, though. Her mother had been pushed because of the pink light. Their father, your father's friend, chose not to acknowledge them either. It seemed to Cotton that it was easy for people to keep their secrets hidden in The Choosing Place, but here, in The Sorting Place, everything became illuminated. She felt compassion for the little lights who had no mother or father. Maybe there would be something she could do for them later. She just didn't know how all this worked.

They continued walking past fields and flowers that vibrated with color. They passed orchards of peaches and pears, their fragrances drifting over her. The two walked on, and they finally arrived.

The well.

The long flowing branches of the weeping willow tree hung down all around the well and swayed in the gentle breeze. "This is for you now," said Mimi. "Go ahead. You may look into it."

Cotton was confused. Why now? She moved aside the weeping willow wisps and bent over the edge of the well that was made of rocks of various sizes—just like the woman had before when Cotton had seen her with the man in the luminous robe.

Bending over slightly, nearly afraid, she said, "I don't see anything. It's just dark." A coolness blew up from deep below. The chill air smelled like fresh rain.

Mimi stepped closer. "As is everything we see at first. You are not looking properly. You must desire to see what is before you. All of it. Even the things that are painful."

Finally, Cotton saw her reflection. "It's just me. I see my blond hair." She unbent her body. "I've always known that I could see my reflection in the water. Is that what I'm supposed to see?"

"You are concerned with you, so, yes…at first."

Cotton was confused and a little wary.

"Now, look again." She pointed to Cotton's heart. "Look from inside there."

Cotton did as she was directed. Again, she saw her blond hair and then her face, but nothing new, nothing profound.

"What do you see?" her grandmother asked, then she bent over the edge, too.

"The same."

"Now look beyond the surface of the water, beyond the apparent, into the depths," Mimi's voice echoed down the walls of the well.

Cotton inhaled. Could that even be done? Cotton tried to do as she was directed. She stared harder and used her heart like when she was trying to divine something from the Rock. The water shimmered. Then she saw darkness. She strained even harder through the depths. She jerked up. "Oh, Mimi."

Mimi stood, as well. "You must look, my child. We all must when it is time."

But Cotton didn't want to. Partly because of what her father had told her yesterday. It had not been decided. Partly because she smelled the fear that was deep below the surface. But what could she do? Mimi said she must. That everyone must. When it was time.

She breathed deeply and bent over the large rocks once again, looking into the depths. It was easier this time.

*Thump*. What she saw was her heart. Every stain. Every sin. Every wish. Every affliction and every affection. Every act of kindness. Every prayer. And there had been too few of those at the end of her time in The Choosing Place. She took all the images in, marveling at the pieces Tsur would admire…and shameful of the pieces He would abhor. The well and all it contained was deep. This needed to be done. She wouldn't shorten the gazing for anything. This was important. So much of what she'd done and wished, she'd even hidden from herself; instead, she listened to her mother's whispering, her mother's leading. She'd listened to the boxes. Because it had fit in with *her own* plan.

Then came the most painful part—the part she'd pretended didn't exist.

She saw it clearly, deeply in the farthest depths of the water.

*Thump.* The fog in her head about her decision rolled up into itself and became nothingness. After Caleb had left that night, after his articulate argument about saving and raising his baby, she couldn't bring herself to make that appointment with that clinic—even though it had made perfect sense to her earlier. Neither could she call the number on the piece of paper he'd left on the table part of the hall tree. It sat there day after day until it became a part of the furniture. Funny how that happens to all sorts of things. Her problem did that, as well. It waited. And became such a part of her life that she didn't even notice or acknowledge it any longer.

If she didn't think about it, maybe it would go away; maybe it wouldn't exist.

She saw herself go to work, day after day, in that box, reporting on stories of interest, people's achievements, people's problems, without much thought of her own.

Her appointments with her manicurist were kept. She shopped online for new clothes that fit her signature style, those expensive red heels and fancy outfits to match—all in the same size her mother had worn—a four. Each day, she would apply the ruby red lipstick to her lips to complete her professional image. Meals were skipped to keep that image as slim as ever.

*The waters shook in waves from the center of her body, her own tummy thumped and jumped, and a white shock of light shot through her.*

There it was. She had to acknowledge it. Like she had with Max, she had starved herself into denying the mirror the right to acknowledge her condition, thus, avoiding taking full responsibility of the situation. Like something or someone other than her would simply take care of the problem.

But that hadn't worked. She was the person fully responsible for the baby. Caleb's baby. The baby that belonged to the Rock Who Begot You.

*The water shook. Her soul shook.*

She saw herself at the church. On that tall ladder. Though she was thinner than she'd ever been, and though she wouldn't let the thought of it dwell in her head, Caleb's baby was still inside her. On that ladder.

Caleb had assumed it was gone. She had pretended it was gone. No one else knew either.

But the Rock knew. Because that baby was His.

And she'd nearly insured its disappearance by all her actions. Had she caused one final little death by falling off that ladder?

What a horrible person she was.

Babies' lives had been jeopardized, traded for her convenience, for her figure, for her reputation, for her career.

She deserved death.

She deserved to be in the dark fog over the cliffs—where

she'd buried the knowledge of Caleb's baby.

She belonged in the black, rolling haze over the cliffs.

"Mimi, I…I…I had hidden the truth from myself."

Mimi nodded. "There is more. The Great Truth is in that well. It is time for you to see it."

Her heart seemed to drop into the water, and she watched the darkness shimmer for the longest time. Until it stilled. But her heart didn't still. Remorse and regret reverberated through it, shook her to her core.

She lifted up again. "It is not there."

Mimi inhaled deeply. "It is deeper. You must want to see it with all that you are."

She drew in a breath that seemed to saw at her lungs. "But how?" The way she had seen the knowledge with her heart just didn't seem to work.

"You must see it with your spirit. If you know how to call upon Him, another Great Spirit can help you."

Could that be done? Where was Cotton's spirit? Had she hidden it away like she had the knowledge that she'd been pregnant when she had fallen off that ladder? She thought hard and remembered some of what they'd taught her in Sunday school—that the Holy Spirit would help with things that were not tangible. Maybe He could help her with this.

Though she'd never prayed for help from the Holy Spirit, she would try.

Deep inside her, where she'd hidden very painful things, she closed her eyes and breathed the prayer.

*Holy Spirit, I desire to know what is deeper inside of this well—what is in the deepest depths of my heart—the things that I've hidden from myself. I pray for knowledge not only for myself, but so that I'll have the information to understand what I must do to repair all the damage I've done to so many. Even if I perish with or because of the knowledge.*

A mighty wind rushed up the well and over Cotton, whipping the tendrils of the weeping willow tree. She heard an echo as it gathered itself together and tunneled back down the well crashing upon the water.

Cotton tentatively placed her hands upon the rock walls, looked into the well, fear flooding her soul. The deep water swirled in a tempest against the sides of the well. The waters made a mighty sound and ran up and down the sides of the well, until the floor of the well was dry, but it trembled and thundered. There, written in the stones at the bottom of the well, were the strange words.

*"God will write His law upon His people's hearts, and it will be a covenant, giving their souls knowledge of His ways."*

*Thump.* All that she'd known in her own core, deep down, the knowledge about right and wrong, the discernment of good and evil, all was written upon that rock. And it had all been inside her, as well. The words and their meanings flowed back and forth between her heart and her hands and the words at the bottom of the well for a lengthy time, an unknown amount of time. All the knowledge. Everything of substance and meaning that was in that mysterious book that she had not bothered to read and claimed to not understand.

She'd known all of it. All along. She simply had chosen not to access it, and had, instead, relied upon the boxes for principles that were too precious to trust to anyone other than Tsur.

*Right and wrong had been written upon her heart from the beginning.*

When the flowing stopped, her hands dropped to her sides, like she'd been released from some electric power.

She drew in a deep breath and stood tall, her eyes trained on the rock. "It had all been excuses. I knew everything that I had done wrong, from the time that I was old enough to know that I shouldn't have climbed that tree after Dad and Mom told me not to. To the selfish decisions I had made about my career and life." She lowered her head. "And my babies."

The Rock that made up the well began shimmering. Words that she couldn't read began to form again. But she *understood* the pure, uncontaminated words.

*"Even when His word is written upon His people's hearts, they turn from the knowledge and excuse their choices."*

She had read those words, assembled in a different way, in the great book when she'd been sitting beside her grandparents in church, waiting for the service to be over so she could go outside to play with her friends or to lie underneath her favorite tree. But she'd never bothered studying them and holding them in her heart to access when she had a decision to make. "When my conscience tried to bubble to the surface, I always turned to a box to help me create an excuse—to not listen to the heart of what was right or wrong. The boxes were easier to look at and to believe. Much easier than that Great Book."

"Yes. Much easier than looking inside," Mimi said.

"It was easier to make excuses for what I wanted to do. I see now. Everything important had always been written in my heart. No box. Or person. Or even textbook could take the place of what the Rock had written in my heart."

Mimi nodded. "You ignored when The Rock of Offense tried to accuse you."

Cotton had the vocabulary now and used it. "And it had become my Stone of Stumbling."

Her grandmother's face showed approval. "You own the truth of it now."

She understood the Great Rock, its words always there, always available when she needed them, even if she couldn't assign numbers to them. And the Great Rock was everywhere…all around her…and inside her. "I understand now. I didn't want to access the wisdom in my heart because I would feel compelled to do what it demanded, and I would feel remorse if I didn't do what my heart told me."

Mimi smiled.

Cotton shook her head in disbelief. "And I really, truly knew better. Deep down inside."

Mimi nodded. "Yes, everything The Rock of Israel had written in the Great Book had always been written upon your heart, as well."

*Thump*…went her heart, and she couldn't breathe for a moment again. *He had.* And how much time did Cotton spend reading that book? Yeah, she'd learned a few stories from it, but the bulk of it was incomprehensible.

"Mimi, so much of it was confusing and contradicting. And I was always put off by all the numbers, the chapters and the verses. I could never learn all those. You know how bad I was at math. I was a storyteller."

"Child, The Rock did not put those numbers in there. Man did. Tsur put the words there, not to be barked and recited over and over with chapters and numbers. He writes his words upon all our hearts so that they are to be understood and lived."

None of the words that Tsur had given her on the Rocks had numbers and verses. They were even in a language not her own. And yet she had understood them. In her own words. Because she had wanted to understand.

"Mimi, this changes everything. What is to become of me?"

Mimi shook her head, seeming to search for the words to say. "Some things have not been decided. Your sorting is problematical."

And now with the awareness that she *had* known better about so many things, that His words *had* been written upon her heart from the beginning, if only she'd searched it. But she couldn't remain stuck at the well. She had to move forward.

*Numbness spread over her and an urging surged up inside her.*

She knew she needed to finish the knowledge the well had for her, so she leaned over the rocks one last time and tunneled into the depths.

This new information was the reason she'd felt her prayer of repentance before Tsur, the great, breathing mountain was incomplete the night she'd tried to settle with her little lights. But they were innocent and didn't know that the knowledge had really been in her heart all the while—all but baby Max. He knew more than the others.

Her heart was heavy with the awareness. She had had all the knowledge all the while. She had just chosen ignorance. It wasn't the world's fault for telling her that she had choices and rights. It wasn't her mother's fault for telling her to think of her career first. It wasn't the boxes' faults for showing her that life is best lived in selfish pleasure. It had been her own fault.

Each moment was laborious as the consequences of that knowledge filled her head with lead. The enlightenment of her understanding filled her with answers. As she stared, she applied her raw, exposed knowledge.

She knew that the two baby souls that had formed inside her were not hers to decide whether they lived or died. She had blocked that understanding so long ago. And there had been consequences. Twelve of them. So many other little lights had been extinguished because of her one, awful decision.

As she absorbed the knowledge, she recalled some of what she'd experienced here in The Sorting Place. She discerned that she had been selfish, but she had excused herself over and over again, just as the boxes had told her was her right. She understood that she should have helped others, but she had discharged her responsibilities, electing to help herself to the pleasures of The Choosing Place. Even if she hadn't read the Great Book, she had the knowledge all the while, secreted in her heart, but opted for her false mantra instead.

*Ignorance can be its own reward.* If one didn't not know better, one couldn't do better. Cotton had lived her life by that refrain, and it had helped her achieve all that she had. Practicing ignorance had been Cotton's favorite way of getting her way. But she hadn't really been ignorant, after all. How very foolish she had been. She had been living a lie.

Now, her fate seemed to be hanging precariously on her irrational practice of feigned ignorance.

When the shimmering was over, she stood and turned. Mimi stepped back into the willow branches.

Love, like she'd never known before, engulfed her. In front of her was the man she'd seen at the well before, dressed in garments, the colors of which amazed her. They were alive with luminosity and grace.

She looked at her own hands. The sallowness of guilt and shame colored them. She'd guess that her face was the color of a yellowed bruise, too. She gazed deep into His eyes. "Jesus, what have I done?"

"What do you want to do now, child?" said the man, his voice echoing through her heart and soul, like the deepest thunder she'd ever heard, leaving behind the knowledge of the Holy Spirit and ribbons of mercy.

Some emotion flooded her that she had never recognized before. *Penance.* No excuses, just pure penance. Her heart was filled with the expectation of punishment. It was also filled with a heavy, foreboding sorrow for all she had done.

"Caleb's baby." The darkness swirled through her brain. "What happened to it?" Guilt gushed from her gut.

But she felt no recrimination coming from Him. In fact, his eyes emanated pure, regal love—love that fully encompassed her. "What is in your heart?" his words swirled the mystery that was in it.

"I would choose to keep it and love it now, but I don't know what happened—how much I may have damaged the baby by all my actions." She panicked. "Whatever happened, it is my responsibility, and I am so sorry."

All the regret in the world pulled her down on her knees, and she wept at His feet beside the well. She wept for her mother. She wept for leaving the church. She wept for all her little lights. She wept for not keeping herself pure for marriage. She wept for Caleb and for not completely recognizing his goodness and for what she'd done to him. She wept for the baby she'd denied and abandoned as she fell from that ladder. She wept because she had nothing to give Him—the man who had nothing but love for her.

*This was real repentance*. True, gut-wrenching, soul-twisting repentance. Not merely words and excuses. It was what regret and sorrow and remorse and shame felt like.

"Oh, Jesus, please forgive me. I *beg* your forgiveness…not to get out of what I deserve. I want your forgiveness because I cannot bear what I have done. I deserve punishment. Those innocent babies were Petra's, not mine." She shook with tears. "I know I am not worth forgiving. I have treated those precious baby souls like they were disposable." More tears came. "I realize that what I prayed to You before was incomplete and imperfect. I will accept what price I must pay."

Still, she felt no judgement or incrimination from Him. Instead, His love overwhelmed her to the point that even His love made her feel more remorse for all she'd done.

She wept until there were no more tears to cry. And still, she did not lift up her eyes. She didn't even deserve to look at the Rock of all Ages.

# CHAPTER ELEVEN

## Leave to Find

Cotton was drained. Of all tears. Of all hope. Even of all fears. She was empty. She eventually used the boulders at the well to help her stand in the dim light.

Looking around her, she realized her grandmother had gone. The Living Stone in the garment of colored lights had gone. She was all alone. That was the state of man. Born alone. Alone responsible for what she does in The Choosing Place. Alone to figure it all out in The Sorting Place. Alone to pay the debts of her life.

*Thump.* Something else hit her. She realized that she'd made many mistakes in her life, but when she'd fallen off that ladder, she'd fallen unrepentant. From what she knew from all the Bible stories she'd once learned, repentance was required in The Choosing Place. Of course, everyone would be repentant in The Sorting Place, when they looked in the well and recognized the whole of the truth of what they'd done.

That knowledge tore her in two. No, she didn't deserve Tsur's forgiveness. She didn't deserve the mountain, The Rejoicing Place. That mountain was eternal. It was a reward. A place to be grateful to the God of all creation—the eternal Rock of Ages, who was the beginning of everything. He was the Word that always was.

The knowledge was all flowing to her now as if from a fountain.

*Thump*.

Somehow, she felt disconnected from it, even though she knew what it was. What was to happen to her? Would she see her mother in The Regretting Place?

Maybe she had no right to tell the Rock of Salvation that she was repentant here. It should have been done before she had arrived. No wonder He was gone. Left her alone with her regrets.

Immediately, she knew she had to get back to her little lights, like she had every evening since she had learned of their connection. She didn't want them to think she had abandoned them again. What were they going to think when they would learn that she would have to leave them? And she had not yet even settled with baby Max. She was worthless and deserved all the devastation that was coming to her.

She pushed aside the ribbons of weeping willow branches and sprinted down the road, running with all she had to get to her little lights. When she finally turned the last corner and saw the tree, she breathed out. There they were. With Mimi and her three little glows, too, still playing, darting around in between the falling leaves like they were tagging one another in play.

When her own illuminations saw her, they glowed even more crimson than when they played. She walked toward them with a heavy heart. She'll have to tell them.

Mimi stood. "I knew you'd be here soon. I stayed with them because I knew you wouldn't want them to go with me tonight."

*Thump.* It may be her last night with them here in The Sorting Place. "Thank you, Mimi." Cotton hugged her, breathing in her syrupy fragrance.

Mimi hugged her back in the ethereal way that they sort of touched, and then Mimi pushed her away and held her by the shoulders. "And one more thing. I have completed all the chores Tsur has given me, and I have led you to all the parables I have been assigned. I don't know how else to help you, Cotton—unless He—" She shook her head. "If there is anything more, look inside the well, deep inside the well. There is always more than water there."

"Oh, Mimi. I don't want to say goodbye." Cotton's heart was so heavy with grief and remorse. Now, it had the sadness of losing Mimi all over again to bear, too.

"Oh, child, not all goodbyes need to be sad." Mimi's expression grew light. "I was relieved to say goodbye to that old wart on my hand. I rubbed potatoes on it for years to make it go away."

Cotton spit out a laugh, not meaning to. Leave it to Mimi to cheer her up with one of her silly old wives' tales in the midst of her most awful grief.

"Your sorting is nearly complicated, and still, all things have not been decided, even though we are at the end." Mimi grabbed her hands and stared into her eyes. "Everything will be as it should be. That is the way of the sorting."

Cotton nodded. She needed to muster bravery. It was what she needed for her little lights.

Mimi walked to Sela' and lifted the two little pink lights that had hidden in the fissure. She placed them in her apron and covered them. Next, she motioned to her little golden glows, and they promptly left their crimson playmates.

Cotton wished she could do something for the little pink lights, but she was in the middle of her own crisis. Still, her heart broke for them—abandoned and alone.

She watched as Mimi glowed radiantly as she walked down the road with her little yellow babes shining and twirling all about her. Cotton couldn't see any glow from the reticent little pink lights that were wrapped in Mimi's apron. They all moved toward the breathing mountain, until they were too small to see.

All about her were her own little lights of varying sizes, all but one. They had waited patiently for her to say her goodbyes to her grandmother with her heart.

Did they know? Would they be as sad as she?

All she could think about was to gather them close to her, to hold them in her arms and in her heart, the heart that she'd seen completely emptied in that well today.

She kissed her own finger again and again and touched each one of the little glows. Over and over again, calling each name as she had christened them. "Willow, Skyler, Sissy, Annabelle and Laurabelle. Hunter, Preston, River. Honey. Harper and Georgia."

She gazed up at Max. She felt her time running out to settle with him. Maybe not everything got settled here. That was disquieting. There were certainly things left unresolved where she had come from—Caleb and the baby she had grown to deny. No one would know its father, if it had lived, which it most surely hadn't.

Was one of her little illuminations here Caleb's child? She shuddered. No, it couldn't be. Even though they were ageless, made of light and spirit, somehow, she knew when they had fallen away from her, and none had recently. But that little light could be anywhere. Maybe it had joined the little pink lights on the mountain. Maybe it was Tsur's baby, too—abandoned and alone.

Every time she had thought of Caleb's baby, shadows swirled inside her head. But that child was still there the day of her fall. Maybe it was on the mountain, angry with her, like Max. Or maybe it was still stuck in the churchyard. The thought of that frightened her.

She looked around for Max. He had slipped silently away from the branches above and was hiding in Sela' again, his faint light glowing dim through the fissure. Finding a spot near the split in the Rock, she leaned on it and slid to the ground. "Come to me, my precious ones," she called to her little illuminations.

She cuddled and nestled with her little glows on the cool ground under the tree. As their glows dimmed, her mind reeled and turned. How many more hours would she have with them?

Where would she go? What would become of them?

The scent of jasmine wafted upon the air in warm ribbons.

Despair wafted through Cotton's soul in icy strings.

There was no fixing what had happened before she'd arrived here—no going back to make amends to people, no going back for her baby, if it were still there, maybe under that old sycamore tree at the church, maybe roaming around, trying to find Caleb, the only person who'd truly acknowledged the little soul—the only one who had fought for it.

Instead, she was here. Stuck between existences. She had sorted things out, for the good and for the bad. She had settled where she could. But there was little Max, still hurting. And she, still filled with an unresolved desire to make him hers again. How could it be remedied?

She thought hard, and got nowhere, then she turned the thinking inward, where she'd learned all the truest answers were. But she found none there either. Because they were Max's answers. She could not find answers for someone else. It had been the way of things here. These little lights, though they were of her, were not her. Why couldn't she see that before in The Choosing Place—that she'd made decisions about others' lives?

*Thump.* She felt the rock against her back warm, and she lifted her head to look at the words being formed above her.

*"You should see that I am He. There is no other god. Only I give life. Only I am to put to death."*

She heard the words, almost like they were spoken, but they were not. Those words were from that book she had not read.

They were the words from the Rock That Begot You.

Those words boomed in her heart like thunder, and time buzzed in her ears, like the kitchen timer Mimi used to set for her apple pies. And she knew they held the key to understanding little Max.

*Thump*. Those last words grieved her terribly. If only God was to put to death, then what had Cotton truly done? The words swirled around in her head until she was dizzy.

Eventually, she regained her thoughts. The little glows all around her slumbered peacefully—except Max. She could see his little luminosity just inside the fissure in the rock. Max was disturbed. He shivered. He turned. She almost thought she heard a whimper from the little glow.

Her heart felt like lead. Could this be one of her last nights? Tomorrow, one of her last days? What if things didn't get resolved with Max?

Something rose up in her soul and pushed itself into her head.

What if she went to the well? Tonight.

# CHAPTER TWELVE

## An Unacknowledged View

Cotton had been warned to not leave the tree at night. Again and again. Though she was afraid to abandon all her little lights, she didn't have any other ideas to help Max. She could be gone in the morning, and Max would be lost to her forever.

What should she do? She searched her heart. Her grandmother had told her that there were more answers in the well, but she'd also told her to stay under her tree in the darkness. What should she do?

Something swirled up in her. She knew that she would do anything for little Max, even give her life for him, if she could. But that was too late. It was probably too late for Cotton, too because her recent repentance had not transpired or transformed her in The Choosing Place where it would have counted. What did she have to lose now? She'd already lost her little illuminations in The Choosing Place. She'd already lost Caleb.

She'd already lost her life.

Though she didn't know how much time she had left here, she instinctively knew it was running out. Quickly. For all she knew, she may not even be in The Sorting Place in the morning.

No matter the cost, even if there was more to lose, she would go to the well. For Max.

She gingerly set each of her little lights inside the base of Sela' and stood. As she headed away from safety, she stared at the place she'd grown to think of as home. Would she ever see it again? Would she ever see her little lights again?

The path that led to the well was lit by some unseen, eerie glow. There was no moon. No orb or rays, no discernable source. Just dimly illuminated.

Everyone had warned her, and she'd never ventured away from her tree after twilight had settled upon it. A malevolent fear rose up in her that she had never experienced in this place. Though she was on the right path, the landscapes beyond the path looked unfamiliar. Objects were moving in the distance upon the hills and fields. Dark, shadowed objects, like unnamed animals that were stalking her.

A knowledge rose up inside her. At night, things in The Regretting Place were somehow unbound.

From the distances she heard callings. She felt presences. She sensed evil. She remembered how the landscapes were always changing. Could the cliff with the dark, roiling fog be near? Would the well be on this path the way it had been twice before? Or, was this a trap? Was she on a fool's errand? And was she the fool?

She doubted her wisdom in embarking upon this task, but then again, she'd used no wisdom on so many other occasions. Tonight, she hadn't consulted her head and all of its learned principles. She'd merely consulted her heart and did its bidding. For the sake of little Max.

Her journey into the night was just like the story she'd remembered from Sunday school, about the shepherd leaving his ninety-nine sheep to go find the lost one. Max was her lost one. She would face whatever she needed to face to bring him to her heart. She could never make up for what she'd done, but if there was any kind of healing or reconciliation that could be accomplished, she would try. Because she had sinned against him.

A light gray fog started rising up from beyond the path she was on, but she walked forward, in the direction she remembered. Oh, how she wished someone else could be with her, like her father, like her grandfather, like her grandmother, like they'd always been when she'd ventured from her home. But she was alone. All alone.

Deep inside, she sensed that this was not something someone else could walk her to…or through. This was her path. She'd made the mistake of Max's abortion alone. She'd have to face this final excursion alone.

The grey mist continued rolling in and as it rolled, it became darker and darker, like the mist over the cliff in The Regretting Place. She had already disregarded the warnings of everyone about leaving her tree at night. She realized it had been her home, her safe place, protected by the light from the Rock of My Strength. Now, she faced the unknown. Maybe this was supposed to happen. Maybe, as so many had said, it is to be decided. Maybe the cliffs and the fog were her fate, like she'd begun to suspect, like she had after she'd seen what was below the surface of the water in the well.

Her feet moved tentatively in the cool sand on the path, making sure the grit beneath them still existed and not some of the grassy or rocky or briary soil on the side. She knew she needed to stay on that path and away from whatever lurked and was calling out from the sides. The cries and the dark forms were getting closer now, closer to her path, closer to her.

Under her tree, she'd never felt the temperature drop like it did now, beyond it in the night. There were no jackets or robes to be worn. In the absence of light, she was exposed.

As she rounded a corner, she looked above her to see if she could discern why the shadowy light was diminishing, but she could discern nothing. The path grew narrower as the briar branches pricked and scratched her legs and arms. The calls from nearby turned into whispers, like the whispers she'd always heard from her mother's urgings.

But they were not from her mother's voice. They were from a deep, dark, echoing voice, speaking a confusing language that she didn't completely comprehend. But somehow, like the way she was able to read the Greek and Hebrew words on the rocks, she understood, albeit faintly.

"You had been raped." The low, echoing said. "It wasn't your fault," it said. They were only cells, blobs, masses of matter. These things are done all the time. You have accomplished great things at the television station that you couldn't have with a child."

The voices went on.

"It was your body," echoed one voice, bewildering and bold.

"It was your choice," called another voice, confusing and confident.

"It was your right," whispered a voice filled with temptation and torment.

The voices were secretive, seductive and deceiving.

*Thump.* Suddenly, Cotton stopped in mid-step and dropped to her knees with a thud, her heart thudding, too.

*The voices had ultimately become her own because she had listened to them.*

She wept for not recognizing the wrong that had been in the whispers, the erroneous information that had been in the whispers, the callousness that had been in the whispers, the deception that had been in the whispers…the sin that had been in the whispers.

And those whispers had become her own, inspired by the boxes, borrowed from others, including her mother, who'd travelled this path before, intent upon misdirecting and misguiding.

Their weapon had been obfuscation of the knowledge in her heart, the knowledge of right and wrong, the knowledge of good and evil. The most dangerous weapon in that abortion room with Max had not been the uterine curette, the perforators and tongs; it had been her. Her willful misunderstanding. Her intended confusion. Her deliberate mystification.

*Thump. Ignorance cannot be its own reward.*

What was to be her reward here? In The Sorting Place?

In The Choosing Place it had been…Impunity. Success. Freedom.

With this heavy knowledge, she stood and continued on, inviting the scratches and tears from the briars and thorns along the way to gouge at her mortal-ish flesh. She deserved them. She didn't deserve little Max. Tears flowed for him now like they hadn't at his death.

She trudged on, defiant against her willful, wanton ignorance. She trudged on, abhorring her excuses and immoral rights.

The fog grew even thicker; the path grew more impaired, and the stench of perfume made from the rotten meat of innocence and old blood was suspended in the fog, but she trudged onward.

Finally, she came to the spot with the weeping willow tree, and the mist melted from around it.

*Thump.*

She pushed past the hanging leaves, eagerly ran to the wall of the well and bent over, hoping to find what she needed to discover. Her eyes first searched the surface for that awful day she was separated from Max. She pressed her vision into the dark, murky waters. A chill breeze blew up at her, and she shivered once again.

Down at the bottom of the well, she thought she heard the faint notes of "Hey, Jude," the song that had played in the clinic that day.

The water shimmered and, at first, she saw the scene as she had before. But that was not what she wanted—what she needed. What Max needed.

There was more. She knew it somehow. Because she could see it in Max—the way he tore at himself.

It was as if the big boulders that surrounded the well were preventing her from really seeing. Lifting off her feet and over the edge, she bent as far as she could to see all that the well may possess—deep into it.

As her feet lifted from the solid ground, she wanted to see that day from the most important perspective…from little Max's eyes.

She sensed that she needed to see *his* pain. Only then would she know what he needed her to know, what he needed her to say.

A feeling of tunneling into the well came over her at the same time a feeling of tunneling inside herself overtook her.

*Thump*. There he was. Little tiny, translucent Max, inside her. He was frightened. His home had…changed. He didn't understand in his small, fragile head. But somehow his home had become…not his home…inhospitable. His home no longer tasted warm. It tasted…harsh and…bitter…no, metallic—and salty. His arms and legs…almost…burned. No longer was the red life inside him making him feel…alive. He was struggling to move.

He looked around his dwelling. Something had changed

physically. The funny little rope that he had played with was still attached to the anchoring on the side, but somehow, the anchor was becoming…detached, was pulling away from the wall of his house. That was not right.

*Buh-bum, buh-bum, buh-bum.* The swooshing sound inside his warm home still comforted him.

He heard the mumbling of many voices, and then a most shiny thing came into his view. It came toward him, and he reached for it to play with it. There was a sort of round handle for him to grab, so he curled his tiny fingers around it. But it moved and jerked him. He was frightened. Then it reached toward where the anchor had once been securely attached. The glossy thing poked and reached all over his…house. Max would have been amused, if he weren't struggling so to feel like he had the day before—hours before.

Suddenly, it was gone, and another, sharper shiny thing entered his home. He was curious as he kicked at it, but then it clipped at his little knee. Ouch! He winced. Fear filled his little body. The shiny things were bad. As quickly as he could, he hid behind the entity that had once anchored him to his home. His knee oozed the red color that was held behind the walls of his home. It was painful, and that bad shiny object had caused it.

As hard as he could, he held on to that anchor, that thing that kept the bad shiny thing away.

The bad gleaming gadget seemed to grow angry as it reached and poked and prodded, nipping away at his room and at the anchor that protected him.

Suddenly, it was gone, too. But moments later, a new, bigger, fiercer burnished device came after him.

He continued to hide, holding on even tighter. He peered from behind and saw the thing slice and pull away parts of his protection, parts of his anchor…and the home in which he was living. That hungry thing seemed…unsatisfied. It needed more. What had he done wrong? Was he to be that more…in order to satisfy it?

Then he saw that same angry metal poke over and over at his home, carrying away pieces of the walls. What was it doing? What was its purpose? Again and again, it pulled away pieces of the round wall. He trembled, his translucent flesh shaking like jelly.

And then it was gone.

But in moments, in its place, entered a double-bladed, even larger metal instrument. It grabbed hold of the anchor and trapped his little arm with it. *Ouwey*. It was crushing his tiny arm.

It was pulling him out. Out of his soft, warm home.

He fell with a thud, into a polished pan with shallow sides. It wasn't soft, like where he had been. It was hard.

Suddenly he felt an…urge. An urge to gasp. He did, and inside him felt different, airy.

Something else had changed, as well. All the soft, pink light had been replaced by piercing, blue light that hurt. He wanted to go home.

The weakness that had been growing inside him was leaving, and he felt…almost strong again. But another new sensation overtook that sense of strength. He was…cold. Really, really cold. A shiver jerked through him.

Not understanding what had happened, he thought that this was the way of things. Maybe the home that had protected him for so long would help him, would give him warmth again. In this strange new place.

He knew his home to be close. He just had to let her know he needed her help. So, he lifted his injured leg, with his bleeding knee. It hurt so badly, but he needed her help. He was strong. He could do it.

It grew so heavy that he knew he needed to find another way. He opened his tiny mouth, but nothing came out. That didn't work either. And he needed it to try to bring in as much of the airy outside as he could because it made him feel almost strong again.

His tiny arm ached, too, after being trapped and pulled with the anchor, but he lifted it. Again and again, he lifted it, sometimes hitting it against the shallow pan. *Tink. Tink.*

Then he saw the others. They came one by one and two by two, looking at him. He flailed his little arms and legs, but no one would help him. He was alone. And afraid. And cold.

It had been awful to be attacked by the shiny thing. It had been strange to not have anyone help him as he struggled.

But the most awful thing was to be abandoned by whom he'd called home.

Maybe, there was something Greater that could help him—maybe, the Something that had formed him. He opened his mouth. Was that a sound? Probably not. Maybe *He Who Had Formed Him* could hear what he was thinking. *Help!*

His silent cry went unanswered.

Eventually, all the others who'd come to look at him struggling left. He was in trouble. Big trouble. Still, he was strong enough to wave his little arm. But the airy feeling inside him was leaving, filling with the wetness that was in his home. The two worlds had different properties, different ways to make him feel strong.

Again and again, he attempted to wave his little arms and legs for help. *Tink. Tink.* Surely someone heard him hit the side of his shiny bed.

There was still some strength left, so he struggled and somehow moved his head onto the anchor. It took all the strength inside him. His head was so heavy. He lifted his crushed little hand again, in one last effort to get help.

And then he saw her! She had seen him! Surely, she would come for him now! Come to help him! She had taken care of him for so long. He instinctively knew he was hers.

He struggled to take a long, deep breath and let out a sound. *Mmmmmm...*

Yes! He'd done it. Though it was faint, he'd called for her. She was sure to come. He rested and waited for her.

His home did not come. He heard noises, similar to the muffled ones he'd heard inside her, but they were clear now. But he didn't understand the meanings of the sounds. He longed for the *buh-bum, buh-bum, buh-bum* he'd heard swooshing through his home for his entire life.

Still, he waited. And he waited, his shallow breaths growing more laborious than the breaths before. And he waited, struggling so hard with the breathing that signaling for help was impossible.

He moved, but ever so slightly. Surly, she would come soon. Time was running out, and he felt the fear of it. She had to know that he didn't have much time in the blue light of the cold room. She had to come.

Finally, someone came. But it was not her.

It was the man with the shiny instruments. He threw a heavy white thing over Max. Maybe that would warm him. Maybe the man would take care of Max.

He wanted to call to the woman who'd been his home. *Mmmmm*, was the sound that he'd named her. He tried to articulate it, but it was impossible now.

Max felt movement. The liquid that had grown even icier in his pan sloshed about him, making him colder. It was even harder to breathe under the cover, and his little head bounced and hit against his hard, stainless bed. *Tink. Tink, tink, tink.*

He so wished for his warm home where he heard the swooshing *buh-bum, buh-bum, buh-bum* of *Mmmmm*.

He lay, nearly motionless for a while, as he listened to the clanging of more of the bad shiny things.

⚜

Cotton jerked her head from inside the well.

*Jesus, no. Oh, no. What have I* really *done?* She crumpled into a pile of regret and remorse and tears beside the well, against the heart-shaped stone. *Oh, Heavenly Father, Rock of Offense, Stone of Stumbling. This is what I've truly done. It is revealed to me now, not shrouded in vague remorse, in medical terminology or feminine rights. It is no longer hidden behind the curtain of the womb. The reality of what I've done is truly unbearable!*

And with that, she knew that she had more to bear. So, she pulled herself up onto the side of the well and regretfully peered into it for the last time, looking beyond the surface, accepting of whatever horror it had to show.

⁂

*Thump.*

Maybe his *Mmmmm* would come soon. Maybe the man had helping instruments this time.

The man uncovered little Max in another place, another room with cold, blue light. Was this to be his home now? He wished he could show that he needed help, but he had so little strength left. The man hovered above with the shiny things. And then he poked at Max with one of them.

Max could only open and close his tiny, broken hand.

Then the man used the two instruments to turn him over. Something hard pressed on the back of his head, and he felt it give in, just a little, he guessed because of its soft composition, made up of that gray stuff that had filled it with understanding about so many things inside his home. Then he felt something sharp slit the base of his neck. He writhed in the most extreme black and red pain. Then he heard a snip.

And everything went dark.

# CHAPTER THIRTEEN

## Staffed with Iniquity

Cotton had no memory about how she'd gotten back to the tree where her little lights were sleeping. She walked straight to Max, almost as if she were in a trance. He had awakened while she was gone and had fallen back asleep in one of the low branches on the tree.

But this was no trance this time. She was fully aware of what she had done to him, awfully aware of her callousness, appallingly aware of her sin.

And what she'd really done to little Max.

She reached out to him, not daring to touch him. That would have to be his decision.

All her other little lights had seemingly forgiven her. But they had not been through what Max had been through. They had not seen what Max had seen. Felt what Max had felt. They had not been abandoned like she had abandoned Max.

Her nearness made him glow. But when he realized how close she was, the little light startled and nearly fell from the low branch of the tree.

"I won't touch you, sweetness," she said.

At first, she stared for the longest time, creating the words and forging the strength she needed to do this. "I know everything now. I sinned against you, my most innocent, precious light. There is no excuse. No words I could say or create to express my sorrow exist. To say I'm sorry is completely inadequate. I saw your pain, inside me, inside that room, inside that pan." She closed her eyes and heaved as tears flowed down her face. "And worst of all. I saw you on that day. I saw you move. But I denied it all. And I did nothing. I realize now that there is no excuse for ignorance. There is no justification for my denial. It was you who had the rights. You whose choice it was. And you made the choice to live. And by what false, godlike, power did I have to take those things away from you?" She paused and gulped. "None. Absolutely none."

Little Max began to shake on that limb.

"Max, I realize that *you* are my Stone of Stumbling. You were the one thing that I always hung onto because it affected me so deeply that I could not move forward. If I could go back in time, you and I would have been together. I would have kept you inside me as long as you needed to grow. I would have rocked you after you'd been born. I would have taken you to the playground and would have swung with you. I would have gone on bike rides with you. I would have proudly watched you walk across a stage at your high school graduation. I would have sat with tears in my eyes at your wedding. And smiled when you handed me my first grandchild." She paused, choking on the words. "If I could now, I would give my very life for you, my strong little boy, my brave little boy, the darling of my life."

Max's light glowed more dimly in the sadness that hung about them, splitting in two and then rejoining.

She stared at the little light and embraced his sorrow for as long as his strength glowed dim. Taking in his grief, she understood even more.

*Thump. Had it not been for him, most of his brothers and sisters would have lived. It was his hiding behind the anchor that had caused all the damage. Had he been really brave when the sharp, shiny thing came for him, the others would have had a chance.*

Even little Max had a Stone of Stumbling. One that was not supposed to be his.

After she dwelled with his Stone of Stumbling for as long as he needed her to dwell, she stood up as straight as she could.

"I know one thing for sure, little guy. You are not to blame for any of what happened. You were perfect and full of love. You didn't know what was happening. I did. I am the only one at fault in this entire situation. I bear that guilt for you and for all my little lights."

Letting those words sink into Max, she leaned against the branch upon which he was quivering. When she thought it was the right time, she said, "And because we cannot go back to undo what I had done in willful oblivion and in secret sin, I can only say to you that I would give whatever it is I have here, whatever goodness that is left inside me, whatever good thing that may be given to me or enjoyed by me, whatever I have left...to have you forgive me."

After a short while, she noted that this was the first time that he stayed whole in front of her, the first time his little light didn't tear away from itself, like he'd been torn up inside.

"You don't have to pardon me because I don't deserve to be forgiven for the horrendous sin I have committed against you, but if you want to, I'd like you to touch my heart to see the Stone that lodged there long ago and never left the depths of me." Tears that weren't supposed to be in The Sorting Place rolled down her cheeks. "Max, my heart belongs to you."

The little crimson light backed away slightly, like it had been startled. She let it be. This would have to be his decision, his choice. It was his right, and he, alone, could exercise it.

She just stood with her head hung. What would she do if they didn't settle? She would never blame him, after what she had seen him go through, deep in that well.

And then he moved toward her, ever so slightly, ever so slowly.

Her head remained lowered in reverence to the moment. Repentance and forgiveness were weighty issues—spiritual passages that held holy consequences.

It took a while, but Max timidly and finally got close enough for his sad little light to touch her heart.

His light searched her core for a while. She felt the tunneling. Then, suddenly, Max began to glow brighter than she'd ever seen any little light glow before. He glowed crimson, and her own crimson light shone brighter and redder than she'd ever seen it glow before, too. She could also feel him warm. She knew. He could see that she saw his pain. Felt his pain. And he could feel her regret, her sorrow, her repentance. What she had put him through had placed a hidden stone in her heart. He was most assuredly her precious Stone of Stumbling.

Did she just hear something? She stilled herself, even more, if that were possible, and she listened with great intent.

"*Mmmmmmmmm.*" The little light hummed.

She knew what that meant. In her last hours in The Sorting Place.

He was calling her *Mmmmmmm* once again. He was hers. Once again.

In the new light, she was alerted by the scent of wood. Her grandfather would be coming soon. She lifted her head to see little Max still upon her chest, her heart, as she still lay on the ground. Her other little lights stirred, brightening their glows to match hers.

"Good morning, all my babes. Little Max awoke and was greeted with joy by his sibling lights, now that he'd settled, too. He, like a child, swooshed toward the others in playful banter, like she'd never seen Max play before. He was now one of them. Hopefully, to never feel the guilt of being the cause of their falling away too soon. Cotton had absolved him of that, taking on the true guilt—her rightfully deserved guilt—herself.

Cotton even more keenly sensed the end of her stay here as the wood fragrance neared. She called out, "I want you all to play sweetly while I'm gone today, and we will rejoice together when I get home." Something inside her, however, feared that she may not return. She didn't know the way of things here, but she hoped Tsur would allow her to say goodbye...the same way He had allowed her to meet and reconcile with her precious baby glows.

The little lights darted here and there, chasing one another up the tall tree, Max as their leader. They'd be fine. They always had been, even before she'd arrived. They would be again, even after she departed.

Poppy finally arrived and stopped just three feet in front of her. He leaned against the cane he'd started whittling some time earlier—the one he'd pulled from her home.

She moved her head forward to get a better look. The oak tree's canopy at the top of the staff was amazingly and complexly engraved—each limb and leaf crisply detailed. The whole cane was beautifully and intricately carved in a swirl from top to bottom, and it looked like he'd oiled it, because it shone brightly in the morning sun.

"Hello, Puddin'," her grandfather said.

"Hello, Poppy," she said as she lifted herself up and kissed at his cheek.

He glanced up the tree at her little lights joyfully playing. "I see you are all settled here now."

She nodded. "We are." She blew out a deep breath, feeling settled also in her soul.

He knitted his brow. "Do you know how risky what you did last night was?" He put his bottom lip over his top, like he used to, trying to make light of the seriousness of the situation.

As she blew out a breath, her shoulders lowered. "I had no choice."

He narrowed his eyes. "Funny thing about choices. Sometimes we have them when we think we don't. And sometimes we don't have them when we think we do." He moved his beautifully carved cane to the right of him and shifted his weight to that side.

She nodded. "I understand that now, Poppy."

"You ready?" He stood straight and tapped the cane upon the ground like a decree.

All the desires for her own well-being were gone. She had given up her final one at the well. The Stone of Israel would decide her fate, and she would accept it. "Yep. Where are we going?"

"To the Great River." He pointed the cane in the direction in which they would travel.

They walked in silence for a while. Soon, they came to the weeping willow tree. Poppy used his cane to move aside the dangling branches for them to walk through. As they passed the well, the skies began to rain, but the sun was still shining brightly.

Poppy pointed at the well. "One time before you were born, my neighbor couldn't pay his water bill, so I sent him a card."

Not another bad joke. But she remembered her promise to

herself. She would not roll her eyes no matter the punch line. "What good did that do?"

"It was a Get Well card." Poppy pulled his bottom lip over his top to create his silly grin. He knew how corny he was and reveled in it.

She giggled. It could be her last joke from him. Ever. "Poppy. Really. I'm surprised they let you register that one at the gate. It's really bad."

Poppy chuckled. Even on a day such as this, he couldn't hide his sense of humor. That was okay, though, because she secretly enjoyed it, no matter how bad the joke was.

They walked on, past all the Rocks.

Soon, they came upon a small pond where shepherds had led all sorts of animals to drink.

*Thump. The Rock provides.*

She didn't even have to struggle for the meaning of it. Had she gotten the hang of it all now—the way of things here—just as she was about to leave?

Poppy led on with his gray eyes and his intricately carved cane.

Then they passed a small stream, shaded by great trees. Many weary travelers were resting beneath it.

*Thump. The Rock will give you rest.*

She knew the way of the knowledge now.

They paused briefly, and then Poppy pointed his cane in the

direction that they were to turn. They continued on.

After they passed a field, they came upon a narrow, nearly still river and a man was standing in the middle of it, motioning for the long line of people in robes of white and khaki and even black, a color of garment she'd not seen in The Sorting Place before.

*Thump. The Rock forgives all.*

Still, they continued to walk. All the pure words in the Bible bubbled and burrowed into her head, without their numbers, until they were all stored in her heart—the place that Tsur had put them in the beginning.

A great lake spread out to her left and men walked upon it. She used her heart to understand it all.

*Thump. The Rock transcends all.*

At one point on their path, they took a right turn that had not been there before. After a few steps, she heard a mighty river, roaring and crashing against rocks in the distance. It made her uneasy. For as she walked, she understood the water that they passed to mean many things. She recalled some of what she'd learned in church with her grandparents.

*Thump. Water is also used to destroy.*

She recalled the great flood of Noah and the covering of Pharaoh's army after Moses had parted the Red Sea.

Nevertheless, it was to be more of her…illumination, and she couldn't resist, didn't want to resist.

*Thump.*

Somehow, she knew the *thumping* was to mark the end of her.

As they neared the river, the thunderous sound of the water, like a great waterfall, became so loud that she could hardly hear herself think, and then it grew even louder than that.

Finally, they came to a swift and mighty river that she could scarcely see across. The waters churned blue and aqua and white and created a cool wind that blew upwards toward them. She felt little sprays, caught up on the winds, hit her face. Her grandfather just stood there for a while, leaning upon the cane he'd carved.

Nothing came to her at first. No knowledge. They just stood and stared.

"Why are we here Poppy? I don't know how long I've been in this place, but I know my time of sorting and settling is nearly over. I have seen, truly seen all I have done, and I know that justice would require that I pay a price for my decisions in The Choosing Place."

"So, you know that as we stand on the high banks of the Great River that we are here for some of the final decisions to be made. Your sorting has been complicated, and the decision has been nearly accomplished. None of us have known what work has been left until each morning, though we have all known that you are nearing the end."

She looked out across the mighty river, the edges alive with the verdant trees, shrubs and flowers that drew living water from the Great River. The knowledge settled in her soul. "Yes. I know, too."

Still staring across the great waters, he said, "And do you

know who it is who judges you?"

She thought intently. "God My Rock is my judge."

"Yes. Ultimately. But who has judged you here? In The Sorting Place?"

She pondered the question for a little while. "No one has treated me judgmentally here. But I have done wrong and I deserve the punishment that I earned when I walked in The Choosing Place. Because I did not repent down there. I committed sins and never felt the sorrow for them, until I came here. I never asked God for his forgiveness where I chose the sin. And even my repentance here took too long because I arrived with all these stupid excuses at the beginning."

He slowly nodded, looking out over the Great River. "And so, who has judged you most harshly here?"

That wasn't difficult to answer. "I have."

He nodded. "And have you felt sorrow here?

"Of course. I'd do anything to change what I did. I made so many bad decisions, decisions that weren't even mine to make." She thought of little Max and all he'd been through. Her heart swelled with love for him. And shame for what she'd done to him.

He scratched the ground with the end of his cane. "Would you choose to make a decision like you made with Max again?"

"Oh, no. Heavens, no."

He nodded, ever so slightly and whispered, "We all know that."

She squinted her eyes. "How would you know that?

"That is one of the problematical parts. Because you actually did make a very good decision…by not making a bad one." He leaned on the intricate staff.

Total confusion came over her. "How? Why would you say that?"

"You will see. Today was to have been your last day. Last night, your last night. But there is a…complication. One that could have affected your sorting. You will spend one more night here, under your tree. You will have to wait until the morning to see your fate. But before we go, I want you to take your cane." He held it out, like he was giving it to her, like he didn't own it. Light seemed to emanate from behind the elaborate carvings. The top of it displayed the complexly carved canopy of the oak that was her home.

She took it from Poppy and looked at the intricate carvings that trailed up, like a vine, from the bottom. They were carvings of her. Of her life. Or rather…of her mistakes. Her sins. How embarrassing that her grandfather knew of every one of them—enough to carve them in the oak staff.

"You know that cane." His brows lifted to fully expose his gray, cataract-covered eyes.

The weight of it was almost too much to bear. "I do. It is my life, and I made a mockery of it, squandered it on things that didn't matter. On being selfish, listening to what the self-righteous, politically-correct culture presented as normal. While in The Choosing Place, I bought into the ideal of being progressive; instead, I had regressed into a self-preserving shell.

I watched the boxes all the time. I even told tales the boxes required me to tell."

She held the staff tightly in her hands, hating the fullness of it, the import of it, the leaden heaviness of it. As it backlit the images, there were no secrets on that staff of her life. "I don't like it, Poppy. It is shameful." She held it back toward Poppy. "I don't want it."

He stepped back. "I'm glad that you feel that way. But you still have two choices—here on the banks of the Great River."

"What could those possibly be? I have been judged, and I'm holding the illumination of all the blackness of my sins in my hands, each sin, meticulously carved for all the world to see." Each beat of her heart stabbed a piercing pain into her chest.

"We have all held crosses or canes or boxes or tablets that have been carved for us at one point," he said, looking at her crooked cane.

"That may be. But most have had the opportunity to be rid of them in The Choosing Place—to make up for the awful carvings." She looked across the mighty waters. "I will not have the chance to restore what I have done."

She ran her hands over the carvings, stopping her finger on little Max in that pan that had been painfully and intricately carved into the wood. "These sins belong to me, with me, and I will have to carry this weighty staff with me for eternity." Her shoulders slumped, regret coursing through her body.

"You have put much thought into this. That is good. Yes, you could carry that staff with you for all the rest of eternity as you deserve…or, you could throw the carnal cane into the Great

River."

She shook her head. "What good would that do here? I've already made my bad decisions." She closed her eyes and ran her right hand down the shameful cane.

Poppy looked out over the water. "It is complicated, and I cannot answer that. It is up to Tsur."

She opened her eyes and looked down at the staff, abhorring all that it depicted, her fall away from the Rock and the little church with its old-fashioned ways, her pursuit of image over substance, her careless disregard for Caleb and others, her former shameful liaisons with the other two men who were not her husbands, her separation from little Max, and so much more.

*Thump.* Something in her broke apart. "I never want to see my awful sins again." With all her heart, she pulled her arm back and threw the blemished staff as far as she could into the river. And where it landed, it stained the waters dark and inky.

*Thump.* She winced, but stared at the cane as it floated fast and bobbed brutally until it was no longer in sight.

Poppy nodded. "That was the chore we had to do here today. Tomorrow, the sorting will be complete."

They stared together in silence at the Great River as it roared and tore at the rocks along its banks.

Finally, Poppy said, "We must go now, Puddin'."

All the way home, Cotton's heart hung low and heavy in her chest, like a lead curtain on a rod.

*Thump.* Her insides jolted as she walked.

*Thump.* Her breath halted as she stared straight ahead.

*Thump.* Knowledge stabbed her heart as she remained silent.

*The end is very near.*

When they arrived at her tree, a strange light engulfed them. Poppy turned to her and said, "Tonight is your last. Spend it well." He looked away as he airily kissed her goodbye, and she hugged him with her heart like she'd never see him again. For a while, she watched him walk down the middle road that led to the breathing mountain.

*Thump.* This was definitely her last night. She would be spending it showing her little illuminations how much she loved them, how much she was going to miss them.

As the evening settled, the crimson glow under the tree grew brighter and brighter in the strange light.

Max and his brothers and sisters chased her, and she chased them, around the tree and up the tree. All her fears of heights…gone.

Because they could not speak, she did all the talking, save little Max when he made his little *Mmmmm* sound.

"I will not be here very much longer, so I need to teach you all that I know," she said. "Let's rest for a while. Mama is tired." She giggled at calling herself that. "First of all, you must always remember how very much I love each of you." She reached out to touch each as she called each name. "Max, Preston, Honey, Laurabelle, Annabelle, Hunter, Skyler, Willow, Sissy, River, Harper and Georgia."

Each brightened as she touched every little light. Laurabelle and Annabelle, the twins, joined, entwined and separated again and again. The little illuminations twirled and twisted, danced and darted. All her little brilliances put on individual shows of radiant light. It made her happy that Max and Preston no longer split and tore themselves in pieces to show their pain.

"Oh, my heart swells with love for you. I love you because you were each created by the Rock Who Begot You. I love you because you are of me. I love you because of how pretty you shine, how sweetly you sleep and how joyfully you play." Tears welled up in her eyes. "And I love each of you because each of you is so different and special. And even when I'm not in your presence, my love will be upon each of you." She looked down and saw herself glowing more than she'd ever seen before. All together they radiated the grandest crimson glow under the tree.

*Thump.*

Time ticked in her ears and heart. There was so much she wanted to tell them and teach them. They were her babies. What to teach them first? *Hmmmm.*

"I want to show you a game." She stood and lined them up. "Okay. This game is called Leap Frog. This is how you play. Max, you jump over Honey first." She stood like a mother on a playground, teaching her little ones to play the game. She taught each in turn to jump over the other. "That was great, little ones!" She thought about the other games she used to play as a child. "Hide and Seek is next. I'll be *it* first. Okay. I have to touch you before you get to be it. Then it's your job to find another and touch him or her."

Max glowed brightly. He was going to like this game.

After endless hours, she said, "Let's sit down again. I have much to tell you about the place we once lived."

After they all settled down again, she gathered them close to her. "I want to tell you about the church I would have taken you to if we could have gone together. It was the same church that my grandparents took me. It was made like a rock, to be immovable. Timeless, a little like Tsur. There was a school where you would have learned about The Rejoicing Place. You would have heard songs and would have learned prayers and verses. Oh, and children. There would have been lots of children for you to play games with on Saturdays when we had children's Bible studies. And you would have learned about Daniel in the Lion's Den, and you would have eaten lion cupcakes." What else did she need to tell them? "Oh, and I would have taught you to make good choices in The Choosing Place." She had so much to tell them, to teach them, and she didn't want the evening to end, but her little ones grew tired and started resting, one by one. So, she lay down against the large trunk of the tree with her little illuminations all about her. Max settled upon her chest and slept upon her heart.

They all buzzed a low, radiant glow under the tree as the night loomed over them and the leaves fell all about them.

Though it had been her plan to stay up all night, she suddenly felt that familiar pulling of her eyelids, and though she fought it for a time, she was ultimately unable to and gave in to what was to come.

Her last…vision. *Thump.*

⁂

Cotton was back under the tree at the church where she'd fallen from the ladder. But how'd she arrive here? She didn't remember soaring back to The Choosing Place. She was no longer under the delusion that she could somehow do something about her situation, though. She was—for all intents and purposes—finished. Sorted. Settled. And judged. There could be no real reason for her to be here.

Except to be illuminated about what she'd missed the first time. But this was somehow different from her other visions. Even the light seemed to be different.

As she leaned against the tree's trunk, she thought she heard a buzz. She dismissed it. But when it buzzed again, she knew it to be real. Far to her right, almost out of reach, wet from the dew that had fallen upon the cool grass, was her old phone.

"That can't be," she said aloud. She'd thought that it had broken into a thousand pieces, hitting the pavement. But, instead, she realized it had hit the branches of the sycamore tree, breaking its fall and causing it to land upon the ground. But what good could her old cell phone be now?

She leaned over as far as she could and reached to grab it from the tall grass. It had two percent of its power left. Time had somehow folded in upon the phone. She didn't understand how long she had been in The Sorting Place, but she knew it to be for quite a while—even though time behaved differently there.

She swiped across it and saw twenty-eight calls, all from a local number that she didn't recognize.

She called her voicemail and heard Caleb's voice. "I am so sorry, Cotton."

She sat up straight and listened to the next one. "I will always love and miss you."

*Thump.*

Her heart sank to hear herself spoken about like that, and she leaned back onto her elbow, the grass wet from dew.

"If I could take back my words, I would. I wish you could hear my words now," Caleb said.

Each message of grief from that sweet, beautiful man, sadder than the one before.

Again, she pressed the arrow to play the next message. "I can't believe this has happened." Someone was talking in the background. It was a woman's voice. Maybe he'd already moved on. Cotton's heart was sad, but Caleb deserved happiness.

She sat up, crossed her legs in the cool grass and pressed the arrow again.

"Why are you are leaving me again and again? Please stay." She heard beeping in the background.

Wait. What?

She held out the phone and realized something odd. In each one of her previous visions, she'd seen the scenes through such illuminating light that it cast no shadows, like it was perfectly illuminated from all sides. She had seen the past in her previous visions. But tonight, the streetlight cast the shadow of her phone and arm onto the new grass. Wait. This was new grass. When she'd lain below the tree the last time, it had been fall, and the grass had been turning brown.

She caught a whiff of jasmine in the air. Jasmine grew in the very early spring. Then this was most definitely not October any longer. How long had she been in The Sorting Place? And why was she back here—in The Choosing Place—now?

The confusion of it all was too much. She looked at the phone again, examining the dates this time. Suddenly, the phone glowed and the battery was at 100 percent. Impossible. But then it was impossible for her to have met her unborn children and to have reunited with her grandmother, her grandfather and her father. Right?

*The Rock transcends all.*

*Thump.*

The truth of it shook her. It had been written upon her heart.

She listened to the next message. Each one as short as the last. "They shocked your heart again tonight. Please don't leave quite yet."

The messages sounded like…she was still alive. Wait. Had she actually been taken to the hospital?

Again, she punched the button. "I will do right by you, but you have to hang on."

Hang on? What was he talking about? She was as confused now as she had been the day she'd arrived in The Sorting Place.

"Just a few more weeks, and I will say goodbye." His voice sounded sorrowful.

Why couldn't Caleb let her go? Why did he want her around for a few more weeks? Why would he still be calling? To acknowledge her death over and over again?

She pressed the arrow once again.

*Thump.*

"It is almost time, but I had to hear your voice once again."

Yep, he'd been calling simply to hear her voice on her voicemail. A warm breeze blew through her hair. She pressed the arrow again for the next message. She felt a simple, clean, unadulterated love for him now—one that she had not felt for him before.

She heard silence at first, then Caleb said, "Cotton," in a most broken voice. Then she heard someone yell, "Code Blue! Code Blue," in the background.

Wait. Why would he be making calls from a hospital? She was dead, had died four months ago.

*Thump.*

She hit the play arrow again.

"Somehow, you've got to know. You've got to be here. For her."

*Her?*

No way!

Cotton's body had been taken to the hospital that night after all. Only her spirit had been left on the pavement at the church.

Summerbrook Hospital was just blocks away. She knew she needed to go there. To figure out what this was all about. She scrambled herself up and started toward the direction of the hospital.

*Thump. She didn't have much time.*

So, she walked and walked, more and more briskly, not feeling tired and surprised that she had been able to cover so much ground in so little time as she sensed the direction to walk and took shortcuts that she hadn't known about previously. She loved walking the slow streets of her quaint little town, and she wasn't even worried about the red sack she was wearing or her bare feet. Who cared about such things of the surface?

If she could, she'd throw away those red high heels that had pinched her toes so terribly, go back to that little church that listened to the Rock and not the boxes. In The Sorting Place, she'd become what Caleb really needed. And—if she could—she'd do good things—for others, not for herself. If she could. But she couldn't. So, she kept maneuvering the streets toward the hospital.

The dogwoods and azaleas were blooming, and she could feel the warm, humid air in her lungs. It felt so good to be…but it wasn't her home any longer. She was a stranger in a once familiar land.

Finally, she arrived at the four-story-tall building. Somehow, she sensed where to go. The fourth floor. She moved through the halls in a way she'd never before moved. No one acknowledged her in the halls, in the elevator, even though she saw her own shadow this time. But it mingled with all the other shadows, and no one deciphered whose was whose.

When the elevator doors opened, she saw the sign. Intensive Care Unit. There was no need to ask questions at the nurses' desk. No one could see or hear her. She knew that, even though she did own a shadow now. But why? Why did she now possess a shadow?

As she strolled by the doors of each room, most were pulled shut, but one at the end of the hall had not been completely closed. It was ajar and bright light was streaming into the hallway.

As she walked the distance to where the light was flooding through, she peered in the door and saw Caleb, standing against the wall, tears streaming down his worried face. That cute furrow in his brow made her want to kiss it.

All about the hospital bed were technicians, doctors and nurses. She heard the buzzing as they worked quickly with a piece of equipment. She slipped through the door and leaned hard against the casing.

"Okay. Back up," called the doctor across the bed from where she stood.

Everyone stood back, and he placed two paddles on the body on the bed. "Clear," he yelled.

*Thump.*

Cotton felt the familiar *thump* jolt through her body as she stood beside the doorway.

*Wait. The body on the bed was hers, too. She was not dead.*

There her body lay on the bed, great with child. Caleb's child. The child that she hadn't made a decision about—the child that she'd grown to put out of her mind—in The Choosing Place...and in The Sorting Place, until nearly the end. But that child's fate had still been a mystery, still covered by the swirling, mysterious light and still hidden from her.

Was Cotton still really alive? Well, her body was, in a way. It had been hooked up to a respirator and feeding tubes and IVs and all sorts of monitors.

"She's still coding," said the doctor. He put the paddles back upon her chest. "Again," he yelled.

*Thump.* The power of the electric jolt lurched through her body once again—her earthly body and her spiritual body.

They were keeping her alive, obviously, until her baby was born. This was why her case in The Sorting Place was so complicated.

*Dear Jesus, have mercy on me!*

# CHAPTER FOURTEEN

## A Decision of Light

Cotton felt her body shaking. She cracked her eyelids. She was under her tree in The Sorting Place. Mimi was awakening her from her sleep—and from her last vision. But it had been a vision like none of the others. Her body had been alive in The Choosing Place all this time, and she hadn't made a choice about the life that had been inside her. She had seen it all so clearly there—in the actual light, not the illuminating light that had been in the other visions—the visions in which she was merely an observer. What did that mean?

*Thump. It is complicated.*

Cotton looked around her, but her little lights were not there. "Where are they?" Her heart panicked. She wanted to spend every last moment with them before she left. "Where are they?"

"They are fine, sweetie. Don't worry about them. We are to

finish your sorting now," Mimi said.

Cotton's heart sank. "Mimi, this is still such a mess. And complicated, like Poppy said—like you've all said."

Her grandmother nodded, her sweet scent wafting all about. "I know, child. I know. I thought I had seen the last of you here. But it will be decided today. It is usually not the way of things, but your falling was convoluted and problematical. You were sort of there and sort of here at the same time."

Cotton nodded. "I know. I thought I had died. And somehow, I had procrastinated figuring things out and had somehow veiled the knowledge about the baby—even from myself. But that was before I had met my little lights—before I had settled with them and had seen what I put little Max through. Oh, Mimi. If I could change what I did to him—alter what he had experienced."

Her Mimi sat beside her and touched her hand. "Aren't babies precious?"

A huge wave of electricity hit her. *Thump.* She knew what that was. Again. She'd been shocked back to life over and over again in that hospital, stuck between The Sorting Place and The Choosing Place.

Tears streamed out of Cotton's eyes. "I didn't want to make a decision about Caleb's baby, so I put it off for so long. That was wrong, too."

Mimi exhaled. "I know, darling. That is a part of the reason why this has been so prolonged and complex." She handed Cotton a new cane. "Here, someone wanted you to have this."

She eyed it suspiciously. "But why did Poppy send me a new

one?" she asked as she ran her hand over the smooth, straight surface.

"Oh, it is not new. This is the one you threw into the Great River yesterday."

The wood was blonde and the length of it had been unbent. "But there are no more of those awful carvings." No notch or scratch could be seen anywhere.

"That's because the Great River can wash away all the awful things we've done. The Rock sees to it when it is…right."

She held the staff close and closed her eyes. "How can that be?"

Her grandmother's eyes gleamed. "You hold it in your hands. It is His way. The Rock is everywhere, even below the treacherous waters, and at every turn and bend, it smooths out what is forgiven, what is eternal. It is all in His power. He has the power to transform all in the world. However, what is written on the Everlasting Rock never changes. Not in The Sorting Place. Not in The Choosing Place. Not through the Ages."

Cotton placed the perfectly smooth cane on the ground beside her. "I understand all that. But I cannot be forgiven because I didn't see my sin until I came to The Sorting Place. Wouldn't everyone be repentant here?"

Mimi giggled. "You'd be surprised. No. Too many still try to justify what they did or didn't do in The Choosing Place. They offer the same excuses they offered on Earth."

"That seems nearly unbelievable to me." But something quickened in Cotton. Hadn't she done the same when she had first arrived, claiming that she hadn't known what she'd done. Cotton closed her eyes. If only she could go back in time, she would have never done the things she had done.

*Thump. Regret, repentance and remorse shocked her body.*

She opened her eyes.

Mimi started picking up the little leaves and sticks that were scattered where she sat. "Your mother did not see when she was here." She put the sticks in a pile.

Cotton squinted in confusion. "Why could I see and not Mother?"

Mimi inhaled. "Because you had already opened your spirit to His words that had been written upon your heart as a child in The Choosing Place. You were receptive. There. And here. You were honest with the sorting. It just took a little time. It is the Living Stone's decision to forgive, to wash away or to drown, or to allow it to flow over the dark waterfall at the cliffs."

Cotton placed her hand on the stick that was on the ground. "I know I chose all the wrong things in The Choosing Place."

"And here is part of the complication. You, because of all you've learned so willingly and because of your tremendous regret, also had and have the final choice."

"How can that be?" Cotton was still confused.

Mimi stood. "Let's get this place cleaned up so that you can leave it like you found it." She picked up several sticks and placed them in the pile she had started. "Did you and your little ones have a party here last night?" She giggled.

Cotton stood and leaned the staff against the tree, not quite sure it really belonged to her. "Sort of," she said, picking up some of the leaves she'd knocked off last night as they played hide and seek through the branches of the old tree. She set them on the pile Mimi had started.

As she picked up the debris under the tree, Mimi said, "Life is messy, but we each have the chance to clean it up." She tossed another load onto the pile. "So, let's get to the heart of this matter. What are your big concerns right now?"

That would be easy. "I did not go through repentance in The Choosing Place, and I have nothing to offer Him. I did nothing that wasn't self-serving."

Mimi inhaled. "Okay, so let's address that first."

Cotton nodded. "Everything that I had learned on those numbered pages with numbered chapters and verses is troubling. Coupled with everything I have learned here. It just seems so convoluted. And it doesn't seem fair that I can be saved on a technicality or because of some kind of accident."

Mimi leaned against the fissured rock. "First of all, He sees no technicalities or accidents. Everything is as it should be."

Cotton joined Mimi against the rock and stared off into the distance. "But I did not do any work or anything for Him."

"Are you trying to talk yourself out of Grace?" Mimi giggled.

Cotton thought. "No, it's just that this is so important. I want to get it right."

Mimi stood in front of Cotton with her hands on her hips. "About your work. What about your series—the one that you'd been planning with the woman from social services, going into the orphanages and the foster homes and showcasing the children's achievements. And then, ultimately, having an awards program."

"But I left it only as an idea—an idea on paper in that binder that never came to fruition," she said, saddened. "And if truth be told, I was planning it as much for me as for the children. It would have brought me more…" She hung her head. "Fame and credits." She was ashamed now for thinking that way.

Mimi shook her head. "It was the intent. It was in your heart. Don't you see? We make imperfect messes out of many things, but the Rock can smooth them all out, turning them into miracles. He turns messes into miracles. That was actually His project. He was just using you to accomplish His will."

Cotton thought about the white binder with all the ideas and information in it, left to be thrown away by some cleaning company. She'd worked so hard on it. "Well, that whole project will never be a miracle, now, unless, I could go back."

"Don't think so highly of yourself. Aaron Brown has already run with that idea. You had it all written out, neatly organized in that notebook he found on your coffee table in your house when he went in with the police to look for something that might tell them who to call. He called the lady you'd been working with at social services. You wrote her number on the first page, and when he called, they hit it off. In fact—" Mimi giggled. "They're dating now."

Hope and joy shot up in Cotton's heart, and she pushed herself off the rock.

"In your honor, he is calling the program, the Cotton Project and the awards program, the Cotton Ball."

"Oh, my. That's funny, but it's nice. And catchy." She wasn't even bothered that everyone would know her nickname. The program titles somehow seemed apropos. Growing real cotton is a process, and the product is turned into so many beneficial things—just like the children in the program.

"Aaron tells people that if you come out of your coma, the program's all yours, but he's going to run with it until then. He tells viewers in his segments that it's his way of keeping the spirit of your work alive."

Cotton could feel her mouth open. Gob smacked. "I feel so…honored…and blessed." She inhaled deeply, still feeling undeserving of her good fortune.

*Thump.*

She bent over at the jolt. This couldn't go on much longer. She glanced up.

Cotton watched as words formed on the rock in front of her.

*"The God in Heaven has sworn, 'Just as I have planned, so it will be done, and as I have intended, it will absolutely happen.'"*

Cotton had *heard* those words before, but she had never *lived* them. God was in control of it all—even everything that He had allowed her to do. The knowledge seemed to come more and more easily now.

"I am so elated that I left something behind…something so important. But that doesn't change the fact that I didn't go through the process of repenting from all that I had done during my adult life." Sure, as a child, she had accepted Jesus, but that was easy because not sinning was easy when she was young. She walked away from Sela' and picked up more leaves and twigs.

Mimi giggled. "Process? My dear, it's more like a choice. You made the choice to follow Him as a child."

Cotton shook her head. "But I made some really bad choices later."

Mimi smiled. "You see, the Rock of Salvation endures all your choices. And respects your final one, even if you repent of those choices by calling on His name with your last breath, with your last word."

Cotton stood still, swallowed hard and closed her eyes. With great emphasis in her voice, she said, "But I didn't repent in The Choosing Place before I came here. I saw my sin, my bad choices, here, in The Sorting Place. While mortal, I chose the way of the boxes, the sand, the earth, the cloth that covered and hid my sin. It was only exposed here." She glanced at the staff leaning against the tree. "Poppy carved each of my iniquities onto that cane."

Her grandmother stopped and looked out beyond the tree. "I know. And did you hold onto it?"

"No. I threw it into the Great River." Such relief had accompanied her release of it.

Mimi straightened the khaki ties on the apron that covered her white dress and started to pick up the leaves again. "Why?"

"Because I never want to touch those sins ever again."

Mimi nodded and walked to the trunk of the tree and grabbed

the cane. "Here. Hold onto your staff."

At first Cotton didn't want to. But that wasn't the way of it here. When something is presented, it must be embraced and understood.

"Do you know how you figured out the meanings of the parables and the messages on the Rocks?"

She inhaled. "Yes, I wanted to know…with my heart."

"You accepted the knowledge. Concentrate on that stick in your hand."

Cotton studied the smooth wood for quite a while. "I can't understand this. How it can all just go away."

"No. You cannot understand it with your head."

Cotton lowered her head and tried to concentrate with her heart, but she saw the pile of sticks and leaves and knew she must hurry. She looked up and said, "Mimi, I am running out of time. Please help me to understand."

"You already do. You simply need to accept. Remember how you instinctively knew the names of Tsur, of Sela', the Rocks."

Cotton thought. "Yes, they came to me because I was open to them."

"That is the way of this. Calm your mind and open your heart to the name of the cane."

Cotton tried hard—to freeze out the urgency she felt in her head. She allowed the flood of all she had learned to wash over her. And then it came. "The Staff of Grace."

Mimi smiled. "Grace is undeserved forgiveness. You did not deserve forgiveness, but the Rock of Salvation met your true remorse with His absolute grace. You, however, feel your remorse so deeply that you don't want to accept Tsur's Staff of Grace."

Cotton tightened her grip around the cane, hoping, somehow, the feeling of being forgiven would transfer from her head knowledge to her heart. "How can I simply rely upon your words? I need to feel it, to know it, like I did when I put my hands on the Rocks."

After a few moments, her grandmother said, "Did you see Caleb at the hospital? With you and the baby girl inside you?"

She jerked her head up. "Yes. It is a baby girl." Sadness covered her heart. "How did anyone know to call him?"

"You'd never moved the note he left at your door on my old hall tree. When the police and Aaron came to try to find next of kin, Aaron found Caleb's note."

"Call me if you change your mind." Those words had haunted her for weeks after he'd left it. "But I never called him."

Mimi nodded. "And though you could have, you never made any bad choices."

"No. I couldn't. I don't actually know what I was thinking. Actually, I wasn't. I put the baby out of my head and continued living like she didn't even exist." She gripped the staff even tighter.

Mimi grabbed Cotton squarely by the shoulders. "I know. But you knew that you were running out of time to make that decision."

"I knew I couldn't decide to let it go, like I had Max." Her love for baby Max welled up in her heart with her regret for what she had done.

"Don't you see? Then *that* was your decision." Mimi let her go.

She nodded. Somehow, she'd always known that in her heart because she'd bought the second binder to organize the *how* of it—of having a baby and a career. She'd left the note by the door on top of the empty binder because she was going to call Caleb. Eventually. But the days turned into weeks and the weeks turned into months, and she never showed any outward signs of being pregnant. So, she assumed she still had time to figure out all the details of it. Her crazy mad organizational skills would help her, too. In fact, the notebook would help her with all the planning. In it, she'd placed the pregnancy test she'd picked up off the floor after Caleb had stormed out of her home that night. On the first tab, she had written "Day Care." She simply couldn't bring herself to finish it—to write all the details in it because it would signify letting go of all that her mother had hoped for her.

She *had* really decided to have her baby. And the incomplete notebook stood witness to that fact. Just because she didn't know the next steps didn't negate the fact that she had chosen life for her baby girl. She wasn't going to be one of Tsur's quiescent lights. She was going to be Cotton's and Caleb's baby—even though it had all started out of God's plan.

Something swirled around in her heart.

*"God arranges all things to work together as a part of His plan*

*for those who love Him and are called to perform His will and purposes upon earth."*

The problem was that she just didn't know *how* she was going to accomplish any of it. How would she tell her station manager that she was going to get huge when she'd carefully cultivated her polished image with her tiny waist, her red shoes and red lipstick? How was she going to get up at 3 a.m. with a baby if she were the morning anchor? Who would take care of her baby when she was working? How could she be up all night and home with her when the baby gets sick? Without a mother, who'd tell her when and how to feed the baby? It was all overwhelming. So, she put it out her mind. Blocked it. In some kind of…coping mechanism.

*Thump. Daniel in the Lion's Den.*

God was going to give her the strength and show her the how of it, moment by moment. It was not going to be something to be organized in a notebook. And just as the Rock protected Daniel, He would have protected her, and He would have delivered her from all her difficulties, all confusion, all her problems—He would have given her all the answers when it was time. *That* was her knowledge.

The only thing that she had definitely figured out in The Choosing Place was that she was going to call Caleb. Someday. When she could also figure out how she could convince him that she had changed. She was imperfectly working on that very thing when she had fallen—and when she had called her friends to reconnect—and when she had worked so hard on the children's project—and when she sat alone in her apartment thinking about how much she loved Caleb and would do anything for him—and the child from which she couldn't separate herself. "Still, how can I be forgiven here? I did not pray for forgiveness at the church, like I'd seen so many do—like we'd been taught to do."

Mimi straightened her apron and shook her head. "You are a difficult case, Cotton. So, *why* did you keep this last baby? Your baby girl?"

"Because I felt so terribly sorry for what I'd done to little Max. Though I had tried to put it out of my mind, too, it haunted me every day of my life afterwards."

"So…you were remorseful for that? Why?" Mimi picked up an armful of the sticks and leaves and took them to the big pile and released them.

Cotton thought and took a deep breath.

*Thump.*

The jolt nearly knocked her off her feet.

"The knowledge of how wrong it was to have terminated little Max had been written upon my heart from the day I did it. That and many other things." She inhaled the truth of that knowledge. "But I never said the words in The Choosing Place. I thought about how I would say them in my head—about how I would say the words to Caleb. But I kept putting it off, and I kept making mistakes."

Mimi stopped with a bundle in her arms. "It is the state of man."

"I don't understand." The language of The Sorting Place still confounded her sometimes, even as she was about to leave it.

"Man sins. He is remorseful. And he sins again. Only one man walked without sin. Without needing to feel remorse. The chain had been broken, and the example had been given." She released the twigs in her arms, making the pile even higher.

"But without the words, it shouldn't count. I've heard people talk about how it's all supposed to happen." All the numbers and the chapters and the verses kept rolling over and over in her head.

Mimi took another handful of leaves to the pile under the tree. "We are told many things, some from the Rock, some not. What about the people who say the words but do not ever feel the remorse? What about the people without voices and without words? Should a stroke victim be denied salvation because he cannot form the words with his mouth?"

Cotton thought. Her situation seemed similar. Her remorse ran through her heart, into her arteries and veins, her bones and muscles, and into her mind and spirit.

"Sometimes we get stuck in the process of it all. And, there were these special circumstances in your case, many of them. Usually, the body and spirit are united until death, but your body and your baby still live in The Choosing Place. It is just your soul that came here to be sorted ahead of time, so that's a pretty special circumstance that needs to be handled differently."

"I never thought about those kinds of circumstances," she said. *Thump.* The jolt hit her harder than the others, and her knees buckled. She nearly hit her head on the tree. *Wow.*

Her grandmother looked at her intently—worried. "It is almost finished," she said. "We haven't much time."

Cotton grabbed the tree to steady the dizzying sensation she had in her head.

"And now we need to iron out your intent in The Choosing Place. At the end. Your intent towards others. To harm others. Do you think that counts at all?"

"I don't know. I suppose so." Too many times she'd been so consumed with herself to think of her intent towards others. But she had intent to repair that in the end.

"Was it your intention to save little Buddy?"

"Yes." Tears welled into her eyes.

"And the very next time in your vision, when you may have had the chance to choose not to, did you do it again?" Mimi looked toward the mountain.

Cotton searched her heart. "I'm not so sure I knew I didn't have to climb the ladder the second time."

"Did you *try* to stay below on the ground?"

Cotton thought for a moment. "No, I didn't think about it. I just ran up the ladder. Again."

She nodded. "Your intent was good. Your heart told you to climb that ladder. Your heart was good and knew the right in it. You intended for him to live, even at your own peril." Mimi smiled.

*Thump.*

The jolt weakened her even more. She grabbed the tree to steady herself. *I did.*

"Little Buddy will be a great man of Tsur's one day. He will stand before boundless crowds of people in many countries and will speak words that will draw many people to the Rock of Ages. You saw a glimmer of that when you saw how humble the little guy was. You knew he could come out of his shyness one day and could stand before people and talk like you did."

*Thump.*

Vibrations rang through her like a bell. It won't be long now. She was weakened further. As she glanced over at Sela', she watched the letters swirl and form words on the great, fissured rock beside her.

*"Even before I formed you in the womb, I knew and loved you. Even before your birth, I designated you as mine, and I appointed you to serve as my prophet to all peoples."*

Those words were for little Buddy. She knew Buddy was special. Somehow, God had moved her where Buddy was concerned. All those feelings that emerged when he was being taken advantage of as the children were playing came flooding back. "I remember feeling empathy for him." She did have good intentions toward him even then.

"It was the same good intent with this last baby. Your heart knew it would be wrong to separate from it, and you chose not to." A huge smile covered her grandmother's face.

Cotton knew that she couldn't possibly have separated from that little soul, even as much as the world continued to tell her that it was her choice, her body, her right.

"All that was a part of what might seem to be a messy process. But ultimately, what were your final words when you were in that hospital room? While your body and soul were mixed in proximity?" Her grandmother carried the last of the twigs to the big pile.

She thought and suddenly looked up.

*Thump.*

"Dear Jesus, have mercy on me!" had been Cotton's words.

*It had been that simple.*

"You called upon The Name of the Lord. And He saw the intent in your heart. Your remorse. In The Choosing Place." Mimi reached down toward the pile and gathered as many twigs and leaves in her arms as she could and threw all them into the air, toward the branches of the large oak. They continued upward, attaching themselves to the branches from whence they came. It was as if they had never been broken or knocked off in the first place. They were simply restored.

Cotton looked amazed at what her grandmother had accomplished. Had all her brokenness and sins simply disappeared and had been restored like that? She grabbed handfuls of twigs and leaves, throwing them up as hard as she could into the tree, and she watched as each broken twig and each detached leaf reattached to the Great Tree of Life as it was being made whole again.

Cotton and Mimi looked at each other and laughed. They took turns picking up the debris, tossing it into the tree and watched as the tree was made perfect and whole again. Cotton felt frailer, however, with each throw.

Had all of Cotton's sins simply been washed away in the

Great River as the Rock wore her sins off the staff? Yes. Had all her brokenness been made whole? Like the leaves and twigs on her big tree? Yes.

*Thump.* Things nearly went black, and she suddenly felt the feebleness intensify. She sensed her time to be close at hand. And something still needed resolution because of her complications. She stared straight into Mimi's eyes. "So, what is left to be decided? And how?"

Mimi nodded. "Ah, there are three choices. Do you see the three roads that diverge just beyond your tree? You may decide which one you should travel on from here."

Hope leapt up in her. A chance to repair all her wrongs perhaps? A chance to actually bring good gifts to Tsur, the Rock.

*Thump.* Cotton's knees buckled, and her vision faded again. Time was running out quickly.

Mimi pointed. "The middle path will lead you back to your life, back to Caleb, back to making decisions, back to doing good things. Or wrong things. You could be at next fall's Cotton Ball. In The Choosing Place."

The hope inside Cotton became brighter. That had been the project of her heart. How could she have possibly hoped for such an amazing ending to all this? Restoration of her life!

Mimi squinted. "It would take God performing a miracle within your brain, but he would, for you, especially for you, because of the work—His work."

*Thump.* Cotton stumbled.

"Oh, Mimi, I would do good things this time. I would work at the church and would make up all this to Caleb. I've been terrible to him, as well. And I have so many more ideas for the Cotton Ball."

"Let me finish." Mimi's face grew serious. "The far right path would lead to the mountain, Tsur, the Rock of Ages, and you would share in the joy of eternity in The Rejoicing Place."

*Thump.* A jolt of knowledge came to Cotton. "But I would have to die." The understanding didn't impact her like she thought it might. Instead, it came with a measure of peace.

Mimi nodded. "Your baby would live, and Caleb would get the desire of his heart."

Cotton drew in a deep breath. She so wanted her baby girl to live.

Her grandmother grew silent for a moment and dropped her head. "And the last path—the left path—leads to your mother and The Regretting Place. It is the path you must take if you wish to stay, but you don't truly accept and apply the Staff of Grace into your heart."

That was a no-brainer. Though she loved her mother dearly, and she knew she actually deserved to be there with the bad choices she'd made, she didn't want to hang on to all that she'd done. She held the smooth cane toward the branches above and allowed the clean, unblemished wood to give her knowledge. *Thump.* Grace was undeserved forgiveness. Though she didn't deserve it, how could she reject it? She couldn't. She squeezed her eyes shut and tightened her grip around the Staff of Grace, allowing the gift to flow into her. As it did, she felt lighter and lighter. *Transformed.* This was her cane now. She fully accepted the smooth staff, accepted her forgiveness. She couldn't throw away something so valuable again. Even for her mother, like she had before in The Choosing Place.

*Thump.* Cotton still needed to know. She needed to know the consequences of what she'd desired the entire time she had been in The Sorting Place. "What if I choose to go back? To take my body back?"

"Then your baby will die. She will become one of Tsur's little quiescent spirits. It is complicated. It would disrupt the spiritual order of things. You would be required to complete the work that she would have accomplished."

*Thump.* The thud hit her again. There it was. Another shock to her system. She felt her body jolt like she had over and over again—like she had under that tree on the church grounds—like she'd felt again and again in The Sorting Place. Everything was making sense.

A furrowed line appeared in Mimi's brow. "There isn't much time. Your baby girl cannot take many more of the shocks from the paddles. They have been restarting your heart for months now. A decision must be made," her grandmother said with a sense of urgency in her voice.

There was really no choice to be made. "It is decided." Cotton will not ever make any other choices ever again that would take another of her babies' lives. Her life was no more important than theirs. She had done so much work to settle with her little lights, so much work to settle with baby Max. How could she make any other choice, now that she knew better? The knowledge brought her responsibility.

A huge smile spread over her grandmother's face and her eyes radiated pride.

Rejoicing rose in Cotton's soul and in her heart. "I choose the Rock of My Refuge. I choose for sweet Caleb to have his baby. I choose my little illuminations. I choose Max."

*Thump.*

Was that her last?

Her grandmother closed her eyes and nodded. "Then, it has been decided." She grabbed Cotton's hands, holding them between hers, the Staff of Grace in Cotton's.

"I must go," Mimi said.

Cotton knew this. She knew she had to face her fate alone. And God would pronounce that fate shortly.

Mimi turned and started walking down the right path toward the breathing mountain with lightness in each step.

Cotton gazed for a while. What was going to happen next? Whatever the answer to that would be fine because she would be fine. It was settled in her soul.

*Thump.*

Then, everything around her went black, and she had the sensation of sinking and falling.

⁂

Cotton didn't know how long she'd been on the ground. Eventually, she saw the light and darkness swirl together behind her eye lids. She slowly opened them. She stood up and sensed something had changed. Suddenly, she heard a slight hum from above, high in the branches. "Mmmmmmmmm," hummed and buzzed a small chorus of…voices. It was almost…musical.

All her baby lights, her little illuminations floated down from atop the very highest branches where they'd hidden. They had probably distanced themselves for fear of her decision. There was really no choice for her after she'd spent time with them, named each one, settled with them.

She lifted her arms and rejoiced at their radiance. Far in the distance, she heard an unearthly song of joy, and she and her illuminations danced around the Great Tree together. They all glowed in the most brilliant crimson glow she'd ever seen. How precious they all were! She lightly touched each, her heart glowing warmer and more crimson with each caress.

She couldn't wait to stand before Tsur and thank him for them, each of them. Even in all her sin, she'd been blessed. It was true.

Sela' swirled the murky depths of its stone façade.

*"Everything did work together for the benefit of those who love The Tested Stone."*

*"Everything."*

All the living parables she had witnessed in The Sorting Place settled in her soul. In her childhood, she had been planted in fertile soil. She had been called, and she loved Him. In her adulthood, she'd tried to ignore him—to tune out the words that had already been written upon her heart, but in her sorting, she came to understand that the words never go away once they have been placed there. The Rock had never abandoned her. He had protected her, even as she had wandered away from Him. He was always there, sometimes disappointed with her decisions...but always nearby.

The little lights darted here and there, playfully, and she joined them. Around and around the tree, they danced and played, joy emanating from each step and touch. Eventually, she glanced down and noticed her earthly red garment had changed. She now wore the white and khaki cloth of the spirit like the others wore. But she glowed more crimson than ever before.

*It is completed.*

After much celebration, she gathered all her precious baby glows together, calling them each by name, noting the subtle differences in their crimson hues. The light beyond the great tree began to dim. Inside, deep within her spirit where Sela had written His word, she knew that tree was not her home any longer, and she couldn't stay there another night. She and her baby souls would join the others on Tsur, in The Rejoicing Place.

She picked up her smooth Staff of Grace, and, without hesitation, with her little crimson radiances frolicking all about her, she started down the path that led to the breathing Rock, the glowing Rock. The Everlasting Rock.

Now, that she was fully and finally illuminated.

# AFTERWARD

Throughout my life, when Jesus placed something upon my heart, I would not dismiss the calling, even though the calling sometimes required waiting. This novel was no different. Although this story had simmered in my heart for years, I struggled with how to construct it. Finally, with much prayer and contemplation, I was inspired to write a rough outline, and it ended up being nothing like I had ever written before.

I knew the major theme was to center around a woman meeting her babies' souls after she had died, but the mechanics of a story like that was difficult because it involved writing about death and heaven, and—of course—I had never experienced either. I knew that if Jesus inspired its telling, He would provide the words—in His time.

Like with all my novels, I avoided the influence of other writers and styles. This was to be my unique story in my unique voice and style. I knew the novel would necessitate breaking traditional writing standards, but the story required it. No one was as surprised as I was at the end when I realized what the final product turned out to be.

Before writing this book, the only thing I knew about Near Death Experiences was that people sometimes died for a short period of time and traveled through a tunnel toward a light. That was it. After finishing this novel, I happened upon a Youtube channel that featured NDEs. I was shocked to realize that although I knew nothing about the topic, my story could be loosely categorized as something similar to a Near Death Experience or maybe—more accurately—an out-of-body experience of sorts.

Though the story defies traditional categorization, it does inspire contemplation about what may wait for us on the other side of the veil of life. I do not claim to know the specifics of the afterlife. This fictious story that Jesus placed upon my heart a long time ago does, however, speculate about those possible details. I cannot escape the impression in my soul that Jesus not only called me to write this parable, but He also provided some of the ideas that graced the pages. One day, I may know for sure.

In the meantime, as I await the end of my journey, I pray for a reunion with the baby that I miscarried. My faith about that meeting rests in the verses of the Bible that give me hope.

Please also pray with me that this novel reaches those who would benefit from the contemplation of the ideas on the pages of this book—about life, repentance, grace, and forgiveness. Most importantly, please pray for the lives and souls of the voiceless unborn.

# Author's Use of Bible Verses in the Text

One of the author's motifs in the novel is the idea that Bible verses need to be internalized and committed to one's heart and not merely memorized for rote recitation. As the Bible verses mysteriously appeared on various rocks throughout the story, she created Author's Versions (AV) of those verses based upon the King James version of the Bible in order to enlighten the main character in a language that she could understand and internalize.

*"Though many hear the call, few prepare themselves to be His chosen." AV based on Matthew 22:14, KJV*

*"In the final days, peril will reign. People will love themselves, will covet, will boast, will be proud, will blaspheme and be ungrateful and disobedient to their parents, and will live unholy." AV based on 2 Timothy 3:1-2, KJV*

*"God will judge all deeds—every good action, every evil work, and every secret thought." AV based on Ecclesiastes 12:14, KJV*

*"You saw the unformed substance that would eventually become who I am, and you saw every day that I would live. My life had already been ordained and written down, even before I was completely formed." AV based on Psalm 139:16, KJV*

*"Just as Elizabeth heard Mary call out to her, the baby inside her turned over in excitement, and the Holy Spirit filled her soul. She then called out to Mary, 'You are blessed above all women because your baby will be holy!" AV based on Luke 1:41-42, KJV*

*"God gave you freedom to choose, but do not use that allowance for the flesh..." AV based on Galatians 5:13, KJV*

*"God will write His law upon His people's hearts, and it will be a covenant, giving their souls knowledge of His ways." AV based on Jeremiah 31-33, KJV*

*"Even when His word is written upon His people's hearts, they turn from the knowledge and excuse their choices." AV based upon Romans 2:15, KJV*

*"You should see that I am He. There is no other god. Only I give life. Only I am to put to death." AV based on Deuteronomy 32:39, KJV*

*"You should see that I am He. There is no other god. Only I give life. Only I am to put to death." AV based on Deuteronomy 32:39, KJV*

*"The God in Heaven has sworn, 'Just as I have planned, so it will be done, and as I have intended, it will absolutely happen.'" AV based on Isaiah 14:24, KJV*

*"God arranges all things to work together as a part of His plan for those who love Him and are called to perform His will and purposes upon earth." AV based on Romans 8:28, KJV*

*"Even before I formed you in the womb, I knew and loved you. Even before your birth, I designated you as mine, and I appointed you to serve as my prophet to all peoples." AV based on Jeremiah 1:5 KJV*

*"Everything did work together for the benefit of those who love The Tested Stone." "Everything." AV based on Romans 8:28, KJV*

## About the Author

293

Vicki is a native of the Charleston, South Carolina, Lowcountry and loves to share her enchantment with the area with readers through her novels. Her faith has always been very important to her, and that faith finds its way into the themes and narratives of every story she writes. She is also a former high school English teacher, editor, and journalist. In her spare time, she enjoys lovingly restoring her Victorian home, traveling, painting, writing and cooking. Visit Vicki on Facebook at https://www.facebook.com/vickiwilkersonauthor.